"What ☑ P9-API-967 beautiful woman you are, especially when you're angry."

Mélissande's eyes sparked, but she restrained her tongue as she rose from her chair.

Catching her hand as she passed him, Gideon pulled her close to him. She drew a quick, startled breath as she looked up at him, suddenly more conscious of his height, the width of his shoulders, his aura of sheer masculine sensuality, than she had been since their first meeting on the rainswept road near Fiesole.

"Gideon, please," she murmured, attempting to pull away.

Ignoring her, he cupped her face in his hands, his gray eyes beneath the tousled dark curls gleaming with a fitful flame as he gazed down at her. "Ever since we first met, I've been longing to do this—again..." He crushed her slight body against him, pressing his lips to hers with an insatiable pressure that grew steadily more insistent as he drained the sweetness from her mouth.

Mélissande made no attempt to break away...

*   *   *

"Highly recommended."
—*Rendezvous* **newsletter on** *Cassandra*

Also by Diana Delmore

Anthea
Cassandra
Dorinda
Leonie

Published by
WARNER BOOKS

ATTENTION: SCHOOLS AND CORPORATIONS

WARNER books are available at quantity discounts with bulk
purchase for educational, business, or sales promotional use. For
information, please write to: SPECIAL SALES DEPARTMENT,
WARNER BOOKS, 666 FIFTH AVENUE, NEW YORK, N Y 10103

ARE THERE WARNER BOOKS
YOU WANT BUT CANNOT FIND IN YOUR LOCAL STORES?

You can get any WARNER BOOKS title in print. Simply send title
and retail price, plus 50¢ per order and 50¢ per copy to cover
mailing and handling costs for each book desired. New York State
and California residents add applicable sales tax. Enclose check
or money order only, no cash please, to: WARNER BOOKS, P O
BOX 690, NEW YORK, N Y 10019

MÉLISSANDE
Diana Delmore

WARNER BOOKS

A Warner Communications Company

WARNER BOOKS EDITION

Warner Books, Inc.
666 Fifth Avenue
New York, N.Y. 10103

 A Warner Communications Company

Printed in the United States of America

First Printing: March, 1987

10 9 8 7 6 5 4 3 2 1

CHAPTER I

Ignoring the sound of Aurore's pleading voice, Mélissande stormed out of the drawing room and through the great front entrance doors of Fiesole, her cousin's Palladian mansion. Angrier than she could ever remember being, Mélissande had rushed halfway down the long driveway of the house before realizing that she would be obliged to walk home, having refused Aurore's offer of a carriage. With a shrug, she continued on her way; after the bitterly wounding words that had just passed between them, Mélissande could not bring herself to accept the smallest of favors from her cousin. The prospect of five miles on foot did not faze her, since she was an inveterate walker; however, as she emerged on the roadway, past the rather surprised gatekeeper at the lodge, she paused to look up at the sky, almost regretting her stubbornness. The light had faded from the beautiful bright autumn day, and a scarcely perceptible mist was falling. Fearing that the mist would turn to rain, she decided to take a shortcut through a woodland bordering the Fiesole estate, which would bring her to her home at the Dower House on a diagonal course without the necessity of returning through Easton village.

Striking into the woodland, Mélissande was so lost in her

dark thoughts that she was paying little attention to her surroundings until, swerving to avoid an overhanging branch that suddenly loomed above her, she lost her balance and fell into a thornbush. Extricating herself with considerable difficulty, she totted up the results of her mishap and discovered that her gloves were in ribbons, her once trim bonnet was crushed out of shape, there was a large rent in the front of her pelisse, and she had twisted her ankle. Favoring her injured foot, she walked gingerly a short distance toward a break in the trees and found herself on the roadway leading to the Dower House, still a mile or more away. She paused, looking up and down the road, half hoping to see a vehicle driven by an acquaintance, for a ride home would be very welcome. At the same time she was apprehensive about meeting a friend in her bedraggled condition.

Hearing the sound of wheels, she looked up with mingled feelings to see a curricle, its hood up against the mist that had now turned into a light rain, coming from the direction of Easton village. She lifted her hand, only to drop it to her side when the curricle neared her, as she recognized that its occupant was a stranger. The driver reined in his team and directed at Mélissande a long, inquiring look. "Good afternoon, miss. You seem to be in some distress. May I be of assistance?"

The speaker was undoubtedly a member of the gentry. He was a tall man with powerful rangy shoulders, handsome, classically severe features, and steely gray eyes. His clothes were modish and expensively tailored but carelessly worn, his cravat negligently tied, his beaver hat thrust back at a raffish angle on his rumpled curly brown hair, the elegance of his many-caped driving coat marred by a slight sprinkling of snuff.

"No, I thank you, sir," replied Mélissande with a polite bow and a smile of dismissal. As she turned to resume her walk toward the Dower House, however, she felt a sharp pain in her injured ankle and regretted her automatic refusal of assistance from a strange gentleman. She turned back, saying hesitantly, "If I might be permitted to change my mind . . ."

"But of course," replied the stranger, smiling. "The privilege of changing her mind—though *not,* one fervently hopes, her feelings—must be an immutable prerogative of the fair sex."

"Oh." Mélissande gazed somewhat blankly at the man. A little quiver of alarm ran through her as she noted that his flashing smile extended none of its warmth into those still gray eyes, but at the same time she became aware of a kind of magnetic current flowing between them, rooting her to the spot. For a moment, his assured gaze seemed no longer faintly menacing but dangerously enticing. To her dismay, she realized that her eyes were locked on his handsome mouth, and she wondered suddenly how it would feel to have those firm lips pressed to her own. Flushing, she beat back such a wildly improper thought and forced herself to say calmly, "I was about to say, sir, that I should be glad of a ride. My home is just over a mile down the road. I have wrenched my ankle, you see, and walking has become rather painful."

"I'm quite at your disposal." The man snapped a peremptory finger at the wiry young groom perched behind him. "Rob, help the lady into the curricle." As the tiger jumped down to extend a slightly grimy hand to Mélissande, his master motioned to his left leg, stretched carefully and stiffly before him. "I trust you'll forgive me for not myself assisting you into the carriage? I, too, am something of a temporary cripple."

As he put his horses into motion—from the ease with which he handled his powerful team, Mélissande judged that he was what her brother Nick would call a first-rate "fiddler" —the man looked her over with a glance of lazy condescension, saying, "Well, now, my girl, are you in service hereabouts?"

After an initial moment of speechless shock, Mélissande

retorted, "No, sir, I am not." She felt a hot surge of anger at being mistaken for a member of the servant class, although the stranger's error was certainly understandable. One did not expect to find a lady of quality traveling a rainy road on foot, dressed in torn and disheveled garments.

The man quirked an amused eyebrow. "What's this, then? Have I wounded a tender sensibility? My dear girl, I didn't for a moment mean to suggest that you were a parlor maid, or a scullery drudge. An abigail, perhaps?" He paused. "No, not an abigail. Wait now—don't I detect the slightest hint of French accent? I have it! You're a modiste, or a milliner. I daresay you're the proprietress of your very own prosperous shop purveying the latest French fashions to the local ladies."

As Mélissande shot him an offended look, the man added hastily, "No doubt we should abandon the ticklish subject of your occupation. What's your name, m'dear? You don't wish to tell me? You'd like to tease me a bit?" Chuckling, he reached over to touch her gently under her chin with a long, slender finger. "Well, Mistress Coyness, if you have no special plans for the evening, might I make a suggestion? As I was driving through, I noticed what seemed to be a very snug little inn in the village. What would you say to having a festive supper with me in the landlord's best private parlor?"

Up to this point, sheer surprise and outrage had been blocking Mélissande's powers of speech. Now she burst out, "The answer is no, a very emphatic no. And I must tell you, sir, that no gentleman of my acquaintance would dream of inflicting his unwelcome advances on a respectable female."

The stranger reined in his horses, leaning back in his seat to gaze at Mélissande, an expression of keen interest replacing his previous air of world-weary amusement. "By George, a lass of spirit, eh? And I note that somewhere you've managed to acquire a certain degree of gentility in your speech. That cozy supper—and other things as well!—begin to seem more and more enticing."

Swiftly the man slipped his arm around Mélissande's shoulders and pressed his lips to hers in a kiss that bruised her lips and left her gasping for breath. He lifted his head to look down at her, his hard gray eyes gleaming now with a flickering little flame, and said softly, "More than enticing. You're as taking a little thing, my pretty ladybird, as I've met in a month of Sundays."

The dazed expression faded from Mélissande's face, and she gasped as if she had suddenly been doused with a bucket of cold water. Pushing the man away from her, she slapped his face with all the force she could muster and scrambled down out of the curricle. She hobbled down the road as quickly as she could move, wincing as she came down on her injured foot, and glanced back to see with alarm that the stranger had started up his horses. As the carriage came alongside her, the man lifted a finger to his hat with an amused little smile, saying, "Calm your fears, my girl. I have no intention of trying to catch you, or, since my leg is hardly up to a pursuit, of sending my tiger after you. I've made it one of the tenets of a misspent life, you see, never to inflict myself on an unwilling female. These little encounters, to be fully enjoyable, should be mutual." Laughing outright at Mélissande's indignant expression, the man put his team to a trot and drove off.

Her face flaming, Mélissande stood motionless on the road for a moment, staring after the departing curricle. Never in her twenty-four years had she undergone an experience as remotely upsetting as this encounter had been. Except for her brother Nick, no man had kissed her before, or held her so closely that she could feel his heart beating through his elegant waistcoat and frilled shirt. Abruptly she sat down on a large rock beside the road, burying her face in her hands as if to hide, not only from any curious passerby, but from herself as well.

She knew that she ought to be feeling both angry and

insulted at the treatment meted out to her by this stranger, this arrogant Corinthian, whom—though she had no direct knowledge of the breed—she would not hesitate to describe as a shockingly loose screw. And yet . . . She caught her breath as she beat back a shaming admission that the stranger's kiss had been exciting, insidiously seductive. From deep within her had surfaced an almost overwhelming desire to respond to those seeking lips. . . .

Mélissande jumped up, the sudden movement driving away her unwelcome memories of the stranger as she felt a renewed pang from her injured ankle. With a weary sigh, she resumed her slow hobble toward the Dower House. As she walked, she reflected ruefully how uneventfully the day had begun.

CHAPTER II

"Mélissande de Castellane! Don't tell me you've forgotten about the parade!"

Startled, Mélissande put down her embroidery and looked up at her sister Cecilia, who had just poked her head around the door of the morning room.

"I fear I did forget," said Mélissande guiltily. "There have been so *many* parades of late. Do you really think Nick would mind if we missed this one?"

"Certainly he would mind, and so should I," retorted Cecilia. "I vow, Sandy, sometimes I think you don't realize what dangerous times we're living in, with that monster Bonaparte about to descend on us with hordes of blood-thirsty soldiers! It seems to me the very least we can do to show our appreciation to the brave men who will soon be defending us is to go watch their parade."

Mélissande threw up her hands in mock surrender at her sister's indignation. "Oh, very well, I'm sure you're right. After all those hours on the drill field, Nick and his men deserve a little attention and praise. Just let me fetch my pelisse and bonnet, and I'll be with you."

As she stepped out of the door of the Dower House a few minutes later, Mélissande thought fleetingly—as she had so often thought during the past year—about the contrast between her present home and Easton Priory, from which she and Cecilia and their brother Nicholas had moved after the death of the sixth Marquess of Rochedale. The Dower House, smallish and undistinguished of architecture, and with a faint air of seediness reflecting the many years it had sat unoccupied, was a far cry from the vast bulk of the Priory, built on lands granted to the Maitland family during the reign of Henry VIII; the original spacious Tudor manor house had been so enlarged and remodeled over the centuries that it was not uncommon for an unwary visitor to become lost in its labyrinth of rooms.

Mélissande smiled at her sister, pacing restlessly on the driveway as she waited for their man-of-all-work and gardener, John, to bring up the pony cart. ''Your hat looks like new, Cecilia. Changing the ribbons made all the difference. You have a real sense of style.''

And indeed Cecilia did look beguilingly pretty in her gown of mauve-colored muslin, topped by a gypsy hat trimmed with matching ribbons. The subdued shade of secondary mourning, so trying to most feminine complexions, only intensified the beauty of her fair skin. Tall, slender, and blond, Cecilia had large blue eyes and a lovely open smile that reflected her friendly, outgoing nature.

The sisters looked strikingly dissimilar. Shorter than Cecilia, though she seemed taller than her actual height because of her gracefully erect carriage, Mélissande had dark eyes and black hair, small, regular features with an elusive dimple in one cheek, and an air of quiet reserve. New acquaintances found it hard to believe that the girls were sisters. In point of fact, they were only half sisters, the daughters of Jeanne-Marie, Duchesse de Lavidan, lady of the bedchamber to Queen Marie Antoinette.

Beautiful and wayward, Jeanne-Marie had abandoned her husband and her three-year-old daughter, Mélissande, to elope to Italy with Thomas Maitland, Marquess of Rochedale, an English nobleman visiting at the court of Versailles. For some years the pair lived a romantic idyll, marred only by the fact that their daughter, Cecilia, had been born illegitimate a year after the elopement. The removal by death and divorce of their respective spouses had enabled Thomas and Jeanne-Marie to marry shortly before the birth of Nicholas, Cecilia's younger brother by two years.

"Thank you, John," said Mélissande, smiling at the handyman, as she and Cecilia climbed into the pony trap. Taking the reins, Mélissande guided the pony down the short, straight drive to the gate in the low wall that encircled the modest grounds of the Dower House. A short drive along a gently rolling road bordered with hedgerows and an occasional pleasant stretch of woodland soon brought the pony trap into Easton, a small East Sussex village nestled beneath a low ridge of the Weald, that irregular plain lying between the chalk ranges of the North and South Downs. The single long street leading to the village green was more crowded than it would normally have been on a quiet Sunday afternoon, with virtually the entire population of Easton and a sizable contingent of farmers and their families waiting expectantly for the Volunteers to appear on parade.

Finding themselves a good vantage point near the green, Mélissande and Cecilia were soon joined by kindly, gray-haired Mrs. Garrett, the vicar's wife, who, as she gazed around at the frollicking children and their smiling parents, said pensively, "I, for one, find it difficult to feel very festive when I consider how grim our real situation is. All summer now, we've been expecting an invasion by the French, ever since the declaration of war in May, and here it is the end of September and still the French haven't come. For weeks now, I haven't stepped out of the house of an evening without glancing up to see if the beacons are lit on the hills, flashing the news that Napoleon has landed."

"Yes, the waiting is difficult," said Mélissande sympathetically. "One almost wishes the French would come soon to end our suspense!"

Mrs. Garrett did not smile at Mélissande's little joke. The

vicar's wife sounded very worried as she said in a low voice, "I fancy we shan't have to wait very long. They say the French dockyards have been busy day and night for months, making barges to transport a quarter of a million men across the Channel." Her voice dropped even lower as she added, "I hear that Napoleon has assigned picked bands of ruffians to murder the gentry in their beds as soon as the landing is accomplished."

Putting a reassuring hand on Mrs. Garrett's shoulder, Mélissande said, "You mustn't pay any attention to these absurd rumors. The French won't be allowed to land in England. If they do land, they will be beaten off. Recall, for months men have been swarming to join the Volunteers, drilling in every town square and village green. Why, even Mr. Pitt has become a Volunteer, a colonel of the Cinque Ports regiment. And the Lord Chancellor is serving as a corporal, and the Duke of Bedford as a private, no less!"

Mrs. Garrett visibly relaxed and Cecilia exclaimed, waving her hand, "Oh, there's Nick with Stephen Lacey. The parade must be about to start."

Responding to Cecilia's wave, the two young men crossed the green to join the sisters and Mrs. Garrett. Both wore dashing scarlet regimentals and rakishly cocked hats.

"Such good news, ladies! The men's uniforms have arrived, and their muskets, too!" exclaimed Lord Nicholas Maitland with a beaming smile. He was rangy and broad-shouldered, taller than his sister, and in him Cecilia's fair good looks had assumed a boldly masculine cast, but otherwise they might have been twins.

"That *is* good news, Nick. I know how concerned you've been, especially about the muskets," said Mélissande.

"Concerned isn't the word for it, Miss de Castellane," said Stephen Lacey, grinning. "I can't tell you how relieved I am, knowing that I'll not be obliged to listen any longer to Nick railing angrily about the pikes that were issued to the Volunteers. Only yesterday he was saying to me, 'Can you imagine what the greenest of French troops would do against our boys equipped only with those flimsy pikes?' ''

Stephen was a tall, slender man who with his curling dark hair and handsome features bore a strong resemblance to his mother, Mélissande's cousin, the Countess of Haverford. He flashed Cecilia an appreciative smile. "I say, what a charming hat."

"Thank you for the compliment, Stephen, even though I sometimes feel like a drab peahen next to you two peacocks in your regimentals." There was an intimate, teasing note in Cecilia's voice, a provocative slant to her head that caused Mélissande to look at her sharply. Stephen and Cecilia were twenty years old, but Mélissande had continued to think of them simply as older versions of the childhood playmates they had always been. Not by any stretch of the imagination, however, could the glances Stephen and Cecilia were now exchanging be described as either childlike or playful.

After Nick and Stephen had gone off to join their men, and Cecilia had moved away to chat with a friend, Mrs. Garrett murmured, "What a handsome pair, your brother and sister."

"Yes. They look like my stepfather. They are both true Maitlands."

"Mr. Lacey, too, is such a fine-looking young man," added Mrs. Garrett. She coughed. "My dear, have you ever thought . . . ? What I mean to say is, since Mr. Lacey's mother is your cousin, I've often wondered if there was a possibility of a match between him and Cecilia."

"Good heavens, no. They're just good friends. They've known each other practically from the cradle," replied Mélissande with a vehemence that seemed to surprise Mrs. Garrett. The latter replied, "Oh, well, I'm sure you know best, my dear—" She broke off to smile and wave at the Countess of Haverford, who had just driven up to the green in her open carriage.

The crowd quieted as the sound of martial music drifted through the air, and soon into the village green marched the

Easton Volunteers, led by Stephen Lacey with Nick as second in command. As the newly uniformed Volunteers, muskets on their shoulders, went through their maneuvers, Mélissande thought with pride about how much these raw village lads had improved since early summer. At that time, clad in their workaday smocks and carrying the clumsy pikes, they had merely stumbled through their platoon exercises, with their young officers only marginally more knowledgeable than their men.

With the parade over and the Volunteers dispersed, Mélissande crossed the green to greet Lady Haverford, still seated in her carriage.

"*Ma chère* Mélissande, what a lovely parade, *n'est-ce pas*? And Nicholas and my Stephen, how handsome they looked in their new regimentals. You would scarcely credit what it cost to have Stephen's uniform tailored by Weston, no less." The Countess of Haverford's charming, deeply accented voice trailed away, and her delicate brows knit together in a tiny frown as she gazed across the green to where Cecilia was hanging on the arm of her son.

Born Aurore de Bouillon, the Countess, at forty, was still a very attractive woman, with a trim figure and dark eyes and hair. A cousin of Mélissande's father, Aurore belonged to a distinguished family, which, like so many members of the old sword nobility in France, had been living in genteel poverty for generations. Her father had been happy to allow his daughter to become the second wife of the much older Earl of Haverford. It had been a successful enough marriage, marred only by Aurore's scarcely veiled discontent that her only child was a mere second son. The Earl's elder son by his first marriage would inherit his title and his entire estate, a situation that Aurore had always found both incomprehensible and grossly unfair.

She said now, "It's been so very long since we had one of our little chats, *ma petite*. Won't you come home with me for a cup of tea or some chocolate?"

"I'd like that. I'll just tell Cecilia that I won't be returning to the Dower House with her."

The Haverford seat, Fiesole, was situated not far from Easton, and soon Mélissande and the Countess in the open landau were heading up the long, winding drive that led to the great Italianate stone mansion built by an earlier Lord Haverford on his return from his grand tour. Not as old a family as the Maitlands, whose founder had come to England with William the Conqueror, the Laceys were nevertheless much more prosperous. The present Earl not only owned vast acreages but had also inherited the immense wealth of his mother, the daughter of an East India Company nabob.

After the footman had served the chocolate and cakes and had left the drawing room, Lady Haverford observed, "*Eh bien,* tell me your news. Have you heard from the new heir?"

Mélissande shook her head. "No, not a word, but then we hadn't expected to receive any news as yet, even though my stepfather died almost a year ago. It would take five or six months for the notification of his father's death to reach Gideon in India. Perhaps even longer, because, for all we know, he may be off fighting with his regiment in the wilds of the interior. And then, of course, it would take another six months for Gideon to return to England, or to send a letter. But we're expecting to hear some news any day now."

Mélissande purposefully kept her tone casual and unconcerned, but, in truth, the subject of Gideon Maitland, the new Marquess of Rochedale and the half brother of Nicholas and Cecilia, had been a source of worry to her for almost a year, since the deaths, just a few weeks apart, of her mother, Jeanne-Marie, and Gideon's father. Unless they could count on the friendship and support of the new owner of Easton Priory, the occupants of the Dower House might face an uncertain future.

"Nick, of course, is especially anxious to hear from Gideon," Mélissande continued. "As you may know, Nick

just celebrated his eighteenth birthday, and my stepfather
had always promised him that when he turned eighteen he
could become Mr. Morris's assistant and then take the
position of bailiff himself when Mr. Morris retired. My
stepfather also promised that Nick could buy some kind
of new breeding ram next spring and try a modern method
of farming. Something called the 'four-crop rotation sys-
tem.' But, according to our lawyer, any changes in estate
management must now wait until the new heir makes known
his wishes.''

"Ciel," murmured Aurore a little blankly. "I had no idea
that Nicholas was interested in such strange things."

"Oh, but Nick has always been a farmer at heart," said
Mélissande with a laugh. "From the time he was a baby,
he's loved nothing better than poking seeds into the ground.
Of course, he always pulled the plants up the next day to see
if they had started roots. He used to drive the gardeners into
frenzies! And now that he's grown, he's constantly reading
long, complicated reports from the Board of Agriculture."

"I see. Well, it's certainly a harmless enough pastime,"
rejoined the Countess, though it was obvious that she was
really not much interested. She looked sympathetically at
Mélissande. "I know your life hasn't been especially easy
since your very first days in England, but I fear your
existence will be much harder when Gideon Maitland returns to Easton Priory."

"What do you mean?" asked Mélissande, surprised.
"I've been very happy living in England. As for Gideon . . ."

"Come now, I'm stating the obvious, surely. The scandal
of your mother's elopement with the late Lord Rochedale has
been a shadow over your life since you were—let me see,
now—how old?"

"I was three years of age when *Maman* went away in
1782," replied Mélissande levelly.

"Yes, I remember. Well, at that time, *your* social position
was not affected by your mother's disgrace." The countess
pursed her lips primly. "My dear, an elopement was bad

enough, but a *divorce*!'' Continuing, she said, ''Your father was still alive then, the head of one of the most distinguished families in France. He was Duc de Lavidan, Lieutenant-General of Berry, Governor of the Palace of Fontainebleau. But the revolution changed all that. When your father emigrated from France, all his estates were confiscated, and then, only a few years later, he died fighting for the King in Flanders.''

Lady Haverford paused, shaking her head mournfully. ''And here *you* are, the daughter of a peer of France, twenty-four years old—and, let us face the facts, almost too old to find a husband, despite your lineage!—to repeat, twenty-four years old, a penniless orphan in a foreign country.''

''Really, Aurore, must you be quite so lowering?'' rejoined Mélissande with a flash of annoyance. ''At twenty-four I don't consider myself to be quite in my dotage. A number of young women in their middle twenties or even older manage to attract eligible husbands, you know. And as for being penniless, you forget the hundred gold louis that *Grandmère* gave me when she sent me to live with *Maman* in England. I still have the gold, safely invested in the Funds.''

''A hundred louis? How much is that, pray? Twenty-five hundred pounds or thereabouts. A mere—a mere one hundred and twenty-five pounds a year. Not enough to support a sparrow.''

Mélissande lifted her chin. ''You forget also the three thousand pounds that my stepfather left me in his will. He left similar amounts to Nick and to Cecilia, plus the right to live in the Dower House until we establish ourselves elsewhere. So there's no need for you to worry about my future. Cecilia and Nick and I will be very comfortable.''

''Don't talk utter nonsense. Everyone knows the late Lord Rochedale left no money in his estate to pay your inheritance. He and Jeanne-Marie lived far beyond their means. They squandered the Maitland fortune, leaving behind at their deaths nothing but the Priory itself, so weighted down with multiple mortgages that it will be a very dubious heritage for Gideon. I'll wager that for the past year you've been supporting Nicholas and Cecilia out of your own income, and how you've managed that I can't imagine.''

''Aurore, can we discuss some other subject, please?''

''I just want to be sure that you appreciate how precarious your situation really is. For example, I shouldn't count on Gideon's permission to continue living at the Dower House. It's common knowledge that Gideon Maitland despised and resented Jeanne-Marie, and her children, too. He adored his own mother, a charming woman, well loved by everyone. All of us in the county were horrified when, as the first Lady Rochedale lay dying, the husband who had deserted her arrived in Easton with his illegitimate daughter and his *very* pregnant mistress and established them in the village inn while he dispatched messengers at regular intervals to inquire about his wife's condition. Then, when Gideon's mother finally died, the Marquess hastily married Jeanne-Marie by special license, and your brother Nicholas was born legitimate by just one week. I was not long married at the time, and a new mother, and I can recall clearly the stories that were flying about: that young Gideon—he was about fifteen—could not bring himself to say a civil word to his new stepmother on those brief occasions when he came home from school, and that finally, the situation being so unpleasant, Gideon was sent to stay with a maternal uncle until he went off to join the cavalry. I must say, I always empathized with Gideon. And after that, I could never bring myself to feel very kindly toward your mother, especially since I was your father's cousin.''

''*Maman* always understood that you couldn't be truly friendly with her because of your relationship to my father,'' said Mélissande hastily, anxious to guide the conversation away from the subject of her future prospects, and from any further speculation on Gideon Maitland's frame of mind, before she and Aurore actually quarreled. "But *Maman* was happy that you and I could be friends."

"I, too. I'm sure you know that I feel for you almost as a daughter of my own. And, oh, the joy of being able to speak French with you!"

"Oh, I agree. Nick and Cecilia can understand French, but they had English nannies and governesses, and they don't speak it well. What's more, they don't *like* to speak French now that we're at war. They don't wish to be considered as anything but thoroughly English these days."

"I can understand that. Doubtless you and I, as French-women, would be encountering some hostility now if it weren't widely known that we came from émigré families that suffered horribly at the hands of the revolutionaries." Lady Haverford's face brightened. "I know you'll be happy to hear that soon you will have the opportunity to speak our native tongue to your heart's content. I've just received word that His Royal Highness, the Comte d'Artois, will be paying a visit to us at Fiesole in the spring."

"What a great honor for you," said Mélissande, suitably impressed. And indeed, she had never expected, in this quiet corner of Sussex, to be in hailing distance of the younger brother of the martyred King Louis XVI. "I remember that Papa used to be much in the company of the Comte before the Revolution. I hope I will have the opportunity to meet him when he visits Fiesole."

"But of course. You shall be first on my guest list!" As the Countess's smile faded, she added hesitantly, "I must confess something, Mélissande. It wasn't just to give you my good news about the Comte's visit that I asked you here today. You see, of late I have become very—very concerned about Stephen and Cecilia."

"What about Stephen and Cecilia?" Mélissande demanded, caught between surprise and defensiveness. Only a few hours earlier, at the parade, she thought uncomfortably, she herself had been aroused to a quick suspicion of her sister and Stephen.

"I am referring to the way they hang all over each other whenever they meet. You must have noticed their behavior at the parade this afternoon."

"Oh, Aurore, they were just chatting, just enjoying each other's company. And why ever not? They've been friends all their lives."

"Today at the parade they seemed more than merely friendly. I fear they are developing a romantic attachment, and I thought I would just pop a word in your ear so that you could speak to Cecilia and nip the situation in the bud before any harm is done. Because I know you must agree with me that *any* kind of relationship between them is out of the question."

Mélissande stared at her cousin in discomfort. She knew that Aurore, perennially discontented with her son's status as a second son, had always planned for Stephen to marry advantageously, preferably to a titled and wealthy heiress. Mélissande tried to sound soothing as she said, *"Naturellement,* I agree with you that Stephen and Cecilia would not make a good match; however, I feel positive that you're worrying unnecessarily, although..." She hesitated. "In the very unlikely event that we should discover that they really love each other..."

Lady Haverford recoiled in horror. "*Ma foi,* you are never suggesting that Stephen should marry the illegitimate offspring of a scandalous liaison involving a member of my own family! I have always thought that Cecilia's bastardy and her total lack of fortune would keep her from even a respectable marriage, and I certainly would not countenance her union with my own son!"

Fighting to keep her temper, Mélissande replied, "You surprise me. I thought you liked Cecilia. Granted she would not be your choice to be Stephen's wife, but surely there is no reason for you to speak of her as though she were common trash."

"But Cecilia's position *is* very nearly that, common trash," retorted Lady Haverford. "You must have been blind and deaf not to realize her true situation over the years. The local county families, not wishing to offend Lord Rochedale, did socialize with your mother, and later they invited Cecilia to their small private parties and balls, but Jeanne-Marie and your stepfather *never* tried to launch her into London society. They knew full well that she would not be welcomed into any aristocratic family in England." Noticing Mélissande's angry flush, the Countess added quickly, "Now I have offended you, and truly, I never meant to do that. I would not for the world do anything to harm our friendship. I hope you will understand, however, when I tell you that, for the present at least, I do not wish any member of my family to associate with Cecilia."

Mélissande jumped up from her chair. "If my sister is not good enough for you and Stephen, then I am not, either. *Au revoir,* Madame la Comtesse." Snatching up her reticule, she stormed out of the room. Behind her, she could hear Aurore's voice, wailing, *"Ma chère,* please do not be so angry. Only wait a moment until I can order the carriage for you."

CHAPTER III

Mélissande breathed a thankful sigh as she turned into the driveway of the Dower House; the pain in her ankle had increased sharply during the long walk from the point where she had taken leave of the obnoxious stranger in the curricle. Entering the house, she handed her bonnet to the one little maid whom they still retained from the large staff that had served the family at the Priory.

"Well, that was a long visit, to be sure. Did Lady Haverford have lots of juicy county gossip?" Stepping into the foyer from the drawing room, Cecilia paused, aghast, as she looked more closely at Mélissande. "Sandy!" she gasped, using, as she habitually did, the nickname that she and Nick had coined as very small children when they were unable to pronounce the exotic first name of their new half sister. "What on earth happened to you?"

"I'm quite all right, Cecilia. I walked here from Fiesole, and I—I fell into a thornbush," replied Mélissande hastily. She had no intention of revealing to her sister any details of her encounter with the stranger.

"But how was that? Didn't Lady Haverford send you home in her carriage?"

"Actually, Aurore and I had a—a bit of a tiff," admitted

Mélissande reluctantly, ''and I foolishly refused her offer of a carriage.''

''You quarreled with your cousin?'' asked Cecilia with wide-eyed interest. ''That's not like you, Sandy. What was the quarrel about?''

Mélissande shook her head. ''It's of no consequence. I'm going up to my bedchamber now to remove all this dirt. I would love to have a cup of tea with you when I come down.''

In her bedchamber, as she changed her dress and arranged her hair, Mélissande's thoughts turned gloomily to her quarrel with Aurore. Though the latter should have phrased her opinions more kindly, Mélissande was forced to admit to herself that, according to all the ordinary standards of good society, the Countess was justified in not wanting Cecilia for a daughter-in-law. And, if nothing else, Aurore's wounding remarks were forcing Mélissande to confront her long-repressed worries about Cecilia's future. What *would* become of the girl, lost in a crack between two worlds? Without at least a modest dowry, it seemed certain that Cecilia's illegitimacy would prevent her, as Aurore had stated, from making any kind of respectable marriage.

The subject of her sister's dowry led Mélissande inevitably to reflect on the return of Gideon Maitland, whom she had never met. Increasingly hostile to his stepmother and her children, he had never visited the Priory after Mélissande's arrival in England. Could she hope that his resentment had lessened over the years? If not, if he were neither willing nor able to pay out the small inheritances mentioned in his father's will, and especially if he did not allow his father's second family to remain at the Dower House, Mélissande did not see how her own tiny income could support herself and Nick and Cecilia.

After her mother's elopement, Mélissande had been placed in the care of her grandmother at the ancestral estates in Berry. Alarmed by the growing violence in the French countryside after the fall of the Bastille, her grandmother had sent ten-year-old Mélissande to the safety of Jeanne-Marie's new home in England, and there, very soon after her arrival at Easton Priory, Mélissande had come to feel an almost maternal love for her new half brother and half sister. It was a love that had only intensified when she discovered that the vivacious and giddy Jeanne-Marie was not an ideal mother on a day-to-day basis. Jeanne-Marie had really had eyes only for her husband, and since the county gentry never fully accepted her marriage, she and Thomas had frequently absented themselves from the Priory on long visits to Bath or Scarborough, or to the watering places of the Continent. There they lived so extravagantly, spent so freely, that Lord Rochedale not only neglected his estates but mired them more deeply in debt with each passing year.

Leaving her bedchamber, Mélissande tried to put her worries out of her mind, and walked into the morning room wearing a more cheerful smile than her feelings warranted. She dropped gratefully into a chair and accepted a steaming cup of tea from her sister. "Ah, *ma petite Cécile, tu es un ange,*" she murmured. "This tea will make me feel like a new woman."

"Sandy, I've asked you time and again not to call me Cécile," said her sister vexedly, a spot of color in either cheek. 'And you *know* I don't like to speak French."

"But you *are* partly of French extraction, *ma chère*—my dear. There's no way that you can wish away half of your heritage."

"No, of course not. I will always be *Maman*'s daughter. But I've never lived in France or associated with French people, and I *feel* English. And now, with that monster Bonaparte about to invade us, I don't want my friends and neighbors to be reminded that I'm not as English as they are."

Shrugging, Mélissande sipped her tea and munched on a biscuit. "Where is Nick?" she asked after a moment. "Did he go out again after he brought you home?"

"Well—Nick didn't bring me home. He wanted to have a

word with the bailiff. Actually, Stephen drove me to the Dower House.''

Putting down her cup, Mélissande stared at Cecilia for a long moment before speaking, picking her words carefully. ''Dearest Cecilia, I hope you won't think that I'm interfering, but—you're not allowing yourself to entertain romantic notions about Stephen, are you?''

''I'm not saying I have any romantic notions about Stephen, but just supposing I did?'' declared Cecilia. ''Why should you object? I don't understand you, Sandy. I thought you *liked* Stephen. Why, he's your cousin. A very distant cousin, I'll grant you, but still a cousin.''

''*Bien sûr,* I do like Stephen. I've known him for most of his life. And I'm very fond of his mother. But *ma petite,* you must know as well as I do that there can be no question of an attachment between you.''

''I don't see why you find it difficult to imagine that Stephen could be in love with me. I think—I'm almost certain—that he likes me very well.''

''I'm sure he does. You're the prettiest girl in the county, and the sweetest. I don't see how any young man could fail to be in love with you,'' exclaimed Mélissande. She added gently, ''However, I must be honest with you. I'm convinced that Stephen's feelings for you will never lead to marriage, and I presume you aren't interested in any other kind of arrangement.''

Cecilia's face puckered, reminding Mélissande of the little girl who, over the years, had so often been comforted by an older sister over a skinned elbow, a broken doll, or a maternal scolding.

''I never thought to hear you speak so cruelly, Sandy. Why shouldn't Stephen and I think of marriage?''

Mélissande eyed Cecilia with exasperation laced with compassion. ''You're willfully playing the innocent, my dear. Stephen Lacey is a younger son, with no prospects of his own. You must have suspected long since that his mother would never countenance his marriage to a penniless and illegitimate girl.''

"You can't be sure of that! Lady Haverford has always been very kind to me. And I'm not penniless. There's my inheritance from Papa's estate. If Stephen should go into the army—and this he's of a mind to do, since he's enjoying his service with the Volunteers so much—why, then, I'm sure that Lord Haverford would grant him a handsome allowance, and I see no reason why Stephen and I shouldn't live very comfortably.''

Appalled to learn that Cecilia's feelings for Stephen went far deeper than she had imagined, Mélissande exclaimed, "Child, you must not daydream your life away. I hadn't meant to tell you, but . . . you asked my why I quarreled with Aurore. It was about you. Lady Haverford asked me to join with her in keeping you and Stephen apart. You will no longer be received at Fiesole, and Aurore will do her best to make sure that Stephen doesn't see you elsewhere. I've already informed Aurore that I cannot associate with anyone who does not also welcome your company, but Cecilia, that doesn't change the situation. You must face up to the fact that Lady Haverford will never agree to a connection between you and Stephen.''

Tears streaming down her suddenly desolate face, Cecilia rushed out of the morning room, narrowly avoiding a collision in the doorway with Nick.

"Good God, why is Cecy making such a cake of herself?" demanded Nick, staring after his sister. "It ain't like her to enact a Cheltenham tragedy.''

"Don't refine on it. Cecilia will soon feel more herself," replied Mélissande hastily "Come have some tea.''

"I need more than tea," retorted Nick, his face darkening. Throwing down his cocked hat on a small table with such force that a china ornament smashed to the floor, he added, "I'd like some Madeira or, better still, a glass of Blue Ruin.''

"Nick, that was too bad of you," protested Mélissande

as she picked up the broken pieces of china. "This piece was one of *Maman*'s favorites. As for strong spirits, we don't have any gin, and our few bottles of wine are reserved for the vicar's visits, or for a special occasion. Why are you in such a taking?"

Throwing himself into a chair, Nick said morosely, "I've just had a talk with Mr. Morris. At the parade today he asked me to come see him. Sandy, he's withdrawing permission for me to purchase those breeding sheep from John Ellman over in Glynde. You recall, I told you about him; he's developed a miracle new breed of sheep called the Southdown. What's more, Mr. Morris told me to forget about planting the north field of the home farm into Swedish turnips."

"But how is this, Nick? I always thought that Mr. Morris was sympathetic to your ideas. What made him change his mind about the improvements?"

"Oh, that's simple enough. He's heard from my brother—the *new* Lord Rochedale, as he keeps saying. It seems Mr. Morris wrote to Gideon right after Papa died, mentioning Papa's desire that I eventually succeed to the position of bailiff. Well, of course it takes months for a letter to get to India, and as many more to receive a reply. It was only yesterday that a letter finally arrived from Gideon; in it he wrote that he wished to postpone any decision about the management of the estate, including any plans for improvements or innovations, until he returns home. Which will be in the very near future, according to Mr. Morris."

Mélissande tried to reassure her brother, whose averted, eighteen-year-old face looked close to tears. "Well, Nick, I'm very sorry about this setback to your plans, which I'm certain is only temporary. We must just wait patiently until Gideon returns."

Nick jerked upright, blinking angrily. "But dash it, why should I wait to do what Papa wished and intended for me to do? It's not as though I wanted to do something purely selfish. All these improvements are for the good of the estate, after all, my brother Gideon's own estate.''

"Papa is dead, Nick. And Gideon *is* the new Lord Rochedale. He has every right to do as he wishes with the estate. But don't anticipate evil. Doubtless he will act just as he ought to carry out your papa's wishes.''

Looking slightly more cheerful, Nick accepted a cup of tea and proceeded to demolish a tray of biscuits, but Mélissande's thoughts were less optimistic. She recalled her conversation earlier in the day with Lady Haverford, a conversation that had dredged up the half-forgotten, unsavory details of the scandal that had blighted a younger Gideon's life. Perhaps his recent curt and noncommittal letter to the bailiff, Mr. Morris, meant nothing, reflecting only a natural desire on the part of the new owner of Easton Priory to avoid any changes until he was on the scene to supervise them personally. But it was equally possible that Gideon's resentment and dislike of his young half brother and half sister had not subsided with the years. In which case—Mélissande shook her head. Suddenly Mélissande smiled wryly. In her intense concentration on Gideon, another subject, which on any other day would have occupied all her thoughts, had completely slipped from her mind. She felt an odd sort of triumph, wishing it were possible for the obnoxious stranger in the curricle to know how slightly his outrageous behavior had affected her.

CHAPTER IV

Mélissande stared at the menacing column of figures in her household account book. Even if she practiced stricter economies, it was difficult to see how she could make her meager funds stretch until she received her next payment from the Funds.

She was glad to be diverted by Cecilia's arrival in the morning room. Cecilia was out of mourning at last, and looked charming in her gypsy hat, which had once again been refurbished, this time with a large rose and a new ribbon to match the deep blue pelisse. "Sandy, do you need anything in the village? I'm off to the linen draper to buy some thread to mend the rent in my pink muslin gown."

Glancing up from her desk, Mélissande narrowed her eyes as she noted Cecilia's air of barely suppressed excitement. It was out of character, too, for her sister, a normally reluctant needlewoman, to be so quick to effect a minor clothing repair. Lombard Street to a China orange, thought Mélissande, Cecilia has arranged to meet, or at least hopes to see, Stephen Lacey in the village.

"I was thinking to going to Easton myself, Cecilia. The vicar's wife has promised me her new copy of *The Lady's Magazine,* and I hear that old Mrs. Andrews has been ill.

I'm sure she would appreciate some new-laid eggs and a loaf of bread. Wait just a moment until I get my hat and shawl.''

"Sandy, dearest, there's no need for you to tear yourself away from your dreadful accounts. I'll be happy to do your errands," rejoined Cecilia quickly. Blowing Mélissande a kiss, she was out of the door before her sister could mount an objection. A troubled frown furrowed Mélissande's forehead as she reflected on how helpless she was to prevent Cecilia's indiscreet meetings with Stephen. Her sister was no longer a child, nor could she be disciplined like one. Sighing, Mélissande returned to her accounts, but was interrupted a few minutes later by the arrival of Phoebe Wright and her father, a stout, graying, shrewd-eyed widower who owned extensive property adjacent to the Dower House.

Phoebe was small and delicately pretty, with soft blue eyes and chestnut curls. Her father, a prosperous yeoman farmer, had contrived to give his only child an education ordinarily enjoyed only by daughters of the landed gentry, and this advantage was reflected in her charming manners. In recent years, Phoebe and Nick had become close friends, since Nick, with his single-minded interest in agriculture, had been spending much of his time with Mr. Wright, learning the routine and absorbing the expertise of a successful working farmer.

"Phoebe, my dear, it's so thoughtful of you to bring us these beautiful flowers. Cecilia and I have often envied you your green thumb," exclaimed Mélissande, gazing with delight at the pretty mauve-pink bouquet of Michaelmas daisies, cyclamen, and pale rose fuchsia. "Oh, and I see some sweet william also. You know, they should have finished blooming long ago, but this exquisite weather simply lingers on. Sometimes I wonder if summer will ever end this year.''

"Aye, we be having fine weather," nodded Mr. Wright,

"but I hear tell that a few thunderstorms and gale-force winds would keep us much safer from Boney."

"Father and I are off to Hastings," said Phoebe, smiling shyly, "to choose a new pianoforte for my birthday. Perhaps, after it is delivered, you'll come play for us, Miss de Castellane?"

"That's very kind of you, but I fear that my playing is very rusty. We have no instrument here at the Dower House."

"That be a shame, miss," declared Mr. Wright. "If I might make so bold, you and your sister and brother shouldn't be living here at all. You belong at the Priory. Lord Nicholas now, he has a real feel for the land, he's a natural-born farmer. If the old lordship's wishes were heeded, Lord Nicholas would soon become bailiff of Easton Priory, and a very good one, too."

"I agree with you. Let's hope that the new Lord Rochedale will give him the opportunity to do so."

Mr. Wright frowned. "I don't know as how I would put too much faith in Gideon Maitland, him as was. I reckon he wouldn't go out of his way to do a favor to his half brother." Mr. Wright paused in embarrassment. "Ah, well," he muttered after a moment, "it's not for me to say, after all."

Mélissande repressed a sudden urge to question Mr. Wright about the details surrounding the death of the first Lady Rochedale. Having been a close neighbor of the Priory all his life, and with sturdy family antecedents reaching back many generations, the yeoman farmer probably knew as much about old county scandals as any man alive.

Nick entered the morning room just then, his face lighting up when he caught sight of Phoebe. "I say, what a coincidence. I was planning to visit you this afternoon to tell you that Justine finally had her pups. Nine of them, and every one of them healthy."

Phoebe's smile was glowing as she said to her father, "Oh, Papa, you won't mind if I go to the stables with Nick to see the puppies? I shan't be long. And Nick, could you come to supper tonight? Cook has baked the most delicious gooseberry tarts.''

Gazing after Nick and Phoebe as they went off arm in arm, Mr. Wright said, somewhat tentatively, ''Don't you think they make a handsome couple, Miss de Castellane?''

''I—why, yes, they certainly do.''

Mr. Wright's manner became more assured. ''Well, now, ma'am, I allow as how we can be frank with each other after these many years. My Phoebe will be a bit of an heiress one day, and I don't mind telling you that I should like to see her well established. What would you say to a match between her and Lord Nicholas? It's plain as a pikestaff that they have a case on each other.''

''Mr. Wright, I hardly know what to say. You've caught me quite by surprise. I must tell you, however, that when Nick comes to marry, he will certainly make his own choice.''

It was clear from Mr. Wright's expression that he was not entirely satisfied with her answer. He stayed only a few minutes longer before going to the stables to retrieve Phoebe for their jaunt to Hastings, leaving Mélissande with decidedly mingled feelings. She had no real reason to believe that Nick was romantically interested in Phoebe, but it was obvious that he no longer regarded her as the often tiresome little girl whom he had patronizingly allowed to dog his heels during his visits to her father's farm.

Mélissande crossed her fingers, hoping that the question of Nick's possible marriage would not become still another item in her pack of troubles. Society would frown on a match between Nick, who after all was *Lord* Nicholas Maitland, with a long and distinguished ancestry on both sides of his family, and the daughter of a yeoman farmer, however prosperous. And yet, Mélissande liked Phoebe very much, and as far as mere appearance and manners were concerned, the girl would not find it impossible to mingle in county society.

When Nick returned to the house a little later after saying good-bye to Phoebe and her father, his thoughts were not on love or marriage. He sought out Mélissande in the morning room, saying, "I didn't like to speak of it in front of the Wrights, but the fact is I have news of Gideon. Mr. Morris has just told me that my brother arrived at the Priory several days ago. I think I should go see him immediately. I know if I can just speak to him personally, not at second hand through Mr. Morris, I can make him understand how essential it is that the estate adopt the new farming methods. Sandy, I'm *so* eager to get started. After all my reading, and observing Mr. Morris and Mr. Wright at work, I want to do something on my *own*."

"Of course you do, but do you think you should besiege your brother at almost the very moment he arrives home after all those years in foreign parts? Recall, he has just undergone a fatiguing ocean voyage of five or six months' duration. Why don't we just send him a welcoming note from the three of us? Doubtless he will contact us when he recovers from the fatigue of his journey."

A shadow crossed Nick's face. "You don't want me to push myself on Gideon. You're fearful that he still bears us a grudge. Sandy, my brother is a grown man now. No matter what unhappiness my parents may have caused to his mother, surely Gideon must realize that Cecilia and I have done nothing to injure him."

"Of course," soothed Mélissande. "I simply think it a bit more graceful, more diplomatic, if we let the initiative for our first family meeting come from Gideon himself. Come help me compose a welcoming letter."

Mélissande drove the pony trap through the gate of Easton Priory and proceeded up the long wooded driveway at a smart clip. A week had elapsed since she had written to Lord Rochedale, and with each succeeding day Nick's face had grown a little more woebegone at their failure to receive a reply from his brother. Without telling either Nick or Cecilia her plan, Mélissande had decided to beard Gideon on her own. If, as seemed probable from his silence, the new heir had retained all his old animosities toward his siblings, then it was better for Mélissande, as a somewhat more detached observer, to explore his state of mind rather than to allow the impetuous Nick to blunder into a fiery quarrel with his brother.

As she continued up the driveway, Mélissande observed sadly the neglected state of the park. Downed trees and fallen branches had not been removed, the grass was unscythed, and there were deep ruts in the roadway, reflecting the lack of funds and the reduction in staff that had afflicted the estate since her stepfather's death. But her sadness faded away in a rush of nostalgia as she swung into the great forecourt and gazed with affection at the house that she considered her true home. Her memories of the ancient stone castle in Berry, which she had left at the age of ten, were now faded and dreamlike.

Built in the last days of the reign of Henry VIII, when the King had granted the abbey lands to the Maitland family, Easton Priory was an immense brick quadrangular mansion, its numerous rooms grouped around a spacious inner court. Off to the side were the remains of the original monastery, roofless now but still imposing in its ruined beauty. The old Tudor house looked hopelessly old-fashioned when compared with the Italianate elegance of Lord Haverford's palatial home at Fiesole. Mélissande loved every aspect of the place, however, from the bristling turrets, ornamental chimneys, and oriel windows of the exterior, to the splendors of the interior: the superb paneled wainscoting, the great marble fireplaces, the ornate plaster ceiling, and the sweep of the stone grand staircase with its ferocious heraldic lions atop the newel posts.

Lifting the heavy bronze door knocker, Mélissande had to wait for several minutes before the housekeeper, Mrs. Stedman, opened the door. It was a delay that would not have been tolerated during the lifetime of the late Marquess, but since his death the buxom, middle-aged housekeeper, who had been in service at the Priory for over thirty years, had been caring for the house with only a skeleton staff of maids. Devoted to the first lady Rochedale, Mrs. Stedman had also developed a fondness for the children of the Marquess's second wife, and especially for Mélissande, whose mother had been totally uninterested in the details of domestic management. From the time Mélissande entered her mid-teens, Jeanne-Marie had largely given over the direction of the household to her elder daughter. During her past year's exile in the Dower House, Mélissande had frequently visited the housekeeper at the Priory.

"Miss Mélissande! How nice to see you." Mrs. Stedman's pleasant, open face displayed a quick delight at Mélissande's arrival, but she also seemed uncharacteristically flustered. "Perhaps—would you care to have a cup of tea with me?"

"I'd like very much to have tea with you, and a long, cozy chat, too," replied Mélissande, stepping into the vastness of the two-story Great Hall. "But first I'd like to see Lord Rochedale. Will you announce me, please?"

"I'm so sorry to tell you this, but his lordship isn't seeing anyone. Since he returned home, I've been obliged to turn away all visitors. I scarcely knew what to say yesterday to Lord Haverford. It seemed very wrong, somehow, to refuse entry to the Lord Lieutenant of the county."

Mélissande lifted an inquiring eyebrow. "Is his lordship ill, then?"

"Well, no, not to say ill, exactly."

Mélissande read the combination of embarrassment and worry in the housekeeper's face and asked, "Has Lord Rochedale been drinking?"

"Well, Miss Mélissande, now that you ask me right out—mind, I should never have mentioned it to you *without* your asking—his lordship's been dipping very deep. Not just a bottle of port after dinner. No, his lordship starts drinking when he arises in the morning, and by evening, most days, he's half seas over. It's none of my affair, I suppose, and it's not that his lordship turns quarrelsome or ugly, but... Miss Mélissande, I remember so well the

clear-eyed, handsome boy that he was before—well, before
all the troubles, you know—and sometimes I wonder if his
lordship is really that boy grown up.''

"I must see him. Where is he, in his bedchamber?"

"No, he's in the library, but really, miss, I can't allow
you to go in there."

"I will take responsibility for the intrusion." Brushing
past Mrs. Stedman, Mélissande quickly climbed the great
romantic stone staircase to the second floor. She walked past
the tapestry-hung withdrawing room and the closed door of
the chapel and opened the door of the library, a finely
proportioned room with a marvelously intricate parquet floor
and an elaborate plaster frieze over the fireplace.

The seventh Marquess of Rochedale sat sprawled in a
wing chair beside a window, a bottle of wine on the stand at
his elbow. He was wearing leather breeches and top boots
and a rumpled, half-buttoned shirt without a cravat. His
gray eyes were bloodshot, and his pale, drawn face showed
plainly the effects of several days of hard drinking. Looking
up scowling as Mélissande entered the room, he barked,
"Confound it, I gave Mrs. Stedman strict orders that I was
not to be disturbed." He paused, his scowl fading into a
cynically amused smile. "So you've changed your mind
about sharing my company, my girl. How did you go about
finding me?"

Mélissande blinked as she emerged from the near-trance
into which she had been thrown by the realization that the
new Lord Rochedale was the man who had accosted her on
the road. Drawing a deep breath to help her regain her
composure, she said coolly, "I fear you are under a misap-
prehension, sir. I am your stepsister, Mélissande de Castellane."

"Mél . . ." The Marquess stared at her incredulously.
"The devil you are. Then pray tell me why I found my
stepsister—not a Maitland, of course, but well-born enough—
walking along a country road unattended, her garments,
such as they were, torn and disarranged looking as though

she had just spent the night under a bush, appearing more like a scullery maid than a lady of quality?"

"Indeed, sir, I am well aware of how unwisely I acted," retorted Mélissande. "Not only did I look a perfect guy, but I put myself in danger of receiving unwanted civilities from passing gentlemen who did not recognize my station in life."

The Marquess's affronted stare softened as he broke into an involuntary chuckle. "Touché, Miss de Castellane." He picked up the bottle to pour himself a glass of wine, withdrawing his attention from Mélissande so completely that she might have been invisible.

After a moment, not accustomed to being ignored, Mélissande asked pointedly, "May I sit down, sir?"

The Marquess shrugged. "As you wish."

Forcing down her temper, Mélissande sat in silence, studying Lord Rochedale's profile as he kept his face averted from her. With his severely handsome features and dark hair, he bore no resemblance to her stepfather or to Nick and Cecilia. His chiseled good looks must be a legacy from his mother's family, thought Mélissande as she noticed suddenly that her stepfather's favorite portrait of her mother, showing Jeanne-Marie in a beribboned polonaise gown with her hair piled high and elaborately curled and powdered, was missing from its place opposite the fireplace. In its place was a picture of a young woman in a charming *robe à l'anglaise,* her dark hair dressed close to her head and lightly powdered. Her resemblance to the new Lord Rochedale was unmistakable.

After a silence of several minutes, the Marquess turned his head to speak to Mélissande. "May I ask the reason for your visit to the Priory? As Mrs. Stedman must have indicated to you, I am not receiving company at present."

"As a member of your family, I've come to welcome you home. I trust you had a pleasant voyage, though I understand the weather is frequently stormy around the Cape."

"No more than usual. In any case, I am not subject to

mal de mer. Also, I broke the voyage with a stay of several weeks on the island of St. Helena. A delightful place, with a marvelous climate. I recommend it to you.''

''St. Helena sounds like a very pleasant place in which to recuperate from a wound,'' said Mélissande, motioning to his leg, which was stretched out on a footstool before his chair, and to the heavy cane leaning against the wall, convenient to his hand.

''I appreciate your kind thought, but I must tell you that my leg was perfectly well during my visit to St. Helena. My injury occurred after my return to England, when my colonel shot me. Quite understandable from his point of view, since I had departed from India in the company of his lovely young wife. Incidentally, she helped make the voyage, and our stay on St. Helena, all the more delightful. Her husband boarded the next available ship to England and actually arrived in London before we did, owing to our dalliance on the island. Naturally, he challenged me to a duel, during the course of which I did the gentlemanly thing and deloped. But Colonel Lee was unable to suppress his bloodthirsty instincts and put a bullet through my upper leg.''

Mélissande was quite aware that Rochedale, for some private reason of his own, was making a deliberate attempt to shock her. Refusing the bait, she said calmly, ''I can readily understand how such an experience would make your life in the regiment very uncomfortable.''

The Marquess poured himself another glass of wine. ''So it would have done, undoubtedly, if I had remained in the regiment. I am now a civilian again, however. The army didn't take kindly to my romantic misadventures, on the grounds that they were rather too public, and requested my resignation—which is really why I am having the pleasure of talking to you here, Miss de Castellane. You see, after the duel, London society as a whole received me with as little warmth as the powers that be at the Horse Guards. Take a valuable piece of advice, my dear, and don't commit adultery unless you can do so discreetly. So, spurned by society, I turned to gambling, only to discover when I had exhausted my own meager purse that no more funds were available. I presume you are even more aware than I am that my late papa shockingly mismanaged his affairs. My solicitor in London informed me that I could wring no cash out of the estate, and not even the seediest cent-per-cent would advance me any money on my dubious prospects. Now, I don't play if I can't pay—about the only virtue I can claim from a thoroughly misspent life—so there was nothing for it but to retire to my ancestral estates and wait for the next rents to fall due.''

More conscious than ever that Rochedale was attempting to goad her into a quarrel, Mélissande replied, ''Yes, I know very well that my late stepfather lived beyond his income. I . . . my main reason for coming here today bears on that situation. I believe your bailiff, Mr. Morris, wrote to inform you that Nicholas would like to succeed Mr. Morris and eventually to improve the estate by using better farming methods. Nick wants to try a new crop, Swedish turnips, for example, to make a start in scientific breeding of livestock. . . .''

There was a hard edge to the Marquess's voice as he interrupted her. ''I received the letter and wrote back instructing Morris to tell my brother that I wanted no part in Swedish turnips or—what was it?—Southdown sheep.''

''Perhaps Mr. Morris didn't express himself very clearly. My stepfather had fully approved these changes, and he was eager to have Nick succeed Mr. Morris. Nick firmly believes that the new methods would increase the productivity and hence the income of the estate, which could work for the advantage of all of us. It may not have come to your attention yet, but the small sums left to Nick and Cecilia and to me in your father's will have not yet been paid, and . . .''

Rochedale raised his hand to cut her off. ''Allow *me* to express myself clearly: I have no interest in my late father's plans for Nicholas—or for Cecilia and you, for that matter—

and no interest in Easton Priory itself. Actually, I'm planning to sell the property. I understand that land values are very high these days. I will realize what money I can after paying off my papa's ruinous mortgages and then move on to greener pastures. Canada, perhaps. Or I might go to the Orient and become a military advisor to some Eastern potentate. No one could deny that I have a good deal of experience to offer in that line."

Recoiling, Mélissande exclaimed, "But you can't sell Easton Priory. It's an entailed property."

"Entails can be broken."

"But not, I think, without the consent of your heir, who, unless you have recently married and fathered a son, happens to be my brother Nicholas. And I can assure you that Nick would never consent to bar the entail. Why, he loves every square inch of this place. The Priory has belonged to the Maitlands for over two hundred and fifty years, and even before the first Marquess was granted the abbey lands, the family had been landowners in the vicinity since the Conquest. It would be like cutting off a limb for Nick to consider allowing the estate to go out of the family. For that matter, I quite fail to understand, sir, why you do not share some of your brother's love and attachment for your ancestral lands."

Shooting Mélissande a contemptuous glance, Rochedale snapped, "My 'ancestral lands' have been neglected for years, while my father took every shilling he could squeeze out of the property and squandered his income on his various whims. The estate is so overmortgaged that I would have to realize a pretty sum just to pay off my father's debts. No, I want to dispose of the Priory with enough capital to begin a new life elsewhere. You see, my father destroyed any sentimental regard that I might have had for my lands and my ancestry when he brought his strumpet and her illegitimate brat to mount a death watch on my mother. I've often wondered why he bothered to stay in the village. With that elephant's hide of his, why didn't he install his mistress right here in the house so that he could receive the news of my mother's death all the more quickly? A crucial point, one would think. I believe my half brother's birth occurred less than a week after my mother died. If she had clung to life for only a few more days, Nicholas would have been born illegitimate, and would not have been eligible to succeed me.''

Mélissande flinched at the outburst of black rage that so belied the Marquess's cynically indifferent veneer. After a moment she said quietly, ''I make no excuses for Lord Rochedale's behavior, or that of my mother. However, it is very unjust of you to blame Nick for what his parents did. . . .''

His eyes blazing, the Marquess was about to reply to Mélissande when he stopped short, clamping his lips together and visibly willing his temper under control. ''My half brother's guilt, or lack of it, is immaterial. I expect him to join with me in barring the entail by participating in a medieval and mystifying legal masquerade known as 'fines and recoveries.' Actually, I'm told the process is really quite brief and simple.''

''Simple or not, Nick will never consent to give up his birthright.''

''Then he will have the empty satisfaction of being heir presumptive to a property from which he can never derive any material gain. He will have no position as bailiff, no opportunity to experiment with his new agricultural ideas, and, indeed, no access to the estate, because he will no longer be living in the vicinity. Consider this a formal notice to you and your half brother and half sister to vacate the Dower House.''

''But . . . my stepfather specified in his will that we be allowed to live at the Dower House until such time as we had established ourselves elsewhere.''

''So he did. But it was only a request. Since the Dower House is part of the entail, I am not legally bound.''

Dazed and angry, Mélissande drew a deep breath, determined not to reveal to Gideon Maitland how shocked she felt. "You may do as you like, sir. You'll find that you cannot blackmail Nick into joining with you in barring the entail. The three of us can manage very well without the Dower House. We'll rent a small house, in Hastings, perhaps, and simply wait you out. Because, until—or if—you marry and have issue, Nick remains your heir. Even if you marry and have a son, you will have to wait eighteen years for him to join with you in breaking the entail!"

His composure fully regained, Rochedale smiled mockingly. "And what will you live on, pray?"

"I have a small income of my own."

"Ah, yes, I recall hearing about the famous louis d'or that your doting grandmother sewed into your petticoats before you fled the revolutionaries. What was it—one hundred louis? Can you really support three people on the income from that sum?"

"There are also the bequests left to us in my stepfather's will."

Gideon Maitland's mocking smile deepened. "I'm perfectly familiar with those bequests. True to form, my wastrel father had no cash assets at his death. He did, however, leave a written request that I honor his intentions."

"I take it you have no plans to do so."

"That is correct. Not unless Nicholas consents to bar the entail. If he does so, I will pay your bequests from the proceeds of the sale of the estate. Now, I don't insist that he agree immediately. He will want some time to consider the proposal, and I will need time to find a suitable buyer. Shall we say one month? If, at that time, your brother does not agree, I will grant you two additional months in which to vacate the Dower House. On the other hand, if Nicholas joins with me in barring the entail, I will make it a condition of sale to the new owner that he allow you to occupy the Dower House until the spring."

"Your generosity astounds me. Fancy allowing us occupancy until the fine weather returns. I'm sure you would much prefer that we move out in the dead of winter. Doubtless you would delight in hurrying our departure by pitching our belongings into the snow!''

The Marquess grinned. ''My dear sister, what a melodramatic cast of mind you have. At a guess, I should say that you've been reading too many of Mr. 'Monk' Lewis's lurid romantic novels.'' Gideon poured himself another glass of wine. ''I've been forgetting my manners. Will you have some claret? Fortunately, there is still a fair-sized supply in the house. My late parent had at least one redeeming quality, it seems. He didn't neglect his wine cellar.''

It was obvious that he was intensely enjoying Mélissande's discomfiture. Suddenly her anger broke through the bonds of her usual quiet dignity. ''Pray keep your wine,'' she blazed. ''I do not wish to drink with a man who has forgotten all the instincts of a gentleman, much less those of a brother. I shall urge Nick *not* to agree to bar the entail, not to sell his birthright for a mess of potage.''

''Let us hope that your brother will seek advice from someone with a clearer head for figures than you possess. Mess of potage, you say? If I read my late parent's will correctly, he left the three of you the combined sum of nine thousand pounds. Presumably that amount would buy a great deal of potage. Whatever that is. My biblical education is somewhat sketchy.''

Meeting Gideon Maitland's assured, triumphant smile, Mélissande turned on her heel and strode out of the library before he could see the tears of angry frustration that were gathering in her eyes.

CHAPTER V

Returning to Easton after a short trip to Battle, the nearest town of any size, Mélissande halted the pony trap at the edge of the village green to watch a group of grammar school children as they drilled with sticks in earnest imitation of their elders in the Volunteers. The glorious weather was still holding, even though it was already early October, she reflected, and yet the long-feared attack by the French had not come. On a nearby tree a brightly colored poster, which she had not previously noticed, caught her eye, and she moved the pony trap closer to the tree for a better look. The crudely drawn poster depicted bloodstained, fang-toothed French soldiers in the act of burning the houses of a small village after massacring all the inhabitants, including a number of babes in arms. Mélissande shivered. Was there even a possibility that such a calamity could befall her adopted country?

She looked up as Lady Haverford's stylish landau came abreast of the pony trap and halted.

"Mélissande, how lovely to see you." Aurore's face wore a pleased smile as she greeted her young cousin, but there was an underlying note of constraint in her voice. "Are you arriving or departing?"

"Good afternoon, Aurore. I've just come from seeing my stepfather's solicitor in Battle."

"Would that be about Lord Rochedale's will?" inquired Aurore, shrewdly reading the signs of strain in Mélissande's face. "My dear, is Gideon Maitland being difficult?"

"Yes," said Mélissande shortly. "You were quite right, you know. Lord Rochedale appears to resent Nick and Cecilia and me as much as he ever did."

"*Ma mie,* I'm so sorry. I would much prefer not to be right." Lady Haverford leaned across the door of the landau to place a sympathetic hand on Mélissande's arm. She added wistfully, "I've missed seeing you this past week or so. Can't we smooth over our little disagreement? Won't you come see me one day soon?"

"I would be delighted to do that, provided that I may bring Cecilia."

Aurore squeezed her hands together in distress. "*Chérie,* I simply cannot welcome Cecilia to my home. You know that I don't dislike your sister. It's just that I cannot countenance any relationship on her part with Stephen."

"How did Stephen react when you forbade him to see Cecilia?" asked Mélissande curiously.

"Oh, as to that . . . He *is* of age, you know. One cannot order him to heel like a naughty schoolboy! My husband and I have made known our views to him, but we feel that our best course at present is to—well, ignore the situation. Not to refine on it overly much. We are confident that Stephen will eventually see where his best interests lie and drop the connection, especially if—pray don't take offense, my dear—especially if you join your efforts to ours. If you will just talk to Cecilia . . ."

Mélissande eyed Lady Haverford coldly. "I shall certainly warn Cecilia again about the danger of friendship with a man whose family is treating her like a pariah."

Looking uncomfortable, but stubbornly maintaining her position, the Countess replied, "Please do that. Because, despite all my talk, all my advice, I believe that Stephen and Cecilia are seeing each other secretly. My housekeeper spotted Cecilia a few days ago as she left your pony trap at the rear of the Easton Arms and stepped into Stephen's curricle."

"If Cecilia is making secret assignations with Stephen, I shall certainly do my best to put a stop to it. Was that all you cared to discuss with me, Aurore? If so, I'll bid you *au revoir*." As she said her dignified good-bye to Lady Haverford, however, and drove away, Mélissande remembered the incident of just over a week ago, when Cecilia, secretive and excited, had insisted on going alone to the village to buy some thread. Mélissande had suspected at the time that her sister's errand was a blind to conceal a meeting with Stephen. Now she knew her suspicion was correct. Worse, the meeting had been spotted by the Haverford housekeeper, and very likely by half the population of Easton. At this rate, Mélissande thought with a troubled frown, it would not be long before the entire county branded Cecilia as Stephen Lacey's doxy.

A short distance from the turnoff for the Dower House, Mélissande met Stephen in his curricle coming from the opposite direction. He smiled and waved as he came abreast of her, but did not stop, rather to her surprise. They had always been on good terms with each other, and usually he liked nothing better than a friendly chat. The mystery was explained after she turned into the Dower House driveway and saw Cecilia about to enter the house. A little later, having driven the pony cart around to the stables, Mélissande found Cecilia in the morning room.

"There you are, Sandy. Back from Battle already? I've asked Sally to make me some chocolate. Would you like some?"

"Yes, thank you. And what have you been doing all day?"

"On, nothing very interesting. I did some embroidery, and I dusted the drawing room for Sally. Oh, and I took a long walk."

"You also went for a drive in Stephen Lacey's curricle, did you not? Did you intend to tell me about that?"

Cecilia flushed. "How did you . . . ? No, I wasn't going to tell you, because you don't approve of my seeing Stephen, and I have no wish to quarrel with you. But I wasn't doing anything wrong, and I don't care to listen to another of your lectures about losing my reputation. Sandy, I'm of age now, and you can't choose my friends for me."

Mélissande gazed at her sister's mutinous profile in dismay. "Cecilia! Is that how I appear to you? Like a dragon governess, always finding fault, always finding new ways to interfere in your life?"

"Well—sometimes you do sound a bit like old Miss Roseberry at the academy. According to her, I rarely did anything right."

Mélissande sighed. "I'm sorry. Of course I don't have the right to dictate what your conduct should be, and I'll try to do better. It's just that I want so much for you to be happy, and I'm so afraid that your friendship with Stephen will bring you nothing but unhappiness."

"There you go again, Sandy," flared Cecilia. "Can you never find a kind word to say about Stephen?"

Mélissande shrugged, feeling baffled and helpless, and a strained silence between the sisters was broken only when Nick entered the room, gun over his shoulder and his favorite dog at his heels.

In the week since he had received his brother Gideon's ultimatum about breaking the entail of the estate, Nick had retreated into himself, spending his solitary days in long, aimless walks about the countryside. Ostensibly he was hunting, but Mélissande suspected that his musket rarely left his shoulder. Today, however, he had found game. As the maid, Sally, entered the room with their chocolate, Nick handed her his single game bag, saying, "Better luck today, as you can see. I got a nice brace of wood pigeon in the copse behind Mr. Morris's house." As he watched Mélissande pour his chocolate, he asked casually, "Was it any good, going to see Papa's solicitor?"

"No, it was just as I thought. The solicitor says that your father's bequests to us—and his permission for us to live here at the Dower House—have no basis in law. Gideon is under no obligation to honor Papa's wishes."

Despite his best efforts to maintain a stoic calm, Nick's face fell. Mélissande hastened to add, "The news isn't all bad. The solicitor also says that, without your consent, Gideon stands no chance of barring the entail. If you choose not to give in to your brother, I—and Cecilia, too, I'm sure—will back you all the way."

"Oh, yes, Nick, you mustn't sign away your rights to the Priory," cried Cecilia. "The Maitlands have been the principal family in this area since the Conquest." She paused, flushing. "I hate the idea of leaving my home and all my friends, but of course the situation is much worse for you, Nick. You *really* belong here."

"Don't talk fustian, Cecy. You belong here as much as I do."

Cecilia shook her head. "Do you remember Lucy, the red-haired nursemaid who came to the Priory when I was about eight years old? When she first arrived, she addressed me as 'Lady Cecilia.' Then, one day, I overheard Nanny explaining to Lucy why she must call me simply 'Miss Cecilia,' or, later, 'Miss Maitland.' That was when I realized for the first time that my birth was different from yours, Nick, and that I wasn't entitled to the name of Maitland except by courtesy. But still, I love Easton Priory as much as you do, and I think it would break my heart to leave."

Putting his arm around his sister, Nick said softly, "I know, Cecy. I feel the same way. Nonetheless, I can't let my actions be ruled by sentiment. My refusal of Gideon's demands won't keep us in Easton. He will simply turn us out of the Dower House, and then how and where would we live? No, I can't let you and Sandy suffer for my stubbornness.

I'll go see Gideon this evening to tell him that I will join in barring the entail.''

"You mustn't give up the Priory for our sakes," protested Mélissande. "Look, we can manage without any income from the estate. We'll take a small house nearby, in Battle perhaps, or even Hastings. I'll give lessons in French and music, and Cecilia might find temporary employment as a companion. And you, Nick, with your experience in farming, may easily find employment on some large estate."

"We've lived too long on your income," said Nick shortly. "I won't do it any longer." Cecilia chimed in quietly, "Nor will I."

Disappointed, but proud, too, of this show of independence by Nick and Cecilia, Mélissande urged, "You needn't strike your colors immediately, Nick. Your brother gave you a month's grace. Take it, if only to make him stew in his own juices. It will do him good," she added, thinking darkly of Gideon's monstrous behavior and wishing desperately that she could think of some way to foil his selfish plans.

Nick shrugged. "Very well, though I can't think what good a delay will do." He excused himself, saying that he was going for a long ride and later to the village for evening drill with the Volunteers. A listless-looking Cecilia complained of a headache and went to her bedchamber, leaving Mélissande alone to sip her lukewarm chocolate and reflect on her little family's uncomfortable circumstances. She welcomed the diversion when the maid, Sally, ushered Mrs. Stedman into the room. The housekeeper's normally sunny face seemed clouded with worry. After Sally had left the room, Mélissande said, "Is something troubling you, Mrs. Stedman? Can I help?"

"Well, Miss de Castellane, I don't like to come bearing tales, and that's a fact, but I just didn't know what to do. It's his lordship, you see. Two days ago, a friend of his, a Mr. Manners, an officer in his lordship's regiment, I believe, came down from London to see him. Mr. Manners brought two ladies with him. Well, ladies is what *he* called them. I say they are nothing but low females, with painted faces and bodices cut so low that you would blush to see them. His lordship said as how I should go off for a short holiday; he and his guests could manage for themselves in my absence, if I left a bit of food for cold suppers. So off I went to stay with my sister. You may recall that she was widowed last year and came to live in the village." Mrs. Stedman's voice trailed away, and she cast her eyes down, fidgeting with the strings of her bonnet. After a moment, she burst out, "I know it's not my place, with his lordship telling me to leave and all, but I do think as someone should look into it."

Mélissande said, "I don't think I understand. Look into what?"

"I can't say exactly. It's just . . . I'm afeared that something dreadful may have happened to his lordship. Jordan— he's the head groom, you know; well, our only groom now that we've had to cut down on the establishment—came to see me last night. Fair worried he was. He'd been walking past the front of the house when he heard shots, coming from one of the upper floors, he thought it was. He said it sounded like a pair of armies shooting at each other, and he heard screams, too, as if someone was hurt mortal bad. So today, more than a bit worried myself, I went up to the house. I just walked into the Great Hall—I didn't like to go any farther into the house, you understand. Not a soul was stirring, it was like the silence of the grave. I thought, what if his lordship has been murdered in his bed? It gave me a real turn, I can tell you, and I came straight here to see you. Miss Mélissande will know what to do, I told myself."

Mélissande reflected scornfully that Gideon and his friend, having caroused the night away with their low female friends, were now probably sleeping off a monumental drunk. Certainly Gideon would not welcome an investigation into his personal affairs, even if it was occasioned by genuine concern. Nevertheless, the groom's story that he had heard repeated gunfire in the interior of the Priory was disquieting. Taking a sudden resolve, Mélissande said, "Would you like me to return to the house with you, Mrs. Stedman?" The housekeeper's response was heartfelt.

When Mélissande and Mrs. Stedman arrived at the Priory, it was already late afternoon, but there was no sight or sound of any of the occupants as they entered the Great Hall. "Miss Mélissande, look," whispered the housekeeper, pointing to an ancient suit of armor that had been moved from its position near the fireplace and thrown violently to the floor. The visored helmet had become detached from the suit and was lying in a corner, impaled by one of the two enormous pikes that normally were affixed to the wall. Overturned on its side was a long trestle table, a vestige of Tudor times when the hall had served as a dining area for the servants. "What can have been happening here?" murmured a wide-eyed Mrs. Stedman.

Mélissande spun on her heel and sprinted up the stairs to the second floor. Following behind her, Mrs. Stedman walked into the withdrawing room. "Well, I never," she exclaimed angrily as she surveyed the havoc that had been wrought in the spacious room. A large platter, holding the remnants of a ham, was upside down in the center of the room, leaving an ugly stain on the faded but still lovely Aubusson carpet. The armrest of one of the massive carved chairs was hanging in splinters, a centuries-old tapestry had been pulled down from the wall, and scattered about the room were numerous empty wine and gin bottles.

Growing increasingly apprehensive, Mélissande returned to the corridor. She briefly glanced into several of the other rooms on the floor, the chapel, the dining room, the library, but they were empty. Then, feeling suddenly cold and clammy, she noticed dark red blotches on the stone steps leading to the third floor. Forcing her reluctant limbs to move, she slowly mounted the staircase.

On the landing, she paused. The doors of all the state rooms on this floor were closed except for those of the Long Gallery, which ran the length of the front of the house.

Stepping into the immense room, flooded with light from its numerous beautiful oriel windows, Mélissande at first could see nothing amiss. Then, from beneath one of the windows, a slight movement caught her eye. Sprawled on the floor beneath the window was a man whose white marcella waistcoat was stained with crimson. Mélissande hurried over to the man. As she knelt beside him, he opened his bloodshot eyes to focus blurrily on her, and a blast of liquor-filled breath informed her that he was not injured, merely very drunk. The red blotches on his waistcoat were port wine stains, spilled from the bottle which lay beside his relaxed hand.

Wincing as the light struck his eyes, the man closed them again, putting his hand to his head with a groan. After a moment, opening one eye to a narrow slit, he muttered, "Hallo, lovely. Be a good girl and fetch me another bottle of wine. My head feels as though a blacksmith were shoeing horses inside it. The hair of the dog that bit will make me feel much more the thing."

Rising, Mélissande looked down at him coldly. "I think you have had more than enough to drink, sir."

At the sound of her voice, the man blinked several times and sat up. He fixed his eyes on her with some difficulty, exclaiming, "You're not Bess, or Lottie either." Essaying a flirtatious grin, he added, "You're a sweet little morsel, I must say. As pretty a wench as I've seen in ages. What's your name, love?"

"I am Mélissande de Castellane, Lord Rochedale's sister." Mélissande jerked her foot away from the man's questing hand, which had fastened on her ankle. "To be more accurate, I am Lord Rochedale's stepsister."

His mouth gaping, the man shook his head, as if to clear his ears. He jumped to his feet, suppressing another groan at the movement. "I beg your pardon, ma'am. I had no idea you were in the house. Matter of fact, Gideon gave me to believe that he lived here alone. But no matter. Allow me to introduce myself. My name is Jack Manners. I served with Gideon in the Nineteenth Light Dragoons.''

At second glance, now that he was on his feet and awake, Mr. Manners appeared to be a pleasant-faced man of medium height, about thirty years of age. ''I'm just down from London for a short visit with my old comrade in arms. We'll certainly miss Gideon in the Nineteenth Dragoons,'' he was saying, when Mélissande's attention was distracted by a flurry of movement halfway down the long room. A young woman, who had apparently been sleeping in a chair near the fireplace, sat up with an audible yawn. Near her, stretched out on the floor, was another woman who was also showing signs of awakening. Turning his head to follow Mélissande's gaze, Mr. Manners smothered a curse beneath his breath and turned an embarrassed red. He was spared the necessity of a comment when Mrs. Stedman, who had followed Mélissande into the room, wailed loudly, ''Look at the portraits, miss! Their eyes are gone!''

Startled, Mélissande glanced at the long row of ancestral paintings that lined the wall opposite the windows. There were holes in the faces of many of the portraits. Some, as Mrs. Stedman had noted, had no eyes.

''*Mon Dieu*, Mr. Manners, what has been happening here?'' demanded Mélissande. ''Who has defaced these Maitland family portraits?''

Mr. Manners gazed at the paintings with an expression of dawning horror. ''Good God, it's true, then. I thought I'd dreamed it. You see, Gideon and I shot the cat last night, and I don't remember very clearly what happened after the second bottle of port. I do recall that we removed the pikes from the wall of the Great Hall and had a jousting match with that suit of armor, pretending, you know, that he was one of those old knights. Gideon had a direct hit on the old fellow, knocking off his helmet, so then I remember saying to Gideon that he might be the best pike thrower in the Nineteenth Light Dragoons, but *I* was the best shot, and *he* said, 'Prove it.' The next thing I knew, we were up here in the Long Gallery blasting away at the portraits. Until this minute, though, I really hoped it was a dream, or perhaps a nightmare.''

One of the strange young women now wandered up to Mr. Manners, laying a familiar hand on his sleeve. "Well, Jack, ye're awake, too, I see." The red-haired girl was pretty in a bold, buxom sort of way, and would have been even more attractive if she had not painted her face so heavily and if her overtight, overskimpy satin dress had been cleaner. She looked past Mr. Manners to Mrs. Stedman, saying haughtily, "Aren't ye the 'ousekeeper? Me and my friend Lottie, we fancy something to eat. See to it, will ye?"

The red-haired girl turned her attention to Mélissande. "And 'oo do we 'ave 'ere, Jack? Ye didn't say as 'ow ye'd invited another friend." She circled Mélissande slowly, examining her with a critical eye. "Can't say as I think much o' yer taste, Jack, and I'll warrant that 'is lordship won't, either. 'E likes a girl what's a proper armful, 'e does, not a scrawny thing like this one. And those clothes!" The girl fingered the material of Mélissande's pelisse, adding disdainfully, "About as much style as a chambermaid in a country inn!"

Shaking off the intruding hand, Mélissande stepped back with a withering stare.

The redhead bridled. "Don't look down yer nose at me, my girl, as if you was too good for the likes o' us." She turned her head to call to her friend, a brunette with an even more opulent figure, who now seemed fully awake. "Come 'ere, Lottie. Cast yer winkers at this fine lady. Wants us to think she's a duchess, or summat just as grand, I'll be bound."

Recovering from a momentary shock, Mr. Manners expostulated, "See here, Bess, you really mustn't talk in that familiar way to Miss de Castellane. She's Lord Rochedale's sister."

"Don't try to gammon me," snorted Bess. "If this bit of muslin is a lord's sister, then I'm a gentry mort."

As Mr. Manners stared at Mélissande in anguished embarrassment, the girl Lottie, sauntering over to join her friend, stumbled when her foot struck a small object, sending it spinning across the polished parquet floor. Picking it up, Bess gazed at the pistol with great interest. "This loaded, Jack? Didn't get my chance to shoot last night, y'know." Holding the gun at arm's length, she closed her eyes and pulled the trigger. "Cor!" she exclaimed in mingled dismay and excitement as the bullet, missing Mélissande's head by a hairbreadth, blew a hole in the lovely paneling of the Long Gallery.

Shaken and momentarily speechless at her near escape from death, Mélissande was suddenly seized with a blind fury at the mindless destruction being inflicted on Nick and Cecilia's ancient home by their brother's vulgar friends. Giving no thought to the question of her authority, she whirled on Bess, exclaiming, "Since you and your doxy friend seem not to know how to comport yourselves in a gentleman's house, I must ask you to go elsewhere. Mrs. Stedman, will you please go to the stables and order Jordan to put the horses to the landau. He will be taking these— ladies—to Battle, where they can obtain seats on the stage-coach back to London."

Bess opened her mouth in a screech of rage. " 'Oo do ye think ye are, ordering me and Lottie out of the 'ouse?"

A little desperately, Mr. Manners pleaded, "By Jove, Bess, watch your tongue. I told you this lady is Lord Rochedale's sister."

"I don't care what she calls 'erself. Ye invited us down 'ere for a week, Jack, and 'is lordship has promised to take us to the seashore tomorrow. No, no, *we* ain't leaving, ain't that right, Lottie?" Bess moved menacingly toward Mélissande. "*Ye* can leave, Miss 'Igh and Mighty."

"Must I call the groom to put you out?" asked Mélissande icily, holding her ground.

"Threatening us, are ye? I'll show ye what's what, I will." Bess advanced on Mélissande with an upraised hand. Without pausing for reflection, Mélissande put out both hands in a powerful shove that sent Bess sprawling. In a matter of seconds, Mr. Manners was in the middle of a wild melee, desperately trying to protect Mélissande from a screaming, finger-raking Bess, who was soon joined by a vengeful and equally vociferous Lottie.

"In the name of all that's holy, what is going on here? I could hear you all the way from the first floor," thundered a voice behind the combatants, who broke off in surprise, turning to see Gideon at the door of the Long Gallery. Shoeless, wearing only a much-rumpled shirt and breeches, his hair tousled and his face pale and drawn, the Marquess bore all the signs of a man who had been sleeping off a long night of drinking. Leaning heavily on his cane, he advanced into the room. He stared coldly at Mélissande. "May I ask why you are here? I am not aware that I invited you."

"I am delighted to tell you why I am here, my lord. I was informed that shots had been heard in the house, and I naturally became alarmed for your safety. I considered it my duty to look into the matter. When I discovered this vandalism"—Mélissande pointed to the ravaged portraits and felt a grim pleasure at the involuntary expression of shock that crossed the Marquess's face—"and when, moreover, this lady—Bess, I believe her name is—found a loaded pistol and resumed her target practice, narrowly missing my person, why then, my lord, I decided to rid the premises of your female guests. I had just ordered them out of the house when they attacked me."

Gideon turned his cold gaze on Bess and Lottie, who shifted their feet in uneasy silence. Mr. Manners, red with embarrassment, said quickly, "Come with me, ladies. Lord Rochedale wishes to have a private conversation with his sister."

Waiting until the trio had left the room, Rochedale barked, "I'll thank you in future not to meddle in my affairs, Miss de Castellane. I trust you don't deny my right to invite whomever I choose to be guests in my house?''

"Not at all. I have no interest whatever in your social activities. Unless, of course, the behavior of your guests threatens the destruction of my brother's heritage.''

"That 'heritage' need not weigh on your mind much longer, if your young brother would stop acting like a paperskull.''

Mélissande bit back an impulse to tell Gideon that Nick had already made his decision to break the entail. She said defiantly, "Unless—or until—Nick decides to join with you in barring the entail, Easton Priory *is* his heritage, every aspect of which he treasures. That suit of armor in the Great Hall, for example, which you and Mr. Manners tried to demolish last night. It was worn by Giles Maitland at the battle of Agincourt. Or take this lovely room, preserved almost unchanged since the visit of Queen Elizabeth after the Armada, until you and your friends engaged in target practice here. Then there is the tapestry that was ripped off the wall of the withdrawing room on the first floor. It was brought from Bruges nearly four hundred years ago by one of your ancestors who was an envoy at the court of Flanders.''

Mélissande glared at the Marquess. "My blood fairly boils when I think how Nick, if he were the owner of the Priory, would protect and cherish this wonderful old house and everything in it, while all you see fit to do, my lord, is to drown yourself in a sea of spirits. In your childish resentment of your father and stepmother, you seem bent on destroying everything that the Maitland family ever stood for.''

A muscle twitched in Gideon's cheek. "Spare me your old-fashioned sentimentality,'' he rasped. "And your opinion of my character is not of the slightest interest to me, either. What's more, I find *your* passionate devotion to Easton Priory singularly difficult to understand. *You* aren't a Maitland!'' He paused, his eyes glazing over in sudden pain. "My head,'' he muttered, sitting down abruptly.

Spying a bottle next to his chair, he picked it up, then threw it away in disgust when he saw that it was empty.

Her lip curling, Mélissande glanced around the room. She spotted a half-filled bottle of port on the mantel and handed it to Gideon. "There, my lord. I believe it is called the hair of the dog that bit. As for my devotion to Easton Priory, yes, I do revere the long service of my brother's family to crown and country, which so resembles that of my own family in France. It is the kind of devotion I pray you will come to feel before you destroy the Priory in a drunken orgy or dispose of it to strangers."

She strode out of the Long Gallery, slamming the doors shut with a force calculated to increase the discomfort of the Marquess's aching head.

CHAPTER VI

"And you will supervise the decoration of the church, Miss de Castellane? Then I believe that takes care of everything," said Mrs. Garrett happily. She and Mélissande were sitting in the vicarage parlor, making the final arrangements for the annual harvest festival. Since Jeanne-Marie had never shown much interest in village matters, Mélissande had become Mrs. Garrett's strong right arm in the parish by default through the years.

"I've been so distracted by this constant worry about a French invasion that I've found it difficult to keep my mind on the details of the festival this year," sighed Mrs. Garrett. "For the first time in my life I am not sleeping well. Many a night I'm obliged to read myself to sleep." She brightened. "My dear, I know you don't care for Mrs. Radcliffe's books, or those of 'Monk' Lewis, but I really do think you might like *Wieland*. It was written by an American. I think you would be interested in the descriptions of a place called—what was it again—oh, yes, Pennsylvania."

Her eyes twinkling, Mélissande asked, "Is it a travel book, Mrs. Garrett? Not a story of the supernatural?" She had always thought it amusing that the quiet vicar's wife

was so fond of bloodcurdling novels, which she was careful
to hide from her pious husband.

"Well, of course, there are mysterious noises, and eventually they drive Mr. Wieland quite mad, and he kills his
wife and children and is clapped into an asylum for the
insane. . . ." Mrs. Garrett shivered with delight.

"It sounds terrifying, just the thing to put one to sleep,"
said Mélissande with a laugh. Sobering, she added, "I have
some news for you and your husband, and I would ask you
to keep it confidential for the present." Briefly, she told
Mrs. Garrett about Gideon's plans to sell the estate. The
vicar's wife was greatly shocked, but Mélissande rather
ruthlessly extricated herself from a discussion of the details
and soon left the vicarage.

Stephen Lacey was riding by as she closed the gate of the
manse behind her. Dismounting, he removed his beaver hat
with a bow. "A pleasure to see you, Miss de Castellane.
And how is Cecilia?"

Mélissande said coolly, "Cecilia is well, thank you. But
I'm sure you are aware of that. You see her quite frequently,
do you not?"

Stephen had the grace to look mildly embarrassed. "Matter of fact, yes, we do encounter each other from time to
time. Easton is a very small place."

"Since I am aware of your mother's strong disapproval of
your friendship with Cecilia," said Mélissande dryly, "I
must assume that all these encounters are purely coincidental."

"Oh—quite so. Perhaps at some later time we might
discuss the matter. But for the moment . . . Miss de Castellane, I
must tell you that I'm a bit worried about Lord Nicholas. I
had thought to mention my concern to Cecilia. If I chanced
to meet her, that is. But then I reflected that it might be
better to bring the problem to you."

"You're concerned about Nick?" asked Mélissande in
surprise.

"Well, you see, it's the Volunteers," explained Stephen.
"Nick hasn't attended a drill for the past two weeks. Since

we've just received word that at any moment, perhaps at the beginning of November, the Volunteers will be ordered to turn out in successive reliefs for permanent duty with the regulars, I really must know if Nick means to continue with us.''

Mélissande felt a twinge of worry. Since he had made his decision to relinquish his rights to the estate, Nick had retreated deep within himself. This withdrawal had become even more pronounced with the dispatch, several days ago, of a short, stiff note to Gideon informing his brother that Nick would join in barring the entail. Mélissande had assumed that Nick needed time and solitude to adjust to the loss of his dreams and to his altered plans for the future, but she had not known that he was missing drills with the Volunteers. To her, this dereliction was almost beyond comprehension, for Nick had been the first and most fiercely patriotic officer to join the Easton company. The fact that he would be leaving the area in a few short months would surely not have dampened his enthusiasm, especially at this time when invasion fears had never been higher; the local magistrates were now sitting daily, issuing orders to cover every possible emergency, from the regulation of alehouses to the registration of enemy aliens.

"Nick has been preoccupied with—with personal matters of late, Mr. Lacey.''

"Yes, I believe Cecilia did mention something of the sort,'' rejoined Stephen hastily. "None of my affair, naturally. But, if you would be so kind, you might just tell Nick that we miss him in the company.'' Bowing, he remounted and rode off. Meeting Phoebe Wright a short distance down the street, he touched a finger to his hat, displaying, to Mélissande's distressed eye, just the proper amount of condescension to a mere farmer's daughter.

"Could I have a word with you, Miss Mélissande?'' called Phoebe. She hurried up, saying, "I'm so glad to see you. I had planned to come to the Dower House today after I finished my shopping.'' She paused, her eyes downcast. "I'd like to know . . . could you tell me if Nick is angry with us? He hasn't come to the farm in such a long time. Father wonders if perhaps he's done something to offend Nick. Papa's new chaff-cutting machine for cattle fodder has just been delivered, and Nick was so eager to see it, and I did just wonder if I should send a message to the Dower House about it, but . . .''

Listening to Phoebe's disjointed remarks, Mélissande wondered if the girl was at all conscious of how transparently she wore her heart on her sleeve. "I'm quite certain that Nick isn't angry with you, or Mr. Wright, either," Mélissande said reassuringly. "He hasn't been very happy of late, however. Just give him time; he'll soon be himself again."

As she drove the pony cart back to the Dower House, Mélissande continued to worry about Nick. If he had been avoiding the company of the Volunteers and the Wright family, then how had he been spending his time? Uneasily, she recalled a recent incident that had made no impression on her at the time. Several days previously, she had been in the kitchen garden, picking the morello cherries that were still clinging to the tree even though it was almost November, when she heard voices from the direction of the stables. Peering over the garden wall, she had caught a brief glimpse of Nick disappearing into the stables with several young men from the village. Mélissande had been mildly surprised to find Nick in such company. When he was much younger, he had been in the habit of slipping away from his tutor to play with the boys from the village grammar school, but her stepfather had discouraged such friendships as unsuitable for the younger son of a marquess, and in recent years Nick had chosen his cronies from the ranks of the county gentry. Was this revival of a childhood association still another problem she must face? Mélissande sighed, thinking back to the time, before the deaths of her mother and stepfather, when life had seemed so idyllic in comparison with those last terror-filled days during the summer of 1789 in the French countryside.

Her thoughts were interrupted when Gideon emerged on horseback from a woodland path into the roadway just ahead of her. "Good afternoon, Lord Rochedale," she said composedly, reining in the pony cart. He lifted his hat a scant half an inch from his head, and for a moment she suspected that he would ride on without speaking. Apparently thinking better of it, he rode over to her, returning her greeting curtly. Mélissande thought it probable that he had embarrassingly vivid memories of their last meeting in the Long Gallery at the Priory.

"Are your guests still with you, sir?" she asked with an air of innocent interest.

"They are not," he said shortly. His color was bad, and he looked tired. Mélissande guessed that he was spending his evenings in solitary drinking bouts.

"I'm happy to see that your injured leg must be greatly improved, since you are riding," she continued with a deliberately exaggerated politeness meant to contrast with his surly manner.

"Much improved. Thank you," he added grudgingly. "I must congratulate your brother on his acceptance of the inevitable. You may tell him that I will be contacting him in the near future to discuss the legal steps necessary to bar the entail."

Mélissande felt her temper rising. "I think you should know that Nick had no thought for himself when he gave in to your demands. He was concerned only about my welfare and Cecilia's."

"You prefer to think highly of your brother, of course. For myself, I've found that sentiment plays a poor second to a full purse. Like any sensible young man, Nicholas would far rather live comfortably than starve genteelly."

"You betray your ignorance, my lord. If you knew Nick even a fraction as well as I know him, you wouldn't allow yourself to say such things. But then, you don't know him at all. You haven't seen him since he was little more than a babe in arms."

"That is the way I prefer it. I haven't the slightest desire to know my young half brother. Good day to you, Miss de Castellane."

Gazing after the Marquess as he galloped away, Mélissande thought resentfully that she had never met a more odious man, or one who so thoroughly deserved to be set down. Moments later, as she drove the pony cart around a sharp curve near the entrance to the road leading to the Dower House, she sawed frantically on the reins to prevent the wheels of the cart from crushing Gideon's limp body in the middle of the roadway. Reins trailing, his horse was grazing unconcernedly on the verge.

Scrambling down from the cart, Mélissande rushed to Gideon. Her heart sank as she discovered that he was unconscious, with blood streaming from a deep gash on his temple. His left leg, the leg injured in the duel with his colonel, lay twisted ominously beneath him. Frantically she attempted to staunch the flow of blood from his wound by pressing her folded handkerchief to his head, but he remained unconscious, his face marked with a deathlike pallor. Kneeling helplessly beside him, she felt a numbing chill creeping over her as she faced the possibility that Gideon might be dying. Her heart contracted painfully. She had known him for only a few short weeks, they had rarely exchanged a civil word, but she thought, stunned, that if Gideon died, a part of her would die, too.

The sound of wheels on the roadway aroused her from her dark imaginings. In a moment a large farm wagon driven by one of Mr. Wright's laborers appeared around the curve. Phoebe jumped down from her seat beside the driver and ran to Mélissande, who exclaimed in a shaking voice, "Oh, Phoebe, I'm so glad you've come. Lord Rochedale is badly hurt. Will you take him to the Dower House in your wagon?"

Phoebe glanced curiously at Mélissande's agitated face, normally so composed, but said merely, "I'm more than happy to help, but shouldn't we take his lordship to Dr. Morley's house in Easton?''

"No, no, the Dower House is just a few yards from here, and Gideon should be moved as little as possible. He may have fractured his skull. See the blood on that large rock next to his head? And I'm so afraid that he may have reinjured his leg.''

With the utmost care, the laborer, assisted by the two girls, lifted Gideon into the wagon. Though the vehicle carried a large load of merchandise that had apparently just been delivered in Easton by the carrier's cart from London— Mélissande noted with a flick of envy a handsome brocaded chair and a bolt of material probably intended for new draperies—there was plenty of room for the injured man and for Mélissande to sit beside him. She guarded him against jolts as best she could during the short journey to the Dower House, where the farm laborer and Mélissande's gardener carried Gideon to an upstairs bedroom. Phoebe left immediately to summon Dr. Morley from Easton.

Cecilia and the maid, Sally, rushed to the bedroom in excitement at this unexpected drama, but soon developed symptoms of hysteria as they caught a closer look at Gideon's bloody head wound, revealed when Mélissande removed the handkerchief with which she had stopped the bleeding. Pushing them out of the room, Mélissande took sole charge of the patient. Cautiously she edged him out of his tight-fitting coat and removed his right boot. She considered removing the other, but thought better of the notion.

Drawing up a chair, she sat down beside the bed. Showing no sign of reviving, Gideon remained deathly pale, and soon Mélissande noticed with disquiet that his breathing had become shallow. She slipped a hand inside his shirt, finding that his heartbeat was slow and very feeble. Fearing that each slow breath would be Gideon's last, Mélissande huddled beside his bed in frozen misery until the arrival of Dr. Morley almost an hour later.

The grizzled, kindly old doctor, familiar to Mélissande

since her first days at the Priory, looked grave as he examined Gideon's head wound. "Miss de Castellane, you say he may have struck his head against a rock? I don't like the sound of that, I'll be frank." Prying open one of Gideon's eyes, the doctor grunted with satisfaction. "That's a good sign. His pupil is reacting to light. Perhaps the head injury is not as serious as I feared."

"I'm so glad to hear that, Doctor. But what about Gid—Lord Rochedale's leg? He suffered a serious gunshot wound to his left thigh a month or six weeks ago, and has not been able to walk without great pain until very recently. I confess that I was surprised to see him riding today. He may have reinjured the leg when he fell off his horse."

"Then we'd best have this boot off. Can you provide me with a stout knife? Though what his lordship will say when he discovers that I've cut up his riding boot . . . ! One of Hoby's more expensive creations, I have no doubt! I'll thank you for water and dressings, too, and could you send your manservant to help undress the patient?" The doctor leaned forward, watching Gideon intently. "I think—yes, I'm sure, his lordship is coming around at last. Miss de Castellane, in such cases, where a patient is recovering from a blow to the head, I find that a basin is often necessary, if you catch my meaning."

After she had filled the doctor's requests and had sent the handyman John upstairs to assist him, Mélissande waited in the corridor outside Gideon's closed door. She listened apprehensively to the sound of someone being very ill, and blessed Dr. Morley's forethought in the matter of the basin. A little later she winced as she heard an agonized groan, almost instantly smothered, and then the low murmur of conversation. When the doctor came out of the room shortly afterward, Mélissande looked at him expectantly.

"Well, Miss de Castellane, I believe we may expect a happy outcome to this affair. Lord Rochedale has come out of his coma and seems to remember all the details of his accident. That is not always the case. Very often the victim of a severe head injury has no recollection of the events of the immediate past. His lordship has a headache, which may persist for some days, but there will be no permanent effects from the blow to his head. As for his lordship's previously injured leg, unfortunately he landed directly upon it when he fell, and there was considerable bruising. No bones were broken, however." The doctor broke into a chuckle. "I find myself in an odd position for a medical man. Though he will be unable to walk without a good deal of pain for the immediate future, my patient informs me he is happy that the accident occurred!"

At Mélissande's' questioning look, Dr. Morley continued, "Perhaps I'm being indiscreet, but, after all, you are a member of Lord Rochedale's family and . . . well, the fact is that he has feared for weeks now that he would end his life as a cripple. When he was shot—it was a duel, I gather, such a mindless way to settle a quarrel—the bullet grazed a bone in his upper thigh. The doctor who treated the wound warned Lord Rochedale that the bone might be permanently weakened, that he might never walk normally again. Happily, I have been able to assure him that his fears are groundless. A man who has been as physically active as he has been since his return from London, and who has survived a very serious fall without further injury to the bone, has excellent prospects for a complete recovery."

Mélissande felt a deep sense of relief. "That is very good news, indeed."

"Yes, his lordship will soon be his old self again. Naturally, he will require careful nursing for a day or so. Now, I have just given him a draught, and I hope he will sleep, but I should like to have someone sit with him throughout the night. He must be kept warm at all costs. If you notice that he has become chilled, if he should perspire heavily or develop a rapid pulse, why, you must send for me immediately."

* * *

Mélissande put down her book and rubbed her weary eyes. It was two o'clock in the morning, and she had been sitting beside Gideon's bed, reading by the dim light of a shaded candle, since Dr. Morley's departure in the early evening. She looked over at Gideon, who still seemed to be sleeping peacefully. In sleep his features seemed softened, younger. With his dark curls disarranged and those hard gray eyes closed, Mélissande thought, he must resemble the boy who had been so stricken by his mother's death. Recalling what Mrs. Stedman, the housekeeper, had told her about Gideon's childhood, Mélissande felt a stirring of pity for the lonely boy who had apparently been unable to relate closely to another human being after the loss of his mother. He could not have grown his hardened shell overnight. At some stage before the solitary, grieving youth had metamorphosed into the indifferent, uncaring, coldly aloof Gideon of today, had he ever yearned to extend his hand for a shred of the affection that he could see his father lavishing on Jeanne-Marie and her children? What if he and Mélissande, growing up together, had been able to break through the wall of resentment and misunderstanding that divided them? For a moment, Mélissande allowed herself to imagine what it would be like to have Gideon's gray eyes meet hers with an expression of loving warmth.

Her mind wandering, she found herself thinking about Dr. Morley's revelation. She wondered if Gideon's fear that he would never be hale again had contributed to his decision to sell the Priory. Perhaps he could not envision a cripple as lord of the manor, unable to ride or hunt, unable to attend to estate duties except from the seat of a carriage.

Lost in thought, she sensed rather than observed a motion, and looked up to find that Gideon's eyes were open. She placed her fingers on his wrist, reassured to feel a steady, normal pulse. His color was good and he did not seem chilled.

"How do you feel, my lord?"

"Like death," muttered Gideon morosely. "I think my

ex-colonel must have sneaked into the room while I was unconscious and emptied a dozen pistols into my leg."

Speaking without thinking, Mélissande said, "But at least you need no longer fear that your leg is permanently crippled."

Gideon's eyes shot sparks. "Dr. Morley blabs too much."

"Here is some medicine the doctor left for you," said Mélissande, hastily changing the subject. Putting an arm around his shoulders to assist him to drink, she drew a quick, involuntary breath as the faint scent of his hair and feeling of firm, muscled flesh beneath her fingers recalled to her the bold embrace in which he had enfolded her during their first tumultuous meeting. Hastily, she smoothed his pillow and straightened his coverlets and returned to her chair, moving it farther away from his disturbing presence.

Gideon was staring at her, frowning. "I understand from Dr. Morley that I have you to thank for rescuing me," he said abruptly. "The last thing I remember is Ajax rearing at a confounded rabbit crossing the road." His frown deepened. "Why did you bring me to the Dower House? It would have been more convenient for you to have carted me straight off to the doctor's house. And why are you sitting up with me? You have servants. Why didn't you order one of them to tend an unwelcome patient?"

Mélissande stammered, "Unwelcome, my lord? Surely not. I had you brought to the Dower House because I feared that a long, jolting journey by farm wagon might further injure your leg. As for sitting up with you, Dr. Morley said it was necessary for someone to stay with you throughout the night in case your condition worsened, and it would have been simply unthinkable for me to ask a servant to care for a member of my family when I was available to do so myself."

"Pray spare me these sentimentalities. There is not the slightest tie between us, not even the tenuous and unwelcome bond that joins me to your half brother and your half sister." Gideon's lip curled into a sneer. "Come now, my dear, why *are* you playing Lady Bountiful? Are you trying to shame me into gratitude? By folding me into your family embrace, are you hoping that I will change my mind about selling the estate?''

Mélissande pressed her lips tightly together to hide their quivering. Rising, she walked to the door of the bedchamber, hesitating an instant before replying until she could be sure her voice was steady. ''Forgive me for inflicting my presence on you. It will take a little while, but as soon as I can arouse our little maidservant, I will send her in to you. Good night, Lord Rochedale.''

''Mélissande, please don't go. I—I'm sorry. I didn't mean what I said.''

Mélissande paused. She could hear the note of grudging reluctance in his voice, and she knew how difficult it must have been for him to relax his stiff-necked pride and make the overture. Slowly she walked back to the bed.

''It's my damned leg,'' said Gideon defensively. ''It hurts like fury. I almost wish Dr. Morley had cut it off. Then I'd be rid of it.''

''I think the draught I just gave you will take effect soon, and you will feel less pain,'' said Mélissande, tacitly accepting his apology. She straightened the coverlets that he had once more disarranged and sat down again by his bedside.

''You'll stay, then?'' he asked, again with that note of faint reluctance.

''Yes, I'll stay.''

Soon Gideon's eyes began to grow heavy, and in a few minutes he drifted off into a somewhat restless sleep. Once he half awoke, groaning in pain, and Mélissande, without stopping to consider, took one of his hands in both of hers and pressed it comfortingly. He opened his eyes for an instant, and then, his lips curving in a little half smile, he seemed to relax completely and fell into a deep sleep.

CHAPTER VII

Finding herself nodding off for the third time in five minutes, Mélissande put down her book, thinking ruefully that not even Wieland's bloody crimes could keep her awake tonight. She had just spent a long, chilled, tiring day in Hastings, looking for a suitable house. She had Gideon's promise that she and Nick and Cecilia need not move from the Dower House until the spring, but the New Year would soon be here, and she was beginning to have a panicky feeling that time was slipping away.

Feeling a draft, she hugged her shawl around her shoulders and moved her chair a little closer to the cozy fire in the morning room fireplace. Violent storms and bone-chilling cold had succeeded the glorious warmth of late summer and autumn, although, paradoxically, the change in weather had not eased invasion fears. The newspapers were reporting increased building activity in the French Atlantic ports, and only recently Napoleon had been quoted as saying that the English Channel was only a ditch that could be "leaped by the bold."

"What were you saying, Cecilia? I must have dozed off," said Mélissande in apology to her sister, whose white silk gown, though not new, was far too fashionable for a quiet evening at home.

"I said it was too bad of Nick not to return home in time to take me to the Lansdownes' ball. He knew how much I was looking forward to it. I never thought he could be so selfish."

"I know Nick wouldn't deliberately deprive you of a pleasure. He must have forgotten about the ball."

"You're always making excuses for Nick," pouted Cecilia. "I don't see why you couldn't have taken me to the Lansdownes', Sandy. You were certainly invited, and you know it will probably be the last party given for some weeks. Everything is so dull right after Christmas and the New Year."

"Come now, Cecilia, you know that I was invited merely for politeness' sake. Lady Lansdowne is giving this ball primarily for her daughter's friends, and while you are a member of Euphemia's circle, I scarcely know the girl," said Mélissande calmly. Having a shrewd suspicion that Cecilia had arranged to meet Stephen Lacey at the ball, Mélissande was not entirely displeased that her sister's plans for the evening had fallen through. "Frankly, I have so many things to think about these days that I doubt I should enjoy a party very much. We must move from the Dower House very soon now, you know."

"Exactly. That's why I wanted so much to go to the ball tonight. We *will* be moving soon, and I shan't have many more chances to be with my friends." Cecilia lowered her eyes, fingering the small gold locket at her throat. "I've been thinking. Must we really move out of the Dower House in the spring? Couldn't you ask Gideon to extend our time here? He hasn't sold the Priory yet, has he? We would have heard of any sale. And perhaps he won't find a buyer, not for a long time. It's not just anyone, after all, who can afford to spend thousands of pounds to buy an estate. So how could it possibly hurt my brother to allow us to stay on, at least until he sells the property?"

"I know nothing of Lord Rochedale's plans. But even if I thought he would agree to such a request, I would not ask him to do so," said Mélissande shortly.

"But why not, Sandy? How can you be so stubborn? All our past differences aside, Gideon owes you a favor. You *did* rescue him from a serious accident. You may even have saved his life."

"I would not ask a favor from your brother if *my* life depended on it," exclaimed Mélissande, experiencing as she spoke a mild shock at her own vehemence. These days her feelings about Gideon were decidedly ambivalent. After her night-long vigil beside his bed, she had naturally expected to observe some change in his attitude toward her, but there was little evidence of any softening in his manner when he awoke the following morning. Certainly he made no reference to his apology of the previous evening nor to the fact that for several hours during the night he had slept with his hand in hers. Instead, he had rather peremptorily demanded that she send for his valet so that he could return to the Priory and, as he put it, rid Mélissande of his inconvenient presence. Leaning painfully on a cane, supported on his other side by his valet, Gideon had taken leave of Mélissande with a stiff bow and an even stiffer speech of thanks.

In the face of such ingratitude, she found it hard to believe that she had ever admitted Gideon into even a corner of her heart, and by the time of their next meeting one and a half months later, at a small dinner party given just a few days ago by Lady Inch, Mélissande's antagonism toward him was again in full bloom.

Her lips curved in a reminiscent smile as she recalled the dinner party. Seldom in these past worrying months had she enjoyed herself so much. All of the guests were old friends, and she had been especially pleased to see Jack Childers, a favorite beau. After the gentlemen had joined the ladies in the drawing room, Jack made straight for her side, murmuring under cover of the general conversation, "I'm dashed if you're not looking more beautiful than ever tonight. Is that a new gown?''

"Indeed not. You've seen me wear this dress a million times," Mélissande replied with a laugh. Glancing down at her high-waisted round gown of rose-colored crepe, made with sleeves of delicate spider net and worn with a small pearl necklace, she was secretly pleased by the compliment.

"Oh, well, m'dear, you have such style that you could wear the same gown every night of the week and no one would ever notice."

Jack Childers was one of several young men in the neighborhood who had been Mélissande's fervent admirers since her seventeenth birthday. All of them, like Jack, were younger sons, and none of them could afford to marry a girl who did not possess a sizable dowry. Her, and their, lack of eligibility had not perturbed Mélissande, since her heart had never been seriously involved, but she enjoyed their company, and it was both flattering and convenient never to lack a dancing partner at a ball. Jack had recently accepted a minor and not too demanding post at the Treasury, and it had been some time since Mélissande had seen him.

Tables for whist and loo had been set up in the drawing room, but Jack, ignoring the beckoning finger of an imperious dowager at the next table, bore Mélissande off to a secluded corner of the room. "There, isn't this much better? We'll have a cozy game of chess."

Mélissande chuckled as she sat down before the chessboard. "Be it on your own head, then. You know that I can scarcely distinguish a pawn from a rook."

"Just move a piece now and then. If we look absorbed enough, nobody will disturb us. I've been wanting to talk to you, Mélissande. When I returned home from London last week, Mama told me about a rumor that Lord Rochedale is planning to sell up the Priory and that you and Nick and Cecilia would be obliged to find another place to live. Is it true?''

"Well—yes. But I don't think Lord Rochedale wishes the

news to be generally known." Mélissande glanced involuntarily across the room to where Gideon sat playing whist. She had been surprised to see him at the party, for he had been a determined recluse since his return from India. They had exchanged cool nods in the drawing room before dinner, but they had not spoken, and they had not been seated near each other at the dinner table.

"I don't care about Rochedale's wishes," exclaimed Jack. "What's he about, not to make adequate provision for you and his brother and sister?"

"Legally he has no obligation to us. Jack, can't we talk about something else?"

"Lord, yes, I'd be happy to do so. Mélissande, why don't we get married?"

Mélissande broke into a surprised laugh. "What's this? Have you just inherited a fortune from a long-lost uncle?"

Reddening, Jack protested, "I wish you would allow me to forget that I ever told you I was too poor to marry you."

"Dear Jack, I don't bear you the slightest resentment for that remark. You *are* too poor to marry me, and I'm too poor to marry you."

"Listen, I've been doing some thinking these past few days, and the fact is, we could muddle along if we got married. You have a little money of your own, and I have this post now at the Treasury. We could take a tiny house, or rooms even, in London, and I'm bound to receive a promotion soon. My father might even come up with some kind of allowance, for all he moans about living too close to the bone."

Mélissande looked helplessly at Jack, searching for words in which to phrase her refusal kindly. After a moment he reached for her hand, saying, "It's no good, is it? Such gall, to invite you to starve with me in a garret! But when Mama told me you were leaving Easton, I couldn't bear the thought of not seeing you here when I returned home for a visit."

"Jack, I like you very well, but—"

"I know," said Jack with a twisted smile. "Fact is, I probably wouldn't enjoy starving in a garret, either!"

The servants arrived just then with the tea trays, and Mélissande and Jack Childers left the chess table to join the other guests. As Mélissande accepted her cup from a footman, Gideon dropped into a chair beside her. An awkward silence followed, until Gideon, apparently snatching at a subject out of the blue, remarked, "So you're a chess player, are you?"

"A very indifferent one, I fear."

"Ah. I used to play when I was a boy. I was never very good."

There was another silence, and then Mélissande asked politely, "How is your leg, my lord? I see you are no longer using a cane."

"The leg is much improved, thank you. I was able to resume riding several weeks ago." He added, a note of unwillingness plain in his voice, "During Dr. Morley's last visit, he informed me that if you hadn't insisted on taking me directly to the Dower House, I might not be walking around unaided today. He says that a long, jostling ride to his surgery might have permanently damaged the leg."

"I was very happy to do what I could."

"It was kind of you." Gideon rose, saying coolly, "I just wanted you to know that I'm aware of the service you rendered me. Good night, Miss de Castellane."

Mélissande stared after Gideon's retreating back, feeling resentful and dissatisfied with their brief encounter. He obviously felt a sense of obligation to her, but she would have preferred no acknowledgment at all rather than his chilly, brief speech of appreciation.

She was aroused from her reverie by a wail from Cecilia. "There! I might have known you wouldn't intercede with Gideon to allow us to stay on. You don't care for my happiness at all, do you, Sandy?"

Mélissande sighed, knowing that her sister's unhappiness

at leaving Easton stemmed primarily from her fear of being separated from Stephen Lacey. She said gently, "Cecy, darling, I want your happiness more than anything in the world, but I'm obliged to tell you that staying on at the Dower House isn't the answer to your problem with Stephen. Aurore is the stumbling block, and I'm sure she will never change."

"No, and you won't lift a finger to influence her to change her mind, will you? Oh, I wish I were dead!" Her eyes streaming with tears, Cecilia rushed from the room.

Instinctively, Mélissande half rose, intending to follow her sister, but sank back into her chair. She could think of nothing to say that would really comfort Cecilia. Mélissande's shoulders slumped. She knew that she must persist in her attempts to find a new home, but she could not delude herself that a move from the Dower House would mark a brighter future for Cecilia—or for Nick, who these days was seldom absent from Mélissande's thoughts. He seemed to have undergone a personality change, from the cheerful, outgoing boy she had known all his life, to a brooding, uncommunicative stranger. For weeks now, Nick had been leaving the Dower House each day in the early morning, not to return—sometimes not to return at all—until dawn. Except for attending an occasional drill with the Volunteers, Nick had abandoned all his usual haunts, had severed ties with all his oldest friends. She could not imagine what new associations and activities were filling the void.

The clock on the mantel struck eleven, and Mélissande rose wearily. She went up to her bedchamber, carrying *Wieland* with her against the possibility that worries about Nick would cause sleep to elude her despite her long and tiring day. After reading only a few pages, however, her eyes grew heavy and she drifted into a sound sleep, from which she was aroused some time later by the sound of loud knocking at the front door of the house. Groping for the "pocket luminary"—a small bottle lined with oxide of phosphorus—she ignited a sulfur-tipped wood splint by

rubbing it against the interior of the bottle, and quickly lit
her candle. She peered resentfully at her bedside clock. Four
o'clock. Who could be seeking admittance at such a ghastly
hour? Putting on her dressing gown and slippers and carrying her candle, she padded down the stairs. "Who is it?"
she called.

"Rochedale. Hurry, open up."

Throwing the door wide, Mélissande stared in open-
mouthed shock at Gideon, impeccably dressed for the evening in black coat, breeches, and pumps. Next to him,
sagging against his arm, was Nick. Her brother's face, what
could be seen of it beneath the grime, was deathly pale, and
around the sleeve of his shabby, nondescript jacket was tied
a fine linen handkerchief, once white, now splotched with
red.

"Good evening, Miss de Castellane," said Gideon calmly. "There was no need to knock, I suppose. I assume this
young man is my brother Nicholas."

"Of course it's Nick, Lord Rochedale," exclaimed
Mélissande in growing consternation. "What in heaven's
name has happened to him?"

Nick raised his head with a jerk, his glazed eyes clearing
as he glared at Gideon. "You're Rochedale? But how did
you know . . . ?"

Gideon shrugged. "It wasn't difficult to guess who you
were. You gave me directions to the Dower House, and I
recognized your ring. My father's signet ring."

A look of violent distaste crossed Nick's worn face. "If I
had known it was you . . . Just go, please. Sandy will give
me all the help I . . ." His head dropped to his chest, and he
sagged limply against Gideon's arm. His brother picked him
up, carrying him into the house and depositing him on a
sofa in the drawing room. As he straightened his back,
Gideon smothered an exclamation of pain, and Mélissande
said quickly, momentarily forgetting Nick's plight, "Is it
your leg, my lord?"

"A twinge only. The leg isn't quite up to Nicholas's

weight yet. What is he, twelve, thirteen stone?'' Gideon leaned over Nick, loosening with long, slender fingers the handkerchief that had been serving as a rude tourniquet around the boy's upper arm. "Good," Gideon muttered. "The wound has stopped bleeding, at least for the moment." He turned to Mélissande. "I found Nicholas walking along the road about a mile from here. I had been dining with friends near Charlmont and had stayed rather late, which was a good thing for our brother. If I had come along earlier, I would have missed him. He has a gunshot wound in his arm, you see, and it's my guess that he would soon have swooned from loss of blood.''

"Nick has been shot? Why would anyone do such a thing to him?'' stammered a dazed Mélissande. As Nick stirred, opening his eyes and struggling to sit up, she said urgently, "Nick, what kind of scrape have you gotten yourself into? Who shot you?''

Nick leaned back against the sofa with a grimace of pain, but stared defiantly at his sister for a moment. Then, his shoulders slumping, he said, "If you must know, I've had a run-in with the excisemen. We—some of the village lads and I—picked up a load of French brandy near Fairlight Glen and brought it to a farm in Medbury where we have a cache site. Someone at the farm must have laid an information, because just as we were unloading our cargo the excisemen arrived. We scattered after a brief firefight. I don't know what happened to the others. I hope they all got away safely. My arm was bleeding heavily, and I must have fainted and fallen off my pack pony. When I recovered my senses, the pony had bolted. I knew I wasn't far from home, so I started walking to the Dower House. That's when my bro— That's when Lord Rochedale found me.''

"I've been hearing rumors about local smuggling for years, of course,'' said Mélissande incredulously, "but how could you become involved in such a thing, Nick? French brandy, and here we are in imminent danger of invasion by Napoleon!''

Gideon spoke from behind her. "Lord, there's nothing to that. A little brandy here and there has nothing to do with fighting a war. But tell me, Nicholas. Were you and your friends known personally to the folk at the farm?"

"Well, in a manner of speaking, yes," replied Nick with a puzzled frown. "They knew we came from Easton, but we were always careful to use only our first names, even though the village lads had been using the farm as a drop-off point for years." He scowled. "I wonder who informed on us? I don't think it could have been Farmer Pruitt himself. The lads tell me that he's always been a sound man, but recently a distant cousin came to live with him, a man Farmer Pruitt hadn't seen since they were small children, so I suppose . . ."

"So you are reasonably sure that the farmer and his family didn't know your identity?" interrupted Gideon.

"Yes. No, I'm not sure, now I think of it. I remember now, one of the farmer's daughters once called me 'my lord,' and then she caught herself, giggling, as if she knew she shouldn't be talking like that. Perhaps one of the Easton lads did a spot of gossiping with a pretty girl, I don't know."

Gideon touched Mélissande's arm. "That's torn it. We'll need to hurry. Miss de Castellane, please fetch Nicholas some presentable clothes. Also some linen for bandages, and Basilicum powder, if you have it, just to be on the safe side. And we will need a pack of cards and a card table. Set the table up in this room, or, better yet, in the library, together with a bottle of brandy or Madeira. I'll go out to direct my tiger to take the curricle to the stables and unharness the horses."

"I don't understand. You're planning to remain here? I had hoped you would drive to Easton to summon Dr. Morley to care for Nick's wound."

"My dear Miss de Castellane, I had given you credit for vastly more intelligence," said Gideon grimly. "The informer will have given the excisemen as much information as he possessed about the identity of the smugglers from Easton, including a detailed description of 'my lord.' Allowing for a certain period of time during which the excisemen mounted a futile search for the scattered smugglers, it's my guess that the riding officers will be at your door at any minute now, and we can't allow them to find a wounded man here. Or to see my curricule and horses in front of your door, giving away the fact that I just arrived here. Nicholas, do you play piquet? A little? Pray hard, man, that you'll be a much better player by the end of the evening. The stakes couldn't be higher!''

A short time later, still breathless from the speed with which she had carried out Gideon's instructions, Mélissande sat tensely on the upper landing of the staircase. She was still wearing her nightcap and dressing gown, and she held a lighted candle. Carefully coached by Gideon, she deliberately waited several minutes after hearing the sound of the door knocker before she slowly walked down into the hall and opened the door. Rubbing imaginary sleep from her eyes, she recoiled in feigned astonishment at the sight of the uniformed excisemen.

''Good evening, ma'am. Is Lord Nicholas Maitland at home?'' inquired a stiff-looking man who appeared to be the senior officer of the group.

''Certainly. Or at least he was here when I retired for the night,'' replied Mélissande haughtily. ''What is the meaning of this visit, sir?''

''At what time did you retire, ma'am?''

Drawing herself up to her full height, Mélissande said coldly, ''I fail to see why you should be interested in my sleeping habits, sir.''

''Nevertheless, ma'am, I can assure you I have a good and sufficient reason for asking.''

''Sandy, is something wrong? Who is making all that noise? And who are these men?''

Mélissande turned with a muffled sigh of frustration. Her fair curls escaping from beneath her nightcap, her dressing

gown hastily tied, Cecilia was peering around the bend of
the staircase.

"Please go back to bed, Cecilia. Everything is quite all
right. It's true, there has been some kind of misunderstanding, but I fancy it will be cleared up immediately." After
Cecilia had disappeared from view, Mélissande turned her
attention back to the excisemen. "Here, what are you
doing, sir, entering my house without an invitation?" she
exclaimed indignantly.

The senior exciseman put his hands to Mélissande's
shoulders and politely but firmly pushed her aside as his
men crowded into the small hall behind him. "We have
information that Lord Nicholas Maitland was involved in a
smuggling incident earlier this evening. If he is here, we
must see him."

"You must be mad," retorted Mélissande. "That, or
deliberately pernicious. My brother a smuggler? Every feeling must be offended at such an accusation. The Maitlands
have their faults, but they are not common criminals!"

"We've found more than one hedge bird among the
gentry, ma'am," replied the officer stolidly. "But that's
neither here nor there. Where is Lord Nicholas Maitland?"
He paused, cocking his head at a sudden burst of laughter
from the rear of the house. "If you will excuse us," he
said, brushing past Mélissande.

"I must protest this intrusion. I know my rights. You
can't enter my house without a search warrant."

"We have a general warrant that allows us to search any
premises on suspicion of smuggled goods," the officer shot
back over his shoulder as he strode down the corridor.
Mélissande trailed closely behind him, still protesting, wring-
ing her hands, raising her voice deliberately in a loud wail
as they approached the door of the library.

Without knocking, the riding officer entered the room just
as Gideon rose to his feet, flinging a handful of playing
cards to the table. His hair was disheveled, his cravat
artistically disarranged, and his voice was slightly slurred as

he exclaimed jubilantly, "Thirty, forty, *and* repique, my lad. That makes, I believe, my partie of five games."

"You've had the luck of the damned tonight," complained Nick, who was sitting with his back to the door. A wine-glass trailed limply in his hand, and there were several empty wine bottles upended on the floor. Picking up a bottle of Madeira to fill his own glass, Gideon paused, seemingly noticing for the first time the presence of strangers on the threshold.

The riding officer advanced several steps into the library. "Lord Nicholas Maitland?" he inquired, looking at Gideon, who raised an affronted eyebrow and replied haughtily, "I'm Rochedale."

"I beg your pardon, my lord. The other gentlemen, then, would he be Lord Nicholas?"

Swinging his chair around so that he faced the door, Nick peered owlishly at the exciseman. "Don't think I know you, sir. Don't recall inviting you to my house, either, but sit down, sit down. We'll have a game of whist, you and one of your fellows and my brother Gideon and I. My cursed luck is out at piquet, so we'll try another game."

Taken aback, the exciseman stammered, "No, no, my lord, you've quite mistaken the situation. I am Riding Officer Hayward, and I've come . . . That is to say, I am here to investigate an incident of smuggling."

"You've come here to investigate an incident of smuggling?" exclaimed Nick incredulously. "Well, you're quite out, my man. I can't help you there. Wouldn't if I could. There's a deal too much government interference in a man's simple pleasures these days. I'll be damned if I understand why they want to make us so miserable by these confounded heavy taxes on our tea and coffee and spirits and tobacco. Not that I use tobacco myself, mind, but it's the principle of the thing. Well then, officer, if that's all, I'll bid you good night. Deal the cards, Gideon. You must give me my chance for revenge."

There was a note of baffled desperation in the officer's

voice as he said, "Lord Nicholas, I don't mean to be discourteous, but I must ask you some questions."

About to pour himself another glass of wine, Nick fixed a belligerent eye on the riding officer. "By George, this is a pretty how do y'do, I must say, forcing yourself into a gentleman's home to pester him with your fool questions." He looked mildly surprised as Mélissande edged around the excisemen and crossed the room to him. "Hallo, Sandy. You here, too? Did you hear this fellow rattle on about smuggling?"

Sounding distressed, as though torn between indignation and a desire to be reasonable, Mélissande said, "Nick, *chéri,* I really do think this officer is simply trying to do his duty. Why not answer his questions? He will see immediately that he is wrong. Perhaps it is merely a case of mistaken identity."

"Oh, very well, officer," said Nick ungraciously. "Ask me your damned questions so I can get back to more important concerns. My brother's luck has to change sometime."

"Thank you, my lord. Were you in the vicinity of Medbury tonight, at a farm owned by one Pruitt?"

"I was not. Who is this Pruitt?"

"My lord, I have reason to believe that you *were* at Mr. Pruitt's farm tonight, in the company of some villagers from Easton, and that you were engaged in smuggling a load of French brandy from the coast to a prearranged cache on the farm."

"See here, that is the outside of enough!" said Gideon in a tone of outrage. "I don't say that my brother would demand to see proof that duty had been paid before buying a bottle of brandy. *I* wouldn't. Confound it, man, at least half the tea and foreign spirits consumed in this country entered England in smugglers' boats. I *do* say that no gentleman in my family would engage in trade, illegal or otherwise, and he certainly would not do so in the company of uncouth village louts!"

"Begging your pardon, my lord Rochedale, I believe my information is correct." The officer turned to Nick. "We might settle this matter very speedily, Lord Nicholas, if you would tell me where and in whose company you spent last night, between the hours of, say, six o'clock in the evening to two o'clock in the morning."

"Let me see now. I was out after wood pigeons until—when was it, Sandy, fivish?—and then I had a short nap before supper, which was at eight, as usual. Around half-past nine or ten my brother, Lord Rochedale, dropped by to see me about an estate matter. I invited him to stay for a glass of wine and a hand of cards."

The riding officer gazed hard at Gideon. "Is that correct, my lord? You have been in Lord Nicholas's company since nine or ten last evening?"

"Certainly. My brother and I have been playing piquet for some three or four hours, from around ten last evening to . . ." He pulled out his watch, his jaw dropping. "Good God, Nick, it's almost five in the morning." Gideon turned to Mélissande. "I do beg your pardon, my dear. I had no idea that I was abusing your hospitality. I should have been gone long ago."

Mélissande smiled politely. "Not at all, dear Gideon. We are delighted to receive you at any hour, for as long as you wish to stay."

Shifting his weight from one foot to the other and looking acutely uncomfortable, the riding officer said, "Well, Lord Rochedale, if you can indeed vouch for Lord Nicholas's whereabouts for the greater part of last evening . . ."

"I trust you are not giving me the lie, my good man," Gideon replied with an icy frown. "In my circle, I am accustomed to having my word accepted without question."

"Quite so, I'm sure," said the officer hastily, retreating visibly before Gideon's glare. "Pray accept my apologies for having disturbed you, ma'am, your lordships. I'll bid you good night. Don't inconvenience yourself, ma'am. We'll see ourselves out."

Mélissande breathed a sigh of relief as the door closed behind the departing excisemen. She murmured, *"Mon Dieu,* I'm so glad that is over. Gid—Lord Rochedale, I never thought your scheme would work."

"We owe no small thanks to your acting ability, Miss de Castellane. And Nicholas, you were perfect, the inebriated young cub to the life. Did you observe the officer's expression when you asked him to sit down for a game of cards?"

Nick did not answer. The color had drained from his face, and now, suddenly, he toppled from his chair to the floor in a dead faint. A moment later Cecilia burst into the room, saying, "Now that those men have gone, Sandy, will you please tell me what is going on?" She broke off with a scream of fear as she observed Mélissande and Gideon kneeling beside Nick's prostrate body.

Gideon glanced up, at first failing to recognize Cecilia, whom he had met briefly as he was leaving the Dower House on the morning after his riding accident. "Be quiet, girl—Cecilia. You're not helping matters with your screeching. Mélissande, can you help me to remove Nicholas's coat? Gently, now." He cursed under his breath at the blood that had saturated Nick's shirt-sleeve. "I was afraid of that. The wound's opened. Here, Mélissande, watch me. I'm going to use my handkerchief again as a rough tourniquet. You must loosen it periodically to allow the blood to circulate. Can you manage while I go for Dr. Morley?"

"Yes. Please go immediately. Dr. Morley lives near the church, the second house from the left." Though her heart was pounding from anxiety, Mélissande's voice was calm, and her slender fingers, already bloodstained, were steady as she held the tourniquet tight.

After Gideon had left, Cecilia knelt beside Nick, holding one of his limp hands. "Sandy, he's so pale. He looks—he looks as if he's dying. Do you think Dr. Morley can get here in time to save him?"

"Tais-toi, tais-toi, Cécile. Tu es un imbécile," Mélissande said fiercely, and her sister looked at her with concern

mingled with awe. "Lord, Sandy, I can't remember the last time you scolded me in French."

"I'm sorry. I know you're distressed, but you mustn't even admit the possibility that Nick will die. We won't let him die. Be a good girl, now. Put some water to boil and fetch some linen for bandages from the armoire in my bedchamber. Dr. Morley will want to remove the bullet from Nick's arm, and we must have everything ready for him when he arrives."

Dawn had long since broken when Dr. Morley and Gideon emerged several hours later from Nick's bedchamber to join his sisters waiting anxiously in the corridor. The doctor placed his hand on Gideon's shoulder, saying, "My thanks to you, my lord, for assisting me to extract the bullet. I could have sworn you were an old hand at the art!"

"Not quite, Doctor. I've seen my share of wounds, naturally, while I was serving with the army in India, but I've never before been called upon to assist the surgeon."

"Doctor, how is Nick?" asked Mélissande, unable to bear the suspense any longer.

Dr. Morley beamed. "My dear Miss de Castellane, Miss Maitland, I am happy to tell you that Lord Nicholas will be hale and hearty almost before you can say 'Jack Robinson.' The bullet missed the bone entirely, and the wound was perfectly clean. I do advise several days of bed rest because Lord Nicholas lost so much blood, so much as a matter of fact, that I decided not to bleed him."

"And a good thing, too," retorted Gideon. "Why bleed a patient whose veins are practically empty of blood in the first place?"

"Spoken like a true layman," said the doctor, chuckling. "In the ordinary way of things, my lord, I can assure you that a good bleeding has brought many a patient from death's door. Miss de Castellane, I know from experience that you are a capital nurse. I leave Lord Nicholas in capable hands."

"There is one thing," said Mélissande hesitantly. "I

don't know what Lord Rochedale told you about Nick's—
about his accident, but . . ."

"His lordship and I are far ahead of you," the doctor
reassured her. "We have already agreed that the details of
Lord Nicholas's *illness* should be kept as private as possible. And so, if someone—an excise officer, for instance—
were to inquire about my visit to the Dower House this
morning, I should say that I was called to attend you, Miss
de Castellane."

"I?" repeated Mélissande in surprise, and Cecilia chimed
in, "Fie, Doctor, you know better than anyone that Sandy is
never ill!"

"Actually, Mélissande, you fell into a fit of the vapors
when you heard shots early this morning and discovered that
Nicholas and I were half seas over and were using the
chandelier in the library for target practice," said Gideon
with a glint of malicious amusement. "Which reminds me,
I must now go downstairs and break a pane in one of the
library windows. I don't like to admit to such poor
marksmanship even while foxed, but there should be some
evidence of bullet damage in the library if anyone cares to
check. It would be far better to put a hole in that portrait
over the mantel, but I feel sure, Mélissande, that you
wouldn't approve of *that* kind of vandalism!"

With this parting shot, Gideon headed for the staircase
while Mélissande stared after his retreating back in speechless indignation. Dr. Morley and Cecilia burst into laughter.
"Oh, Sandy, I almost hope that my brother *will* be obliged
to tell such a whisker," gurgled Cecilia. "I haven't laughed
so much in ages."

A little later, after Dr. Morley had departed and Cecilia
had gone to sit at Nick's bedside, Mélissande saw Gideon to
the door. Noting his slight limp and the lines of exhaustion
in his face, she said quickly, "I hope you didn't overexert
yourself this evening. Your leg . . ."

"I'm back to being a Hopping Giles temporarily, Miss de

Castellane, but the leg will be as good as new after a proper night's rest.''

"Oh." Mélissande told herself firmly that it did not matter in the least that Gideon had reverted to using a formal salutation rather than her given name. "I won't keep you from your rest, then, my lord, but before you go, please accept my thanks for coming to Nick's rescue.''

"No need for thanks. Like any proper Englishman, I feel it my duty to do anything I can to keep open the lines of supply for importing French spirits.'' With a cool nod, Gideon adjusted his hat and left the house.

CHAPTER VIII

As she came down the staircase, carrying a heavy tray, Mélissande heard the sound of voices and peered into the drawing room.

"Good morning, Miss de Castellane," said Stephen Lacey with an easy smile. "I've come to inquire about Nick. It's all over the village that he had a clash with the excisemen last night, and now Cecilia tells me that your evening was even more exciting than the gossips would have it."

Turning pale, Mélissande set her tray down on a table. "All over the village? But this is frightful. I'd stake my life that Dr. Morley would never say a word about Nick's injury, so . . ."

Stephen interrupted her. "Please forgive my fool tongue. Yes, Nick's escapade *is* common knowledge, but there's not the slightest reason for you to worry yourself about it. Not a soul in the village would blow the gab to the excisemen about Nick. For one thing, virtually every family in the vicinity is neck deep in the smuggling trade. For another, an informer's life expectancy would be very short."

Not entirely convinced, Mélissande said, "I do hope you're right. It was kind of you to call. Nick seems to be resting comfortably. He has no fever, and he just took a little gruel.''

"I'm happy to hear it. I will, of course, be calling again to keep myself informed about his condition, but for now I'll leave you to minister to the patient.''

"Let me show you out," offered Cecilia with alacrity, and Mélissande frowned as she listened to the long drawn-out murmur of voices from the hall. She picked up the tray and was about to take it to the kitchen when Cecilia returned to the drawing room with Phoebe Wright and her father. "More visitors to inquire about our invalid," Cecilia announced merrily.

Observing the quick cloud that crossed Mélissande's face, Mr. Wright hastened to say, "Miss Maitland tells me that you are concerned that too many people will learn about Lord Nicholas's accident. Have no fear. No one in Easton would lay an information against him. Lord Nicholas is safe as houses.''

Breaking into her father's kindly speech of reassurance, Phoebe exclaimed, "Is Nick truly going to be all right? Cecilia has just told us he had lost so much blood that he fainted dead away.''

It was obvious, thought Mélissande, that Nick's neglect of Phoebe during these past weeks had not diminished the girl's attachment to him. Phoebe's pert little face was drawn with anxiety, and her hands were clenched together so tightly that the knuckles showed white. Smiling sympathetically, Mélissande said, "Yes, Nick was very bad last night, but he seems to be making a miraculously swift recovery. Only fancy, he felt so hungry that he actually gulped down some gruel a few minutes ago, though he pronounced it the vilest tasting stuff he had ever eaten! Then he demanded something civilized to eat, but of course he can have only the lightest of diets for the next day or so.''

Phoebe's face brightened and she said eagerly, "I'll be so happy to make him some calf's-foot jelly as soon as I return

home. But for now . . . do you think I might see Nick? I
promise I won't stay long.''

"I'm sorry. He's asleep now. I don't like to disturb his
rest.''

"There, Phoebe, it's just as I told you," said Mr. Wright.
"The last thing a sick man needs is a horde of visitors to the
sickroom. Miss de Castellane, pray give Lord Nicholas our
best regards and our hopes for a quick recovery. Come
along, Phoebe.''

Observing Phoebe's disappointment, Mélissande said, "I
have an idea. Cecilia and I would both be glad to have the
opportunity to rest for an hour or so. We've been away from
our beds since the early hours of this morning! And yet, someone should be with Nick in case he should awaken and need
something.''

"Oh, Miss de Castellane, I should be delighted to sit with
Nick,'' said a beaming Phoebe, and her father, shrugging,
took his leave, promising to send the gig back for his
daughter.

Several hours later, feeling very much more the thing
after a nap and a change of clothing, Mélissande entered
Nick's bedchamber to find him awake, his shoulders
solicitously supported by Phoebe as she held a cup of water
to his lips. Nick's color was good, and his eyes held a glint
of his usual sparkle. "I say, Sandy, it's almost worth a bullet
in the arm to be surrounded by beautiful females, all of
them clamoring to fulfill my slightest wish!''

"Beautiful females, my eye and Betty Martin," retorted
Mélissande. "Phoebe, we're well aware, aren't we, that
Nick is trying to turn us up sweet?'' She left a blushing
Phoebe and a grinning Nick to return downstairs, where her
little maid was just ushering Gideon into the foyer. Frankly
surprised to see him, Mélissande said politely, "Good afternoon, Lord Rochedale. Won't you come into the drawing
room?''

"Thank you, yes." Gideon handed his beaver hat and
caped driving coat to the maid, who murmured to Mélissande,

"The gig's just come for Miss Phoebe. I'll go up to tell her."

As they seated themselves in the drawing room, Gideon said, "I won't keep you long. I came merely to inquire about Nicholas."

"He's very well. Surprisingly strong. I suspect it will be difficult to keep him in bed for as long as Dr. Morley recommends."

"I'm very glad to hear it." Gideon lifted a quizzical eyebrow. "You seemed a bit surprised to find me visiting the sick."

"Well, not surprised precisely, although I admit to thinking that it was more noblesse oblige than brotherly regard that prompted you to help Nick. You dislike your father's second family, but you would not care to see your half brother in jail." Mélissande paused, biting her lip. "Will you overlook that ungracious remark? Whatever your motive, you did bring Nick safely back to us."

"No need to feel guilty. Considering our past family history, I certainly can't claim to be a paterfamilias! But I box a little, and there is nothing I admire more than excellent bottom. If I may say so, you and Nicholas both displayed that quality last night. You might call this visit a tribute. Well, I said I would not stay long, and now that I've established Nicholas's flourishing state of health, I will say good-bye."

Stung by Gideon's frankness, and determined to match his cool courtesy, Mélissande protested, "Oh, but you must let me take you up to see Nick. I know that he will want to thank you for his rescue in person."

"That's not necessary. Just tell him I called."

"No, no, I insist. Nick will have my head if he learns that I deprived him of the opportunity to thank you."

Giving in with a shrug, Gideon followed Mélissande out of the drawing room. As they mounted the stairs, he asked casually, "Have you been able to find a suitable house in which to move when you leave the Dower House?"

"No. It's very difficult to find a place that suits both our purse and our desire to remain near Easton. You need have no concern, however. We will certainly meet your ultimatum of a spring moving date."

Gideon cleared his throat. "Please disregard that 'ultimatum,' as you put it. I haven't yet sold the Priory, though I have had a number of inquiries. I believe you can count on as much time as you need to find a house."

Surprised but gratified, Mélissande felt herself in much greater charity with Gideon as they arrived at Nick's door. Phoebe was just leaving, blushing prettily when she was introduced to Gideon.

"Well, Nicholas, you're looking pretty stout," said Gideon with detached politeness as he sat down beside Nick's bed. "The arm giving you much pain? I can feel for you. It wasn't too long ago that my colonel put a bullet through my thigh."

Nick's smiling animation had disappeared with Phoebe's exit from the bedchamber. "How are you, sir? Good of you to call," he said stiffly. "I should like to thank you for coming to my assistance last night. I'm fully aware that, but for you, I might have bled to death on the road. Failing that, the excisemen would have rumbled my lay, and I'd have been up before the beak this morning and in a jail cell by afternoon. And after the next quarter sessions, no doubt, I'd be dangling from the gallows or deported to the colonies."

"Come now, don't let your imagination run away with you. I'm delighted to have been of service to you, but let's have no more morbid talk of the gallows."

"I wouldn't be honest, however, if I didn't tell you that I wish it had been anyone but you who rescued me," Nick burst out. "I despise the very idea of being beholden to a man I dislike so much!"

Mélissande gasped. "Nick, you haven't thought . . . You can't mean . . ."

Interrupting her, Gideon said coolly, "Let the boy have his say."

Nick hesitated for a moment, but he was far too angry to keep silent. "Yes, I will have my say," he began defiantly. "I want you to know what I really think of you, my dear brother. You've forfeited my respect on every count. You've callously disregarded the terms of our father's will, forcing my sisters to leave their home and their friends. You have no regard for family tradition and no love for a grand old estate that has belonged to the Maitlands for generations. And do you know something else, my lord Rochedale? You are stupid. By selling the Priory, you will be throwing away far more money than you will gain from the purchase price. If you would only take steps to improve the estate, it would be worth so much in just a few years that there would be no need to sell it."

His anger evaporating as he warmed to his subject, Nick continued, "Take Lord Coke in Norfolk, for example. In the past thirty years he has improved his land so much that he's been able to double his rents, and still his tenants prosper. A modern estate owner should use modern methods: rotate crops, marl the land, grow root crops and grasses for better livestock. Above all, he should be *buying* land, not selling it. Mr. Wright, whom you may remember as the farmer whose holdings adjoin the Dower House on the east, has been using the new methods for many years now, and he has been constantly acquiring more land. He's by way of being a very rich man, richer by far than many of the neighboring gentry who wouldn't dream of inviting him to dinner."

As Nick paused, Gideon asked calmly, "Is there anything else you care to say to me?"

Nick lowered his head, muttering sullenly, "No, I've said everything I wish to say."

"Then I'll take leave of you, Nicholas, with my best wishes for a speedy convalescence." Nodding to Nick and making a formal bow to Mélissande, Gideon left the room.

Mélissande caught up with him at the foot of the stairs, where he was being helped into his greatcoat by the maid,

Sally. "Please excuse Nick's rudeness," she exclaimed. "When he reflects on what he said, I know he will want to apologize to you."

"It won't fadge, you know. Nicholas meant every word he said. Be assured I bear him no ill will for his little speech. After all, aside from any assistance that I was able to render him last evening, I'm not conscious of having done anything to make my young half brother love me." As he paused to take his hat and stick from Sally, he frowned, saying, "Incidentally, that young woman to whom you introduced me in Nicholas's bedchamber—Phoebe Wright, is that her name? Is she the daughter of the yeoman farmer about whom my brother was waxing enthusiastic?"

"She is. Why do you ask?"

"I have no interest in the young woman at all, but I do marvel at your shortsightedness."

"Indeed? I fear I must ask you to explain."

"Come now, it must have at least crossed your mind that you were unwise to encourage a friendship between Nicholas and Miss Wright. Unless I miss my guess, the girl has a *tendre* for Nicholas, and even though her father is one of the wealthiest men in the county, the daughter of a yeoman farmer is hardly a suitable match for a Maitland."

"I trust you will excuse me if I find your sudden concern for your family name very difficult to understand," retorted Mélissande in a rush of resentment. "Phoebe may not be a member of the gentry, but if she and Nick should decide to marry, I will gladly give them my blessing!"

Gideon's eyes glinted with a sudden anger. "How you can bring yourself to condone such a gross mésalliance—" He paused, shrugging. "I fancy you are about to suggest that Nicholas's marriage plans are none of my concern, and you would be quite right. Pray excuse my impertinence!"

"Oh, thank you, Sally. I shall be glad of the lap robe. It looks very chilly outside." Dressed in a velvet bonnet and a warm pelisse, Mélissande took the lap robe from the maid and walked to the door. She paused in surprise as she saw Nick making his way slowly down the stairs. He was dressed in shirt and breeches, with his heavily bandaged arm in a sling, and he looked very pale and weak.

"Nick, should you be out of bed? It's only a week since your accident. Dr. Morley advised complete bed rest for several more days."

"I'll go mad if I stay in that room one more minute. Don't worry about me, Sandy. Except for being weak as a kitten, I'm practically recovered. And I won't get my strength back lying in bed."

"I was just off to the village, but . . . Nick, if you're truly feeling better, could I talk to you for a few minutes? Come to the morning room. Sally will bring us some chocolate."

In the morning room, Mélissande watched Nick with some misgivings as he sat down abruptly, leaned his head against the back of his chair, and closed his eyes. Clearly the short walk from his bedchamber had exhausted him. "Fire away, Sandy," he murmured. "You haven't said a word of reproach since Gideon hauled me into the Dower House like a bag of old bones, but I know you've been longing to rake me over the coals."

"Nick, dearest, that's too bad of you! I wouldn't dream of raking you over the coals, but I would like to clear the air. You see, I think I know why you joined the smugglers. You had just signed away the Priory forever, and your world had collapsed around you. I suppose in some obscure way you felt that you were getting back at a malign fate. But now that you've escaped unscathed from the excisemen, surely you don't mean to resume smuggling?"

Nick stared sullenly at Mélissande. "Why not? If you must know, the village lads have been after me for years to join them. I didn't do so, not because I thought smuggling was criminal, but because I didn't want to risk disgracing the family if I were caught. But now, why not? I see nothing very enticing in my future. What am I to do with the rest of my life? I might go into the army, I suppose. I can't afford to buy a commission, but I could enlist as a common trooper in the cavalry. I *can* ride.''

Mélissande was appalled at the depths of Nick's hopelessness and resentment. ''You mustn't even consider enlisting as a common trooper. It's absurd to think that your life has ended at the age of eighteen! You could turn your hand to a score of things. What's to prevent you, for example, from becoming a bailiff on a large estate?''

''And who, pray, would have me at my age, with my lack of experience? Look, Sandy, my only possession of value is an empty title. Perhaps I can become famous, if not rich, as the 'Smuggler Lord'! The situation would have one advantage: if I were eventually caught and hanged, I would have made the Maitland name infamous. I presume that brother Gideon, even if he doesn't care a fig about the Priory, would not enjoy being known as the brother of an executed felon!''

About to protest Nick's outburst of black humor, Mélissande bit back her reply as Cecilia tripped into the room with Stephen Lacey trailing along behind her. ''Look who I found as I was coming up the driveway from my morning walk,'' said Cecilia merrily, her pretty face glowing from her exercise in the brisk air.

''By Jove, Nick, I was hoping to find you out of bed,'' said Stephen. ''I have a famous scheme. How would you like to go with me to Sir Harry Jernigan's estate at Cross-in-Hand? Harry is selling off his hunters. You recall, he took such a bad toss several months ago that he'll never ride again. I thought you and I might make a day of it. The Black Horse Inn at Cross-in-Hand makes a mouth-watering pot pie, and they have a cellar full of French wines.''

Nick's reply was listless and barely polite. ''Thank you for the thought, Stephen, but I'm not up to it.''

''Nonsense, the excursion would do you good. It would do *me* good, for that matter. Next week I'm off with the Volunteers for seven days' relief duty with the regulars at Folkestone. Lucky you, Nick, to miss it. We're to carry field equipment, you know, and sleep and eat with the men.

I confess I'm not looking forward to it. One wants to serve his country, but not if it means rotting in the fields with the sheep!''

"I'm happy you're being sensible, Nick," said Mélissande. "It would be much too tiring for you, a long drive in such cold weather.''

This sisterly approval provoked an imp of perversity in Nick, who said instantly, "I believe I'll change my mind, Stephen. I've been cooped up in this house for so long that I feel like one of your father's hothouse pineapples.''

Cecilia said with an air of bright discovery, "What a capital idea! Could I come along, too, Stephen? You don't have anything pressing for me to do today, do you, Sandy?''

Mélissande stared at her sister. It was transparently clear that Stephen and Cecilia had concocted this invitation to Nick as an excuse to spend the day together. Chaperoned by her own brother, Cecilia would escape any censure for sitting in a young man's pocket. Mélissande lifted her shoulders in a shrug of resignation. Her sister was of full age to do as she liked. Mélissande was unwilling to let the pair off the hook completely, however. She remarked to Stephen with a hint of malice, "As you know, your mother and I have not been on the best of terms of late, but we are certainly not enemies. Pray convey to Lady Haverford my affectionate respects and my hope that someday we can be friends again.''

"Oh, indeed, I shall be most happy to—to convey your greetings to Mama," stammered Stephen, turning an embarrassed red. As well he might, thought Mélissande with a quickly suppressed smile. A meeting with Cecilia, let alone a visit to the Dower House, would be the very last thing Stephen would see fit to report to his mother.

After waving good-bye to Nick and Cecilia and Stephen, Mélissande walked to the stables, feeling suddenly more depressed than she had been for some days. Nick's steady recovery and Gideon's extension of their stay at the Dower House had temporarily lifted her spirits, but now her problems were weighing her down again. Her reference to Lady Haverford had made her realize how much she missed the company of her cousin Aurore, and Cecilia's unwise association with Stephen was a continuing vexation, but it was Nick's dangerous state of mind that concerned her most. How could he put his disappointments behind him and look to the future while he was consumed by his bitterness and his near-hatred of his half brother?

Her thoughts shifting to Gideon, Mélissande was mildly shocked to find herself defending the man. Of course, he *had* risked his own liberty and reputation to save his brother from the excisemen, and he *had* come around to the Dower House next day to inquire about Nick's health, only to be met by a tirade that now struck Mélissande as the rankest ingratitude. For that matter, she mused, she herself had never adequately expressed her thanks to Gideon for his rescue of Nick, even though it might be argued that Gideon's own cool arrogance—his reference to Nick's "gross mésalliance" still rankled—had distracted her fom the standards of polite behavior demanded of a Castellane.

As John, the handyman, handed her up to the pony cart, Mélissande came to a quick decision. At the intersection of the side road with the main road, instead of turning right to go to Easton village, as she had originally intended, Mélissande reversed her direction and turned left toward the Priory, where Gideon's housekeeper, Mrs. Stedman, greeted her warmly as she entered the Great Hall and inquired for Gideon.

"No, I'm that sorry, Miss Mélissande, but his lordship isn't at home. He has a guest, a gentleman from the north of England, I believe, and his lordship is driving this gentleman around the estate. But there, I'm sure the pair of them will be returning soon, and meanwhile, won't you let me give you a cup of tea and a slice of my plum cake?"

"I'd be more than delighted to have some of your famous cake, but no standi   on ceremony, mind! Can't we have a cup of tea in your sitting room, as we used to do in the old days?''

A little later, peering over her teacup with an expression of inquisitive interest, Mrs. Stedman said, ''Well now, I hear that you've had very exciting doings at the Dower House.''

After she had given Mrs. Stedman an account of Nick's escapade with the excisemen—though it was apparent that the housekeeper had already learned most of the details from her contacts in the village—Mélissande said casually, ''And now you must tell me all your news.''

''La, Miss Mélissande, *I* don't have any news. I just go about carrying out my duties as I've always done. Though I must say, those duties are lighter now than they were awhile back, when his lordship first arrived home.'' Mrs. Stedman nodded meaningfully at Mélissande and launched herself on a long, gossipy monologue. ''Yes, indeed, we've had no more drunken parties at the Priory. His lordship packed off those lightskirts once and for all, and they haven't been back, or that Mr. Manners, either. But my heart still bleeds when I look at the damage to the portraits in the Long Gallery. Can you imagine how anyone, let alone a woman, could shoot a hole in a painting? But there, his lordship has promised that he will have the portraits repaired as good as new.''

''Lord Rochedale seems to have mended his ways,'' said Mélissande lightly.

''That he has. Of course, while his lordship drank perhaps more than he ought, it's only fair to remember that he was in great pain from his wounded leg. But now he drinks only a glass or two of wine with his meals. No more solitary, daylong drinking bouts. These days he spends most of his time out-of-doors, riding that great gray hunter of his. Or he goes off on long walks about the estate. I'm reminded so often of how it was when his lordship was a lad, before his mother died; how that boy delighted to be out-of-doors, tramping about the countryside day after day, gun on his shoulder and dog at his heels. All alone, of course. The poor lad never had any brothers or sisters.''

"A lonely existence, surely, for the master of Easton Priory today.''

"So I would have said, until recently. But I'm happy to report that his lordship is becoming positively social! You'll recall that I had orders to turn away all visitors when he first came home. Well, the vicar and Sir John and Lady Layton called this week, and only last evening he had dinner with the Haverfords at Fiesole.''

Somewhat surprised to hear of Gideon's newfound conviviality, Mélissande also felt a momentary pique at the thought of his dinner party with the Haverfords. If she were still on friendly terms with Aurore, she, too, might have been a guest at Fiesole. Not that it was of any great moment, she told herself hastily, and finished her tea.

Returning to the Great Hall, she found Gideon in the company of a stout, florid-faced gentleman in early middle age. "Oh—Mélissande—I didn't realize you were here. Allow me to introduce to you Mr. Josiah Redfort, who is interested in buying Easton Priory. Mr. Redfort, Miss de Castellane is my stepsister.''

Mr. Redfort's small, shrewd eyes bored into Mélissande. "I have it, you're the sister of the young man who's agreed to oblige his lordship by breaking the entail. Your father was a French swell, a real dook or some such.''

"That is correct, sir. My father was the Duc de Lavidan,'' replied Mélissande a bit stiffly.

"The Duc de Lavidan. Yes, it's coming back to me. When I heard about the goings-on between your noble mother and Lord Rochedale's father, I was fair bowled over, but there, I allow as how you can't judge the gentry by ordinary standards, now, can you? You take your ordinary man, if he runs on tick he'll likely as not end up in debtors' prison, but the late Lord Rochedale, when *he* was in the basket, he just slapped another mortgage on his property.''

Biting her lip, Mélissande tossed a glare of outrage at

Gideon, but it was immediately clear from his expression of
frozen hauteur that he had not been exposing family skele-
tons to Mr. Redfort. The latter's familiarity with the Maitland
and Castellane families was undoubtedly the fruit of his own
research, which Mélissande acknowledged would not have
been at all difficult. The two families had certainly conducted
their scandals in the full light of public scrutiny!

"May I offer you a glass of wine while we continue our
conversation, Mr. Redfort?" asked Gideon, in what Mélissande
suspected was an effort to divert his guest from further
personal comment.

"That you may, and thank you kindly. Miss de Castellane,
you'll join us?"

"Oh, no, I won't intrude on your—your business discussion. Gid—my lord, I came on a trifling errand. I'll return
to see you another day."

"Nonsense, ma'am. His lordship can have no objection
to your sharing a discussion about selling the Priory, since it
touches so closely upon you and your younger brother and
sister. Ain't I right, Lord Rochedale? Since the young lady
is now occupying the Dower House, any sale of the estate
must involve other living arrangements for her and Lord
Nicholas and Miss Cecilia Maitland."

An irritated expression crossed Gideon's face at this latest
revelation of Mr. Redfort's knowledge of his affairs. "Since
you know so much about my situation, Mr. Redfort, you
must be aware that Miss de Castellane has no direct interest
in the estate. Now, if my brother Nicholas were here . . ."

"But of course Nick can't be here because he's ill.
Perhaps I should remain to act as his representative," said
Mélissande. Confronted at last with the nightmare actuality
of the loss of the Priory, she was seized by a sudden angry
resolve to add as much discomfort as possible to Gideon's
sale of his ancestral acres.

Gideon shrugged. "You must please yourself. Stay if you
like."

Seated in the withdrawing room on the second floor,

Mélissande was heartened to observe that the gracious room bore no scars from Gideon's recent entertaining. The stain had been removed from the soft, faded old carpet, and the great tapestry once more hung on the wall.

"I understand you are from the north of England, Mr. Redfort," she said politely as Mrs. Stedman brought in a tray containing glasses and a bottle of Madeira.

"That I am, ma'am. I own a cotton mill in Manchester. The biggest, most prosperous mill in all of Lancashire, if I may say so. Now that I've earned all the money I can ever spend, however, I think it's time to turn to something else. I've long been interested in politics, but there's no future for me along those lines in Lancashire." Mr. Redfort's expression turned angry. "Would you believe that the county gentry there have connived an unofficial rule that no mill owner can be a justice of the peace? So, since my good wife Bessie fancies a softer climate anyway, I've decided to come south and buy an estate, so that I can take a seat in Parliament. As a landowner, I can also enter county society, perhaps even obtain a title. I rather fancy the sound of 'Sir Josiah.' Or even better, 'Lord Redfort.' "

Mr. Redfort paused to consider with pleasure his future ennoblement. "Then, too, as a property owner and member of Parliament, I'll be in a position to place my younger boys in the church or the army or the civil service. You see, I don't want my children to work as hard as their old father. I want all my boys to be gentlemen, and I want all my girls to marry gentlemen."

As she tried to concentrate on Mr. Redfort's relentless monologue, Mélissande noticed that Gideon's eyes had glazed over, almost as though he had pulled down a curtain between himself and his guest.

Having satisfactorily arranged for his future and that of his numerous family, Mr. Redfort remarked to Gideon with an air of decision, "I'll be frank with your lordship. I'm very favorably impressed with your property. The size of your holdings appears about right, and I'm pleased to see that parts of the old abbey buildings are still standing. My wife Bessie tells me that artificial ruins are all the crack these days, but as a man of business I'm delighted to avoid the expense! Of course, the main house is hopelessly old-fashioned. I plan to tear it down and build something on modern lines, like Kedleston Hall in Derbyshire or Harewood House in Yorkshire.''

Appalled, Mélissande exclaimed, ''But Mr. Redfort, it would be almost a sacrilege to pull down this beautiful old house. Are you aware that Queen Elizabeth stayed here on several occasions?''

''Bless your heart, ma'am, that was an impressive honor indeed, and I'm sure Her Majesty was entertained as royally as the circumstances of the times would allow. But if I should ever have the pleasure of receiving King George under my roof, I vow I should blush to welcome him into a house as old-fashioned and shabby as this one.'' Mr. Redfort turned to Gideon. ''Begging your pardon, your lordship, I know your late father was at point-non-plus, or I fancy he would have torn down this old pile himself, or at least he would have maintained it properly. And speaking of money, I think it's time to discuss the terms of the sale. I believe your solicitor mentioned the sum of two hundred thousand pounds. If that's agreeable to you, I'm prepared to make the offer.''

During this conversation, Gideon's face had been assuming the rigid contours of a marble sculpture. ''No, Mr. Redfort. The offer is not agreeable to me.''

''I was sure I understood that that was your asking price. Oh, very well. Say two hundred and twenty-five thousand.''

Gideon shook his head, but before he could say anything, Mr. Redfort said with a forced smile, ''You drive a hard bargain, your lordship. Perhaps you missed your calling. Perhaps you should have become a man of business like myself. Look, I'm not a man to waste my blunt, but I like this property. What do you say to a quarter of a million pounds?''

Mélissande gulped, but Gideon again shook his head. "It's a handsome offer, Mr. Redfort, but the fact is, I've decided not to sell. Not at this time, at any rate."

Mr. Redfort turned a dark purple. "Now, see here, your lordship, I don't appreciate being invited down here under false pretenses. I know you need money. . . . Well, the state of your house and grounds would tell me that, even if I had no other source of information! So if you've refused my offer, it can only mean that another buyer has nipped in ahead of me." Mr. Redfort's brow furrowed in thought. "As I was saying, I like this property. I'll match any offer this other buyer made to you up to—what would you say to three hundred thousand pounds?"

"I hardly think I need discuss with you my reasons for not selling the Priory," said Gideon coldly. "Let me see you to the door, Mr. Redfort. My compliments to your good lady." Placing his hand on the shoulder of Mr. Redfort, who was speechless from chagrin and shock, Gideon virtually propelled his unwanted guest from the room.

When he returned to the withdrawing room a few minutes later, Mélissande exclaimed, "Thank God you sent that man packing, Gideon." Not noticing that she had used his Christian name entirely unself-consciously, she went on, "I don't like to think of myself as a snob, but one simply could not countenance the prospect of a man like Mr. Redfort living here, even if he abandoned his scheme to tear down the Priory. I feel confident you can find a more suitable buyer, someone with at least some pretensions to gentility."

Gideon's normally assured expression was curiously hesitant. He said abruptly, "All my neighbors would have wanted to burn me in effigy if I had sold the Priory to Redfort, but the fact of the matter is that I've decided not to sell at all. Three hundred thousand pounds would have made me a wealthy man on paper, but after I had paid off the mortgages, my net sum would have been much more modest."

Mélissande was too surprised to make an immediate comment. She had been watching his face while Redfort was speaking of tearing down the house, and his quickly erased wince of pain had reflected her own feelings. Was it possible that, during those recent long, solitary rides and walks about the estate, Gideon had rediscovered his boyhood love for the Priory?

Still abruptly, Gideon asked, "Do you think Nicholas might be interested in becoming bailiff of the estate after all?" At her sudden stare, he nodded, saying, "Old Morris came to me last week when he heard a rumor that I was selling. He wishes to retire immediately, since the work is getting beyond him, and in any case a new owner would want to install his own man. He also said it was a shame that Nicholas would not succeed him, because the boy had already served his apprenticeship for the position. Also, though Morris considers himself too old to engage in the newfangled agricultural methods of Farmer Wright, he feels Nick has learned a great deal from the man. By coincidence, several days later I chanced to dine with Lord Haverford. I believe his wife is some sort of cousin of yours, is she not? Lord Haverford strongly advised me against selling my estate during wartime, since both the price of land and the income from it are rising dramatically. Did you know that the price of corn has jumped from under fifty shillings a quarter just a few years ago to over ninety-six shillings today?"

"Yes, I did know it," replied Mélissande dryly. "I marvel at your interest in such a subject."

"I don't pretend to many virtues, but not even my worst enemy would call me a total fool. I'm beginning to think I would be a fool to sell the Priory during a period of prosperity. Tell Nicholas to come see me if he would like to be bailiff. I don't promise anything, but if his new methods seem to be successful over—say a two-year trial period—I will reconsider selling the estate. You and Cecilia and Nicholas may continue living in the Dower House during the interim, of course. However, I won't pay your inheritances. For one thing, I don't have anything like the cash required, especially since I suspect that Nicholas's new methods are going to put me out of pocket! For another, you must allow me some leverage. With you three in possession of your inheritances, you would have no reason to oblige me if, at some time in the future, I should again ask Nicholas to bar the entail.''

Feeling almost too dazed for words, Mélissande mumbled, ''I'll go straight home to tell Nick the news,'' and turned to go. As she reached the door, Gideon said politely, ''Didn't you come to see me about something?''

Mélissande turned around to face him. ''Why, yes, I . . . You see, I felt that I hadn't thanked you properly for saving Nick, and also I wanted to apologize for his ingratitude, for which I fear he will never wish to apologize himself, because he—he . . .''

Gideon cut through her floundering remarks. ''Because he hates and resents me? Don't distress yourself. I'm employing Nicholas for my own self-interest. I don't require gratitude or liking from him, or indeed from any of you. As a matter of fact, I anticipate little contact with my father's second family, except when I must see Nicholas on business, or when all of us chance to be thrown together publicly. At which times, if I may make the suggestion, I think we should unbend sufficiently to allow a mutual use of Christian names.'' He smiled slightly. ''I see no reason why the county should be treated to the continuing spectacle of our lack of fondness for each other, do you? It certainly won't hurt me to say 'Mélissande,' and I've observed that you have already called me Gideon without undue pain.''

Ignoring the cold, hard lump in the pit of her stomach, Mélissande said coolly, ''You relieve my anxieties no end, my dear Gideon. Now that we perfectly understand each other, we will all of us be so much more comfortable. There is nothing quite so fatiguing as the necessity to pretend to feelings that one doesn't have!''

CHAPTER IX

A sharp gust of wind tugged at Mélissande's bonnet, and she hugged her arms closer to her body against the raw chill of the late February day. After many weeks of interminable cold and gales, it was difficult to believe that March was almost here and spring just around the corner. She banished her discomfort to the back of her mind and fixed her attention on the Easton Volunteers as they conducted their Sunday afternoon drill over the winter-ravaged grass of the village green.

Beside her, Lord Haverford murmured with a smile of self-satisfaction, "Observe, my dear, how strikingly the company has improved in the past several weeks. This is a professional body of men now. If I may say so, it was a stroke of genius on my part to ask Lord Rochedale to assume the command from my son Stephen."

The Earl of Haverford was a pleasant but rather dull man, whose chief interests in life were riding, hunting, and shooting. He had always been kind to his wife's young cousin, and Mélissande was fond of him.

Even to her inexpert eyes, it was clear that the Volunteers did indeed present a more crisply military appearance than ever before. Her eyes shifted to the three mounted men at the head of the company. Nick and Stephen were gallantly handsome in their regimentals, but Gideon wore his uniform with the grace and élan of the born cavalryman. Even from a distance, Mélissande could see that he was in magnificent health. His color was good, the dark circles beneath his eyes had vanished, and he sat his powerful horse with a steely poise. That he had elected to join the Volunteers had come as an acute surprise to Mélissande when she had learned of it several weeks previously, until she reflected that Gideon had probably viewed this assumption of civic responsibility as a necessary part of his duties, now that he had decided to remain, if only temporarily, as master of Easton Priory.

"Yes, the Volunteers do look wonderfully professional, Lord Haverford, but do you really think that Napoleon still intends to invade England? We've had so many long months of waiting, and there have been so many alarms."

Casting a quick look around, Lord Haverford lowered his voice confidentially. "Let me assure you that the invasion danger is very much present. Just the other day I had lunch in Brighton with the Prince of Wales, who told me that French activity in the Channel ports has increased vastly in the past several weeks, and many in the government actually fear that Napoleon is preparing an expedition to Ireland as a diversion from his main invasion flotilla."

Lord Haverford stopped, looked embarrassed. "My dear, I fear I've been very indiscreet. You'll not mention my reference to Ireland?" Quickly he changed the subject, glancing across the green to his carriage, in which his wife was sitting with a strange young woman. "Won't you come along with me to say a word to Aurore? Only this morning she was telling me how much she has missed your company. You are her only relative in this country, you know."

Mélissande took the Earl's arm. "Why, of course, I had every intention of greeting Aurore. But as for resuming our old closeness . . ."

"I know, I know," said Lord Haverford uncomfortably. "I do admire your loyalty to that pretty sister of yours, but I think in time you will come to see that she and Stephen just won't do." At Mélissande's quick frown, he added hastily, "Well, enough of that. I'm most anxious for you to meet a visitor to Fiesole, my goddaughter, Augusta Millard. Poor little thing, both her parents died of the fever not long ago. I was appointed her guardian, and I'm happy to have her under my wing because she has inherited a very tidy fortune, and I've no doubt that when she comes out in the spring she will be the object of every gazetted fortune hunter in town."

At the carriage, the Countess greeted Mélissande with a warm smile and a clinging handclasp. "*Ma chère*, it is pure heaven to see you again. I must present to you Edmund's goddaughter, Augusta Millard, who has come to stay with us."

Augusta Millard was a pretty girl, small and graceful, with waving brown hair, bright blue eyes, and a demure, pleasing manner. "Lady Haverford has been telling me such tales, Miss de Castellane, about how you and she barely escaped with your lives from revolutionary France."

"Aurore's stories become more dramatic with each telling," said Mélissande, laughing.

"Nevertheless, I should so enjoy hearing about your experiences from you personally."

"There, you see, Mélissande, you must come back with us to Fiesole for tea so you and Augusta can become better acquainted," declared Lady Haverford. "She knows no one in the county, and I want so much for her to have some new young friends."

"Among whom you cannot include Cecilia?" murmured Mélissande. She turned away from Aurore, whose face had tightened with discomfiture, and smiled at Augusta. "I can't come to Fiesole this afternoon, Miss Millard, but I hope to see you soon."

Excusing herself, she moved away from the carriage, thinking with some regret that Augusta appeared to be a charming addition to county society, a girl she would have liked to know better if circumstances had been different. Mélissande looked across the green to see Nick in animated conversation with Gideon. Waving her over, Nick exclaimed exuberantly as she came up, "Guess what, Sandy? We're getting those breeding sheep from John Ellman after all. Wait until Mr. Wright and Phoebe hear about this!"

Mélissande smiled at his enthusiasm. Her young brother had metamorphosed once again, to become the eager, energetic Nick of old. Initially, on hearing of Gideon's offer, Nick had been reluctant to take the position of bailiff. He had insisted suspiciously that Gideon might change his mind about remaining at the Priory if a new and unusually wealthy buyer appeared, and then he and his sisters would be no better off than before. But eventually he had given in, applying himself to his new duties with a single-minded devotion and an infinite capacity for hard work. His opinion of Gideon had softened, too, largely owing to the fact, Mélissande reasoned, that Gideon had accompanied the Easton Volunteers on field exercises with the regulars some weeks before, during which he had camped in a muddy field with his men and had had his uniform cut to ribbons while charging a vicious briar hedge.

After Nick had left to search out Phoebe with his news of the breeding sheep, Mélissande said pleasantly to Gideon, "The experiment seems to be working out well. I'm very pleased to see that you and Nick are on better terms."

"My dear Mélissande, as I informed you some time ago, my feelings do not enter into my arrangement with Nick. We are simply working together to our mutual advantage. To date, as far as I can judge, he seems to be carrying out his duties very well. For example, he has persuaded John Oliver, our principal tenant, to share the cost of draining the field adjacent to our north meadow. He has also succeeded in doing the near impossible by raising the rents of the tenants without antagonizing them at the same time. He's done this by promising the tenants longer leases on condition that they put a larger share of their arable into artificial grasses and root crops so they can feed more and better livestock. On the basis of these developments, I've been able to obtain a substantial loan, despite my heavy mortgages, part of which will go to purchase Nicholas's breeding sheep. Very little has changed as far as our personal relations are concerned, however. Provided I give him free rein to put into practice his theories about farming, Nicholas wouldn't care if I were Napoleon himself. For my part, as long as he furthers my interests, the fact that he's my father's son is irrelevant.''

''Have you never thought that you might be missing a great joy by shutting Nick and Cecilia out of your life?'' blurted Mélissande.

There was a long pause, and then Gideon, his eyes suddenly bleak, said shortly, ''I haven't really thought about it. As you are well aware, I've had little experience of close family life.'' He cleared his throat, motioning to Cecilia, who was standing close by, talking to Stephen Lacey. He tossed Mélissande a challenging look. ''For a lady who pays such lip service to family ties, Mélissande, you seem singularly blind to the inappropriate friendships of your sister and brother. I've already given you my opinion of Nicholas's relationship with Miss Wright. Now let me warn you—and this is not an opinion, but a fact—that the Haverfords will never consent to any union between Cecilia and Stephen Lacey, licit or otherwise!''

Mélissande replied, her eyes kindling, ''I believe we've already agreed that the personal lives of Nick and Cecilia can be no concern of yours. And while we are being frank, my lord Rochedale . . .''

''I thought we had agreed that we were now on a first-name basis,'' Gideon interrupted her.

''I was about to say, *Gideon,* that I admit to wishing in idle moments that Nick was his father's only son!''

Gideon's lips curved in a crooked little grin. He reached out his hand to stroke Mélissande's cheek gently with his forefinger. ''That, of course, is your privilege.'' He touched his hat in farewell, his smile deepening at Mélissande's expression of startled surprise.

Later that day, after the evening meal at the Dower House, Mélissande was unusually quiet and thoughtful, causing Cecilia, who had persuaded her and Nick into a game of Dummy Whist, to scold her for lack of attention. "You look positively blue-deviled, Sandy. I saw you talking to Gideon this afternoon. Is he being difficult again?"

"Oh, no. But I don't feel in the mood for cards tonight, Cecilia. I believe I'll go up to my bed early." But sleep that night was elusive for Mélissande, whose dark mood persisted after she went up to her bedchamber. As she shifted restlessly in her bed, she found herself wondering about the future. As Nick had once suspected, Gideon's mercurial resolve to keep the Priory might change at any time, and then she would be obliged to find another place to live. In any case, she and Nick and Cecilia would not be sharing a household forever. Nick would probably marry Phoebe, and Cecilia might well find a suitable husband, once she recovered from her hopeless attachment to Stephen. Mélissande thought gloomily that she had been shortsighted not to plan for some kind of independent life of her own. She was twenty-four years old now, and—according to Aurore, at least—getting along in years!

After she had finally drifted into a light sleep, Mélissande was aroused by a sound that she could not at first identify. It came again, followed a few seconds later by the noise of breaking glass. In a moment, from Nick's adjoining bedchamber she heard a muttered curse and a sharp thud as his feet hit the floor. Then came the sound of a window being opened and the murmur of Nick's voice as he called softly to someone below. Shortly afterward the slight creaking of Nick's door was followed by the sound of his cautious passage down the stairs. Mélissande reached for her pocket luminary and lit her candle. Then she shrugged herself into her dressing gown, thrust her feet into her slippers, and slipped down the stairs. There was no one in the hall, but beyond the closed front door she could hear the muffled sound of voices. She opened the door, shivering in a sudden blast of frigid air, to find Nick confronting a small knot of men grouped around a lantern.

"Well now, that's torn it," said Nick in disgust as Mélissande appeared in the doorway. "Why did you lads have to wake up my sister?"

One of the men behind the lantern—Mélissande recognised the voice of Nat Grayson, the blacksmith's son—said aggrievedly, "Well, my lord, we didn't know just where you slept, so we threw pebbles against *all* the windows on this side of the 'ouse. Begging yer pardon, Miss de Castellane, was it yer window we broke?"

"No, it was mine, you idiot," exclaimed Nick. Clad only in shirt and breeches, he hunched his shoulders against the cold, saying, "As long as the fat's in the fire, you might as well all come in before we freeze to death."

As the little group of six or seven men filed past her into the hall, Mélissande grasped Nick's arm, asking urgently, "Nick, it's not the smuggling again, is it?"

"No, of course not. I've learned my lesson. I don't know what the lads want. They hadn't had time to tell me before you came down. Something about finding a stranger."

Closing the door and turning to face the group, Mélissande spotted one face that did not look even vaguely familiar. She was looking at a tall, slim man with very black hair and eyes, dressed in a sodden dark coat, breeches, and caped greatcoat.

"Now then, lads, out with it. What brings you here in the middle of the night?" demanded Nick.

"Well, me lord, we was down in Fairlight Glen earlier in the evening—" Nat Grayson broke off, flashing a sideways glance at Mélissande, who did her best to keep her face expressionless. But even she had heard that Fairlight Glen, with its cliffs and underground caves, two miles by the cliff path from Hastings, was a prominent gathering place for smugglers.

Nick said hastily, "You needn't go into the nature of your doings at the glen. That's none of our affair."

"Very good, me lord. Well, when we was finished unloading our ponies with our—er—cargo, we heard the sound of oarlocks. A minute or two later we saw this fellow 'ere"—Nat jabbed a finger at the dark stranger—"wading through the water to the shingle. Like as not, 'e'd tranferred to a small boat from a seagoing vessel anchored farther out, and then, when 'e got close to shore, 'e set 'is boat adrift so there'd be no trace of 'is landing. It was a bit suspicious, we thought, and then when we discovered the man was a Frenchy—leastwise, 'e can't speak the King's English proper like, *that* I know—we was mortal sure the French fleet was 'ere at last, and this cove 'ad come ahead to spy out the best landing places. So we was about to light the beacon on the cliff and 'and the spy over to the army or the militia when the cove burst out, very excited, that 'e warn't a spy or any kind of enemy at all. 'E said 'e 'ad a cousin in Easton, a Mademoiselle de Castellane, a daughter of Lord Rochedale, and if we would just take 'im to 'er, 'e was sure she would vouch for 'im."

Grayson looked expectantly at Nick. "So there ye are, me lord. We brought the Frenchy here, but if ye tell us 'e's lying, why, we'll 'and 'im over to the justice of the peace forthwith, or better yet, we could string 'im up as a French spy and save everybody a bother of trouble."

Grayson leered at the stranger, who, to Nat's obvious disappointment, showed no sign of intimidation. He returned Grayson's look with a silent, disdainful stare and turned to Mélissande, speaking in French. "You are—you must be— my cousin Mélissande, *n'est-ce-pas*? We have not seen each other for many years, but you still look exactly like the beautiful child that I remember. I am Bertrand de Castellane."

Too shocked to speak, Mélissande stood frozen in place as she returned the stranger's intent gaze. A vagrant memory stirred, and suddenly there flashed into her mind the image of a much prized miniature of her father's that was among the few treasured belongings she had brought from France. The face of the stranger was very like the face in the painting—pale skin, intensely dark eyes, straight, regular features. Very like her own also, she thought, startled. She stammered, "I don't understand, sir. You say you are my cousin, Bertrand de Castellane?"

"I am. My father is Guillaume de Castellane, second cousin of your late father, the Duc de Lavidan. My father was the Duc's nearest relation in the direct male line, the last surviving Castellane of that generation."

Mélissande's expression changed slightly, and her voice turned cold. "Then, monsieur, if you really are who you say you are, your father is the present Duc de Lavidan, the man who slavishly followed the example of the Duc d'Orléans and saved his skin and fortune by voting with the other regicides to execute King Louis XVI. Your father was more fortunate than Orléans, *bien entendu*. Guillaume de Castellane escaped the guillotine and lived to prosper under the Revolution. He not only inherited my father's title as the nearest male kin, he was able to buy the Castellane family property confiscated by the revolutionary government when the Duc de Lavidan was proscribed as an émigré."

Mélissande flashed the stranger a tight smile. "With your background, monsieur—assuming that you truly are Guillaume de Castellane's son—you surely are a very odd visitor to England at this point in history, with your country's armies poised to invade us. Under the circumstances, you can hardly expect me to welcome you. In fact, I daresay Nat Grayson is correct. You probably *are* a spy for Napoleon."

A muscle twitched in the stranger's face, but his voice was calm as he replied, "If I were a spy, I would certainly have tried to arrive more secretively, don't you agree? *Not* at a place well-known on both sides of the Channel as a gathering point for smugglers. And why would I ask to be taken to the home of a relative whose sympathies—or at least those of her parents—are solidly antirevolutionary and anti-Bonaparte? Cousin Mélissande,'' the man added urgently, ''can't we talk privately?''

As Mélissande hesitated, Nick walked over to the villagers, who had been listening intently but with frustrated curiosity to the incomprehensible French conversation. Nick himself was far from fluent in French, but he understood the language well enough, and now he said to the villagers, ''It's all right, lads. This fellow may actually be my sister's cousin. She would like to speak to him alone, so you can go along. Those pack ponies of yours will be getting cold and tired and restless.''

''But Lord Nicholas,'' protested Nat Grayson, ''this Frenchy may be Miss de Castellane's cousin right enough, but 'e could still be a spy, couldn't 'e? What if 'e should turn violent like? P'raps we'd best stay for a bit.''

Turning suddenly, Nick ran swift hands over the body of the man who called himself Bertrand de Castellane, whose startled face reddened with resentment.

''He's not armed, Nat,'' Nick said to Grayson. ''You go along with the lads. I don't look for any trouble with the man, but you might give me that pistol of yours, and then if anything should develop, I'll pop him along to the magistrates.''

Slowly Nat Grayson drew out an ancient pistol from the capacious pocket of his homespun jacket. '' 'Ope as 'ow ye're doing the right thing, Lord Nicholas.'' Reluctantly he walked to the door with his followers. As the door closed behind them, Mélissande said, ''Come with me this way to the drawing room, monsieur. Nick, would you light the candles in the sconces over the mantel? And perhaps we should have a fire.''

The flickering light of the candles softened the shabbiness of the drawing room, but the room was very cold. It was seldom used by the family, who preferred the coziness of the smaller morning room, and except for formal occasions, the fireplace was never lit. But Mélissande had noticed the stranger's involuntary shivering as he moved past her into the drawing room, and a certain compassion stirred within her as she looked at him more closely and realized that his breeches were wet almost to the hip and that the skirts of his greatcoat clung damply to his legs. After splashing ashore at Fairlight Glen, he had undoubtedly had a cold, hard, and unenviable journey from the coast astride a mule.

"Nick, please bring our—our guest a glass of Madeira."

After Nick had lit the fire, the stranger went straight to the fireplace, extending grateful hands to the welcome blaze and accepting eagerly the glass of wine that Nick silently handed to him.

"Thank you for allowing me to talk to you, Cousin Mélissande," the stranger said after he had drained the glass. "It may surprise you, but I can't quarrel with your opinion of my father. He *was* a regicide, and he *did* buy the family property. In his defense, however, I might add that he was the last of his line and believed that the estates should be kept in the Castellane family. In any event, while I was growing up I never questioned my father's conduct. I believed in the revolutionary cause as fervently, I am sure, as your father clung to his allegiance to the King. I joined the revolutionary armies at seventeen, in 1793, serving in Colonel Moreau's volunteer battalion. I was fortunate enough to continue serving with Moreau through his subsequent promotions to command the right wing of the army in Flanders."

Mélissande said with stiff lips, "Then you must have fought in the battle of Turcoing, where my father was killed?" At the stranger's slow nod, she added bitterly, "But with this difference, that my father fought for the old monarchy, and you fought for King Louis' murderers! Why are you telling me about your republican military service, monsieur? Surely you cannot hope to influence me favorably toward you by such a revelation."

Displaying no anger, the stranger said patiently, "I'm trying to explain to you why I came to England. You see, I became a close friend of General Moreau . . ."

"I fail to see . . ."

"You must understand that General Moreau is not an ardent republican, as most people believe, but a man of strong royalist sympathies. Over the years, as he saw the excesses of the Revolution, he began to yearn for the return of the monarchy. Over the years I came to share his views. We have been especially distressed in recent months by widespread rumors that Napoleon plans to make himself king, or even emperor. Our disillusionment became complete a scant two weeks ago, when General Moreau was arrested, falsely accused of taking part in a conspiracy headed by the longtime royalist conspirators Cadoudal and Pichegru to kidnap and assassinate Napoleon. Much as he sympathized with the conspirators, the general could not bring himself to act against the head of the French state. Nevertheless, my innocent friend is in prison and headed for the guillotine."

The stranger spread his arms wide in a rueful gesture. "The general's arrest convinced me that I could no longer live in a country ruled by Napoleon. I decided to come to England and offer my services to the Comte d'Artois. I was able to contact a band of smugglers bound with a cargo of brandy to the Romney marshes, paying them to drop me offshore near Hastings. From there, I intended to make my way inland to Easton. As your kinsman, Mélissande, I thought I might be safe from arrest as an enemy alien, and I also hoped your mother might give me an introduction to His Royal Highness the Comte d'Artois."

"*Maman* is dead," said Mélissande blankly.

"Oh, I'm so sorry, I had no idea. . . ."

Nick, who had been listening in silence, his expression growing steadily more skeptical, broke in impatiently, "Look here, Castellane, or whatever your real name might be, I've never heard such a wild tale. I think Nat Grayson's instincts were right. You really are an advance agent for the French invasion forces. Of course, if you could persuade me that you actually are Sandy's cousin, why then I might be more disposed to believe you."

With a faintly amused smile, the stranger said to Mélissande, "*Ma cousine*, do you remember a tiny gray kitten with three white paws—her name was Minette, as I recall—who climbed high into a tree and then was too frightened to come down by herself? Climbing the tree to rescue the kitten, Minette's mistress caught her dress on a dead branch and could not extricate herself. So then her cousin, a small boy of about— let me think now—of about twelve years of age, scrambled up the tree to help her, only to lose his balance and fall to the ground, breaking his arm."

Mélissande broke into a delighted smile. "But even though you were in pain from your broken arm, you ran back to the château for help. And *Grandmère* was so angry because I had been such a hoyden and had torn my best gown that she sent us both to bed without supper. Bertrand! It *is* you!"

His dark eyes lighting with an answering smile, Castellane threw his arms wide in a beckoning gesture. Without hesitation, her doubts unreservedly dissolved, Mélissande flew into his embrace. After a moment she lifted her head, a worried frown replacing her smile of joy. "Bertrand, you know you must register as an alien with the authorities? Oh, I do hope there won't be any trouble about that, but since you arrived as you did, in the middle of the night from an enemy smuggler's boat . . ."

"But your stepfather, Lord Rochedale, must be a man of great local influence. Couldn't be vouch for me?"

"My stepfather is dead, too."

Totally won over, Nick clapped a hand on Bertrand's shoulder. "Never fear, cousin, Sandy and I will vouch for you. *We* still amount to a little something in this county. If there are any problems, Sandy, we can always go to Gideon."

Stiffening, Mélissande said, "I'm sure that won't be necessary." Her smile reappeared as she said to Bertrand, "I can't quite believe it. I really thought I would live out my life here in England with only Nick and Cecilia and my cousin Aurore for family, but now I have you, too. But enough of my blithering. You're wet and cold, and probably hungry also. We must make you more comfortable.''

"*Eh bien,* I won't say no to a hot drink and a bite to eat," said Bertrand frankly. "But first let me restore to you a piece of your property." Reaching into an inner pocket of his greatcoat, he brought out a small, padded silk bag. Untying the drawstring, he emptied the contents of the bag into his palm.

Her eyes mesmerized by the shimmering green fire of the emeralds interspersed with the glitter of diamonds, Mélissande murmured, "They look like . . . Could these be *Grandmère*'s emeralds?''

"They are. A parure of necklace, earrings, and bracelet in emeralds and diamonds.''

"I thought they must have been lost after *Grandmère*'s death, when the château was looted and partially burned.''

Bertrand looked acutely embarrassed. "When my father heard of your grandmother's last illness, he went down to see her at the château in Berry. Since your father was serving abroad with Condé's army, and she had no other immediate family in France, your grandmother confided the emeralds to my father, asking him to find some way to deliver them to you in England. She had always intended that the emeralds should go to you as her only granddaughter. I think my father really meant to give you the jewelry—oh, sometime when the war was over, when the situation in France was less chaotic!—but in the meantime, he allowed my mother to wear the emeralds. And as the years went by . . ." Bertrand shrugged. "*Maman* came to think of them as her own property." He carefully put the jewelry back into the padded bag and handed it to Mélissande.

She hesitated. "I don't know if I should accept the emeralds, Bertrand. Your father may not have acted very honorably, but I dread to think of what his reaction must be when he discovers that you've taken them.''

"Don't worry about me," replied Bertrand with an edge to his voice. "His reaction when he misses the emeralds will be as nothing compared to his feelings when he finds that I've defected. No, I insist that you take the emeralds. They are yours because your grandmother always meant them to be yours."

It was dawn before Mélissande could finally go to her bedchamber, after cooking a hot meal for Bertrand, finding him some of Nick's clothing to replace his wet garments, and preparing a bed for him in the room next to Nick's. Tired as she was, however, she could not resist taking another look at the emeralds. Clasping the necklace around her throat, she looked at her reflection in the mirror. Soon she could see only indistinctly, her eyes misting over as the glittering green flash of the stones reminded her of the long-gone days when her grandmother, her gown of rustling brocade enhanced by the emerald parure, had presided over a gala gathering at the château in Berry.

CHAPTER X

"Mélissande? Mélissande? Oh, there you are."
Bertrand peered around the door of the library, where
Mélissande, her hair enveloped by a mobcap and her dress
protected by a large apron, was busily wielding a feather
duster. "*Ma mie,* I hate to see you at such a menial task."

"I don't relish it myself, Bertrand," said Mélissande,
dryly. "But as I've told you, we keep only one servant, and
I cannot ask Sally to do all the cooking and housecleaning.
Did you have an enjoyable day in Hastings?"

Bertrand beamed. "*Vraiment.* Thank you so much for
allowing me to use the pony cart. I hadn't driven one since
I was a little boy visiting your grandmother's château. Do
you know, now that it is the middle of March, I really think
spring is coming at last? I saw a crocus in bloom as I turned
into your driveway." He unwrapped the parcel he was
carrying. "Look, don't you think the frame looks well?"

"Yes, it's beautiful, and the painting even more so,"
replied Mélissande, looking with a pleased smile at her
portrait, a small painting of oils showing her head and
shoulders. It was a good likeness by any standard, and a
truly remarkable likeness from the hand of an amateur

artist—Bertrand—who had not touched a brush and palette for a number of years.

To Mélissande, it often seemed that Bertrand had been a houseguest for a much longer time than the three weeks that had elapsed since his arrival at the Dower House, so easily had he fit into the life of the family. After registering with the authorities, he had been given permission to remain for the time being at the Dower House, and he quickly settled into a role as unofficial elder brother of Nick and Cecilia. He had also become a familiar sight in the village of Easton, where, during the course of his leisurely strolls, he indulged in long, friendly chats with the tradespeople and often played with the children on the green. Soon into his stay at the Dower House, declaring that he was not used to being idle, he had purchased a modest amount of painting supplies and had persuaded Mélissande to sit as his first subject.

"Perhaps you missed your calling when you became a soldier," said Mélissande, still admiring the portrait. "Perhaps you should have been an artist."

"Well, as a matter of fact, the proprietor of the artists' supply shop in Hastings told me I would have no difficulty obtaining commissions in the town if I cared to paint professionally." Bertrand shook his head ruefully. "It may come to that, though I've always considered my painting as a youthful pastime. Eventually, however, I will be obliged to earn my living in this new country."

"Oh, I didn't think . . . But of course, whatever money you were able to bring with you won't last forever. Bertrand, you shouldn't have gone to the expense of having my portrait framed."

"*Ça ne fait rien.* Don't trouble your pretty head about me. I have plenty of money for my needs for the time being. Later, if the Comte d'Artois accepts my services, my financial problems will doubtless be over."

"I shouldn't count on that," said Mélissande doubtfully. "I believe the Comte has no funds of his own. The English government makes him an allowance of some hundreds of pounds each month, but I'm told that His Highness donates most of this income to charitable causes and to help support the poorer émigrés in England.''

Bertrand shrugged. "*Eh bien,* I must cross that bridge when I come to it. I know I can't stay here indefinitely, imposing on your hospitality. Soon I must go up to London, or wherever he is staying, to offer my services to the Comte.''

"Bertrand, don't ever feel that you are outwearing your welcome. We want you to stay here for as long as you care to do so.''

"Thank you, *chérie,* but I can't allow myself to forget my true reason for coming to England.''

Just then Cecilia burst into the room. "Sandy, Bertrand, guess what? Napoleon sent agents across the Rhine to kidnap and arrest the Duc d'Enghien in Baden. The Duc was accused of complicity in the Cadoudal-Pichegru plot, and when that was proved untrue, he was accused of bearing arms against the Revolution and was sent to the firing squad!''

Pale with shock, Mélissande sat down abruptly. The Duc d'Enghien was a "prince of the blood," a member of that semiroyal branch of the French aristocracy that ranked just below the members of the royal family. To a convinced royalist, the execution of the Duc would be only a little less shattering than the executions of Louis XVI and Marie Antoinette.

For the past several weeks, the English newspapers had been full of reports about added arrests in the Cadoudal-Pichegru conspiracy to kill Napoleon, and Mélissande had been following the news with an interest heightened by her knowledge that Bertrand's friend, General Moreau, had been unjustly implicated in the plot. Now she said, stiff-lipped, "Papa lost his life fighting under the Duc d'Enghien's father.''

Taking Mélissande's hand in a gesture of mute sympathy, Bertrand asked Cecilia, "Where did you hear the news?

There was nothing in the *Morning Post* that I collected at the receiving office this morning.''

"Oh—Stephen Lacey told me," replied Cecilia, blushing slightly. "I just happened to meet him while I was out walking. He says his father arrived from London last evening with the latest edition of the *Times*." Obviously happy to change the subject, she picked up Mélissande's portrait. "The frame is perfect. You're a man of many parts, Cousin Bertrand. Nick and I want you to know that we're very happy that you've come to stay with us."

After Cecilia had left the room, Bertrand turned to Mélissande with a smile. "What a charming girl, your little sister! I must confess that I've been wondering why such a beautiful young woman is neither married nor betrothed. But—forgive me if I'm intrusive—did I perhaps detect behind Cecilia's blush an attachment to this Stephen Lacey whom she mentioned?"

"Not a suitable attachment, no. Stephen is the son of Lord Haverford. Stephen's parents are both opposed to any connection between him and Cecilia.''

"Lord Haverford. He is—how do you call it?—the Lord Lieutenant of the county, *n'est-ce-pas*? Lord and Lady Haverford oppose the match because of Cecilia's birth, perhaps? I hate to say it, but illegitimacy *is* a handicap, especially since your sister has no fortune, and I understand that younger sons in England inherit *nothing*, which seems very unfair. I will say this, that laws passed under the Revolution provided that all children should share equally in an inheritance, including illegitimate children.''

"Well, yes, there is a lack of fortune on both sides, unfortunately. I've sometimes thought that if only Cecilia were an heiress . . .'' Mélissande's voice trailed away in a sigh.

Bertrand gave her shoulder a gentle pat. "*Pauvre petite,* Cecilia's situation is a great worry to you, *non*? By the bye, I heard in the village that Lady Haverford is French also. Do you know her well?"

"Why, yes, I'm surprised the village gossips didn't tell you. Lady Haverford is my cousin. I suppose she must be a very distant relative of yours also. She was Aurore de Bouillon, the daughter of the Comte de Vallery."

"Aurore de Bouillon. Now that I think about it, I recall hearing my father speak of her. She was a famous court beauty, a lady-in-waiting to Marie Antoinette. Why haven't you mentioned the relationship, *ma mie*?"

Mélissande hesitated. Her natural reticence had always prompted her to keep her affairs private, but she had found, since Bertrand's arrival, that his ready sympathy and quick understanding made it easy for her to discuss problems with him that she would normally have kept to herself. "Oh, there's no reason why you shouldn't know about it, Bertrand," she said, and plunged into an account of her quarrel with Aurore.

"*Quel dommage*," exclaimed Bertrand. "*Ma chère* Mélissande, your life is certainly not an easy one, beset as you are by the rascally tricks of the new Lord Rochedale on the one hand and on the other by the slights of your unkind cousin Aurore. How I wish I could wave a magic wand and make all your difficulties disappear!"

"It helps a great deal just to be able to talk to you, Bertrand," replied Mélissande, feeling warmed and comforted by the unfamiliar sensation of having someone interested in taking care of *her*, reversing her usual role of provider and nurturer. Bertrand's arrival had filled a void in her life that she had not even realized existed.

"Oh, Miss de Castellane, I was hoping to see you here tonight. You look simply beautiful."

Mélissande smiled her thanks to Augusta Millard, Lord Haverford's visiting goddaughter, who had just come up to her as she sat to the side of the dance floor in the Easton Assembly Rooms, waiting for her partner to bring her a glass of ratafia.

Mélissande experienced only a mild surprise at Augusta's

burst of admiration. As she was dressing for the Assembly ball tonight in her simple, often-worn gown of yellow sarsenet, Mélissande had decided to wear the Castellane emeralds, and a glance in her mirror had given her a sudden fancy that she had become an entirely different person, glamorous and beautiful and worldly-wise, not an obscure provincial with an uncertain future.

Recalling this foolishness, she laughed secretly at herself and said merrily to Augusta, "Thank you very much for the compliment, but I fear I must give all the credit for my dazzling appearance to my emeralds! I'm sure they would make a washerwoman the equal of a queen."

"You're much too modest," Augusta hastened to say. "The emeralds are certainly magnificent, however. Lady Haverford called my attention to them. She told me they are a family heirloom. By the way, the Countess—and I, too—has been very disappointed that you haven't come to visit her."

"Well, perhaps one day . . ." Mélissande shrugged. "How about you, Miss Millard? Are you enjoying your stay in Sussex?"

Augusta's face lighted up with a smile of pure joy. "Oh, yes, I've never been so happy in all my life. Lord and Lady Haverford have made me feel like a member of the family, and Stephen—Stephen is the kindest person I have ever met. Oh, there's Stephen now. I must go; we have the next dance. I hope to see you soon, Miss de Castellane."

As Augusta left, Phoebe Wright took her place. She stared at the emeralds. "Nick has been telling us all about your cousin's gift, but I never imagined anything like *this,*" she said in awe. She herself was looking very charming this evening, in a gown of white crepe trimmed at the hem with flounces of lace festooned with tiny bouquets of pink roses.

Mélissande said casually, "Do you see much of Nick these days, now that he's so busy with his new duties as Lord Rochedale's bailiff?" She waited for the faint blush that usually tinged Phoebe's cheeks at any mention of Nick, but it did not come. Phoebe was quite self-possessed as she replied, "Oh, yes, he comes to see Father almost every day. He says Father's advice is very helpful."

Nick came up just then to swoop Phoebe away to join the country dance that was about to start, and as Mélissande watched them go off together, she realized that there had been a subtle change in Phoebe's attitude toward Nick. The shy girl who had vainly tried to conceal her worship of Nick under the guise of childhood friendship had become a confident young woman who accepted Nick's attentions as her due. Could it be, Mélissande wondered, that the pair had made a secret committment to become betrothed, contingent perhaps on the outcome of Nick's service as Gideon's bailiff?

Watching the dancers, Mélissande sipped her ratafia and chatted idly with Jack Childers, who was here from London on one of his frequent visits home. They were back on their usual easy, friendly terms, with Jack, to Mélissande's relief, making no reference to his recent impulsive proposal of marriage.

Out on the dance floor, Phoebe and Nick were going down the line, happily oblivious to everyone except themselves. Elegant and handsome in a new coat, Bertrand was dancing with a pretty girl whose company he plainly relished. Stephen Lacey's partner was Augusta Millard, and Cecilia, rather to her sister's surprise, was standing up to Major Francis Chilton, a middle-aged officer with a slight limp whose determined gallantries Cecilia had always previously discouraged. To Mélissande's relief, Stephen had not yet asked Cecilia to dance this evening; his parents' presence at the ball had doubtless inhibited his usual inclination to keep Cecilia in his pocket.

Also taking part in the country dance was Gideon. As he came off the floor with the handsome daughter of a neighboring baronet, Mélissande observed that the girl was clinging to Gideon's arm, looking up into his face with an expression of near adoration. Watching him as he bent his head attentively to speak to the girl, Mélissande for the first time found herself viewing him with a sense of detachment. Reluctantly, she acknowledged to herself that he was an immensely attractive man with an effortless personal magnetism, and just for a moment there surfaced the ghost of a wish that they might have been better friends. Almost as though he had read her thoughts, Gideon bowed to his partner and strolled over to Mélissande, greeting her with his by now familiar air of faint indifference. "Those are very fine stones, my dear Mélissande, unless I miss my mark. Did they belong to your mother? I was under the impression that my father had been forced to sell most of the jewelry he gave to his second wife."

"That is correct," replied Mélissande, stung. Had Gideon decided to speak to her merely out of curiosity about the emeralds, a concern that in some way part of his inheritance had been diverted to his despised stepmother's children? Her voice was cool as she continued, "Your father did sell most of *Maman*'s jewels during the last two years of their lives. What remained, a few trinkets of sentimental value, came to me and Cecilia, who, as you may have noticed, is wearing a modest string of pearls tonight. These emeralds were never *Maman*'s property, however. They are a Castellane heirloom, bequeathed to me by my grandmother, the Dowager Duchesse de Lavidan. My cousin, Bertrand de Castellane, brought them to me recently when he arrived in England."

"Ah, yes, I believe Nicholas did mention that a cousin was visiting you. Castellane. Surely not a connection of the man who bought your father's estates? The regicide who voted for the deaths of the King and Queen?"

"Well, yes, but . . ." Briefly Mélissande described how Bertrand had become disillusioned with Napoleon's rule, especially after the arrest of his friend and superior officer, General Moreau.

"If your cousin was involved in the Cadoudal-Pichegru plot, I would say he was very fortunate to have escaped from France. All the suspects arrested in that case face almost certain execution."

"Now, wait, Gideon. I didn't say that Bertrand was involved in any plot, or General Moreau either, for that matter. . . ."

"*Ma chère* Mélissande, my partners must be the prettiest girls and the best dancers in all England!" Bertrand came up to Mélissande, his smile fading to an expression of polite inquiry as he looked at Gideon, to whom Mélissande quickly introduced him.

Returning Bertrand's punctilious bow with his usual negligent grace, Gideon observed, "Mélissande has been telling me about your decision to seek political asylum in England, monsieur. Since you are a military man, it must have been a particularly painful action for you at this time, when your country is preparing to invade mine."

Bertrand's face reddened faintly, and there was a hint of sharpness in his voice as he replied, "It must *always* be painful to leave one's country, whatever the reason, milor' Rochedale. In this instance, I could not remain in France without sacrificing my principles. But I hope soon to serve my country even more worthily by offering my sword to the Comte d'Artois."

"A laudable sentiment, monsieur. Mélissande also tells me that you served for many years under General Moreau, whose present situation seems so precarious. As it happens, I have a very good friend who served as an observer with the Austrian army at the battle of Hohenlinden, which he considered General Moreau's masterpiece. Did you serve in that campaign?"

"Why, yes. I will always consider it a privilege to have been there. As you said, the victory was a masterpiece."

"My friend considers that General Moreau was nothing less than brilliant in ordering General Richepanse to turn the enemy right flank, a turning movement that was the key to a tremendous victory."

"Yes, it was a stroke of genius. I was acting as ADC to

General Moreau during the battle, and it was I who delivered his orders to Richepanse to begin the turning movement."

"Indeed. You were very close to the action, then. My friend also admired General Ney's magnificent stand at the center, when the Austrians attacked in force at the village of Erding."

Bertrand smiled. "You are very well informed. But then, I understand that you, too, are a military man."

"Was, monsieur. Was. The Nineteenth Light Dragoons have dispensed with my services." With a cool nod to Bertrand and an easy bow to Mélissande, Gideon announced that he was engaged for the next dance and moved off.

"So that is the wicked Marquess." Bertrand shook his head. "I find it difficult to understand how a man in so exalted a position can have so little polish. He spoke to you, his own stepsister, with little more than bare civility. But enough of this fellow Gideon. Tonight is a gala affair, and I intend to have the next dance with my beautiful cousin." As Mélissande took his arm, Lady Haverford came up to them. She greeted Mélissande affectionately, commented on the emeralds, and then turned to Bertrand with a trace of unease. "You must be Mélissande's cousin, monsieur. I am the Countess of Haverford."

"Bertrand de Castellane, *à votre service, madame.*"

"We are old acquaintances. I was at your christening."

Although taken aback for an instant, Bertrand broke into a charming smile. "I am so sorry that I do not remember our first meeting. I do recall my mother telling me, however, that she once saw you performing in a play at the Petit Trianon. *Maman* said you looked absolutely ravishing."

Aurore's rather strained expression softened. "Oh, that was—it must have been—a performance of *La Gageure Imprévue*," she said with a gratified little smile. "The Queen played a maid, and I was her scheming mistress. I had almost forgotten about our playacting at Versailles, but it all comes back." Aurore sighed, adding wistfully, "The Queen was so lovely. It is very hard to believe she has been dead for over ten years. But, of course, monsieur"—Aurore's voice hardened—"I cannot expect you to feel as I do about Queen Marie Antoinette, since your father voted to send her to the guillotine."

"Believe me, madame, I regret the fact that my father was a regicide as much as you do. At the time, you know, he was completely under the influence of the Duc d'Orléans. At any rate, I have come to England to attempt to make up for what my father did, by serving the cause of the old monarchy under the leadership of the Comte d'Artois."

"You needn't prove yourself to me, at least, Bertrand," exclaimed Mélissande. "*You* weren't a regicide." She looked reproachfully at Aurore, and after another tense moment Lady Haverford visibly relaxed, smiling at Bertrand. "Mélissande is right. I shouldn't judge you for what your father did. Shall we forget about the Terror and the September Massacres and all the rest, and agree to be friends?"

Bertrand bent over Aurore's hand to kiss it. "With all my heart, *ma cousine*."

"Mélissande, you must bring Bertrand to call," said Lady Haverford happily. "Oh, it will be so lovely having another member of my own family near me. And I must tell you, Bertrand, that you need not wait as long as you might have imagined to present your sword to the Comte d'Artois. His Royal Highness will be coming to visit us at Fiesole next month. I will be happy to present you to him."

"What wonderful news. And how gracious of you to offer me your hospitality, Cousin Aurore. Please excuse me," Bertrand added as the music struck up again, "a beautiful young lady, a Miss Grove, has promised me this dance, and I must not destroy her image of French gallantry!"

Gazing after him, Aurore said, "I really do want you to bring Bertrand to Fiesole for a visit, Mélissande. Promise me you'll come." At Mélissande's silent, uncompromising stare, Aurore bridled, her expression a mixture of annoyance and an urge to conciliate. "It's Cecilia again, isn't it?

Well now, your sister is no longer an issue. Bring her with you to Fiesole, by all means."

Mélissande raised an inquiring eyebrow. "Are you going to tell me the reason for your volte-face?"

"Well..." Aurore hesitated. "It's not official yet, so I must ask you not to mention it publicly, but... Mélissande, Lord Haverford and I will soon be announcing Stephen's betrothal to Augusta Millard. You remember her, I'm sure. My husband's goddaughter?"

"Indeed I do remember Miss Millard," replied Mélissande quietly. "I understand the situation very well. Now that Stephen is leg shackled, as Nick would say, you feel it would be quite safe for him to meet Cecilia, even within the sacred confines of your home."

Mélissande's cool cynicism caused Aurore to bite her lip. "That was unkind."

After a moment Mélissande shrugged. "I'd like to be friends again, too. I know you never meant to hurt Cecilia, and I wish Stephen very happy. Now then, tell me all about your daughter-in-law-to-be."

"*Eh bien*, you already know she's Edmund's goddaughter. Her mother was his cousin, her father a wealthy corn merchant with extensive shipping interests." Aurore paused, looking faintly uncomfortable. "*Ma foi*, no need to tell me what you're thinking. Our son to marry the daughter of a tradesman? But England is not at all as France used to be. Here being in trade doesn't automatically bar one from good society. Many of the most noble English families are only a generation away from *very* humble origins. Consider Samuel Whitbread; he is the son of a brewer, but he married Earl Gray's sister!"

"Believe me, Aurore, I'm not sitting in criticism of Stephen's bride. I only think it a bit unjust that poor Cecilia's birth tells against her mostly because she's poor!" Mélissande smiled, extending her hand. "But come, let's be friends again. I promise faithfully to bring Bertrand to see you, and I look forward to being invited to meet the Comte d'Artois.''

The mending of her rift with Aurore gave a lift to Mélissande's spirits, and she enjoyed the rest of the evening with a lighthearted abandon that she had not felt in months. I might almost be the belle of the ball, she thought with a quiver of amusement in one of those rare intervals between her dances with Bertrand and one or another of her usual swains. Toward the end of the ball, Gideon sought her out, saying, ''Shall we display our newfound family solidarity by dancing together?''

Mélissande's mood was so ebullient that she felt not a twinge of resentment at the offhanded casualness of the invitation. Her eyes glinted with a spark of wicked irony as she replied, ''I would be delighted—nay, flattered—to stand up with the most remarked-upon man at the ball,'' and she chuckled inwardly as Gideon's expression lost something of its usual lazy self-possession. ''You must have noticed that you were the object of all eyes as the new Marquess of Rochedale,'' she exclaimed kindly, ''although I must confess that *I* was surprised to find you participating in what a traveled man of the world like yourself must consider a dull-as-dishwater provincial assembly. But doubtless you feel an obligation as master of Easton Priory to show an interest in our local concerns.''

Quickly recovering his aplomb, Gideon replied, ''Yes, that's it precisely. I find that I'm acquiring a touch of noblesse oblige. Perhaps the example of your own selfless devotion to duty is rubbing off on me, my dear stepsister.'' As they walked to take their places for the country dance, he added, inclining his head toward a corner of the ballroom, ''Speaking of duty, I'm happy to see that Cecilia apparently is becoming aware of the conduct proper to *her* station in life. Frankly, I came here tonight expecting to see her in young Lacey's pocket. On the contrary, I've observed that she has spent most of the evening in the company of the gentleman with whom she is sitting over there. Fellow by the name of Chilton, I'm told."

Mélissande gazed at Cecilia, seated in a corner in a serious conversation with Major Chilton, and felt a touch of guilt compounded with uneasiness. She had been too absorbed in her own quite unaccustomed pleasure to note Cecilia's preoccupation with such an unlikely partner as the prosaic, middle-aged retired officer.

"Someone was telling me that this Chilton has a nice little property and a decent income," Gideon went on. "If his intentions are serious, Cecilia would be well advised to accept him, since . . ."

"Since without birth or fortune, Cecilia cannot afford to be fussy?" Mélissande retorted, her eyes flashing.

Gideon lifted his eyebrows. "My dear Mélissande, *you* said that, not I. I'm not always trying to denigrate Cecilia, you know. But yes, I do feel that Chilton would be a good catch for a girl in Cecilia's circumstances."

What she considered to be Gideon's unfeeling remarks put Mélissande so out of charity with him that she did not address another word to him as they went down the dance, and her enjoyment of the rest of the evening was quite spoiled. After the ball, as they drove home in their carriage behind the job horses that Nick had hired from the village livery stables—for reasons of economy they had retained in their own stable only the pony and Nick's hunter—Bertrand was the only lively member of the Dower House party. He bubbled on about what a festive time he had had, without seeming to observe that Mélissande was abstracted and unresponsive, or that Cecilia sat in huddled silence, her head turned away from her companions. Nick, who Mélissande was sure had had access to something more powerful than the innocuous punch served at the ball, was sound asleep in his corner of the carriage.

A little later, as Mélissande put down her hairbrush and took off her dressing gown, she hesitated before climbing into bed. After a moment's thought, she slipped back into her dressing gown and slippers and padded softly down the corridor to Cecilia's bedchamber. She tapped lightly on the door and, receiving no response, was about to turn away when she heard the sound of muffled sobs. Squaring her shoulders, she marched into the room to find Cecilia, still fully clothed, sprawled across the bed with a pillow jammed over her head to smother the sound of her wild weeping.

"Cecilia, *chérie*, can I help?"

Slowly Cecilia rolled over and sat up, using a corner of the bedcover to wipe away the tears that still flowed down her face. "No, you can't help, Sandy," she sobbed. "No one can help. I wish I could die. Stephen told me tonight that he's going to marry Augusta Millard."

"Yes, I know. His mother told me about it. I'm so sorry, but I did try to warn you that you and Stephen had no future together. You must just accept the fact that Stephen is going to marry someone else. Actually, Augusta Millard seems to be a charming, very pretty young lady who will make Stephen a good wife. Try to be happy for them both."

Cecilia's tears abruptly ceased. "Don't you moralize at me, Sandy," she said angrily. "Wish Stephen happy with that odious little dab of a creature? Never! Not when I know that his parents are *forcing* him to marry Augusta—that, or be sent to his uncle in the West Indies to learn to be a planter!"

CHAPTER XI

"Bertrand. Come drink tea with us," Mélissande called to her cousin, hesitating at the door of the drawing room.

"With pleasure, if you are sure I don't intrude. Perhaps not tea?" he implored with a grimace. "But I would love a glass of claret. Major Chilton, I am delighted to see you again." Bertrand bowed with exquisite grace to the major, sitting beside Cecilia on a sofa.

"M. de Castellane." Major Chilton nodded stiffly to Bertrand. The retired army officer who had monopolized Cecilia's attention at the Assembly Ball had been a daily caller at the Dower House for several weeks. He always seemed mildly uncomfortable, however, under the onslaught of Bertrand's formal Gallic courtesies, and now, after the exchange of a few labored commonplaces, he soon took his leave.

"*Chère* Mélissande, I had such an enjoyable visit with our cousin Aurore this afternoon," said Bertrand as he accepted a glass of wine and a biscuit. "What a lovely estate, Fiesole. *Bien entendu,* it does not have the historic significance of Easton Priory or the château in Berry. Aurore was disappointed that you didn't come with me today. With the Comte d'Artois due to arrive soon, she wanted to discuss with you the arrangements for his visit."

"Oh, I'll visit her sometime soon," said Mélissande with a quick glance at Cecilia.

"My dear Sandy, please feel free to see Lady Haverford as often as you like," exclaimed Cecilia with a scornful smile. "You needn't feel the least embarrassed on *my* account."

Forgetting momentarily that Bertrand was in the room, Mélissande said to her sister in distress, "I know this is a difficult time for you, but . . ."

"You mean because of Stephen's betrothal? You're quite mistaken, Sandy. I have no intention of wearing the willow for Stephen Lacey. Actually, I'm thinking of getting married myself."

"If you will excuse me," said Bertrand, rising hastily.

"Don't leave, Cousin Bertrand. You're a part of our family now, and there's no reason why you shouldn't know that Major Chilton proposed to me today while we were strolling in the garden." Cecilia gazed defiantly at Mélissande. "The major wondered if he should first have asked Nick's permission to address me, but that would have been absurd, don't you think? Nick is eighteen years of age, years younger than the major. And you aren't my guardian either, Sandy. So Major Chilton decided it would be best just to speak to me about his intentions. I told him I would give him my answer soon."

Mélissande was appalled. "Cecilia, what can you be thinking of? Major Chilton has been calling here often during the past few weeks, and of course I've long suspected that he's trying to fix his interest with you—but marriage! Whatever *his* wishes, I never thought you could be considering such a match."

"Why should I not? The major is a gentleman of good family. He has a snug little estate, a pension, and a small fortune of his own. If I married him, I should be living near you and Nick. What more could I wish for?"

"He's years older than you are. Old enough, in all probability, to be your father. And you've never before paid the slightest attention to him, though he's been hovering around you since he arrived in Easton. I should have said that he is just the quiet, dull sort of man that you've never fancied."

"Perhaps my tastes are changing," Cecilia replied. "I'm getting older, too, you know, so perhaps an older man would be more congenial to me! Yes, the more I think about it, the more I should like an establishment of my own. When next you visit Lady Haverford, Sandy, be sure to tell her I'm contemplating matrimony. It will relieve her mind from worries that I might still have designs on her precious son. Better yet, I'll drop a note to Stephen so that *he* can give the news to his mother!" Her blond ringlets fairly quivering with wounded anger, Cecilia flounced out of the room, leaving Mélissande staring after her in helpless concern.

In an attempt to comfort her, Bertrand said, "I can see you are very upset, but consider: it would be no bad thing for *la petite* to marry, *n'est-ce pas*? And I know you always believed that a match between Cecilia and young Stephen would be unwise on both sides."

"Of course there was never any real possibility that Cecilia would marry Stephen. And of course I would like to see her married to someone else. But I don't want her to marry simply because she is disappointed in love, or because she wants a home of her own, and I don't want her to choose a husband who is old enough to be her father, a man whom she doesn't even like."

"Forgive me, but are you being quite sensible about this matter? This man, this Major Chilton, he is a respectable man of good family, *non*? He has a competence, an estate? He can provide for Cecilia, give her a comfortable home? With your sister's lack of—ah—background, you know, she may not receive many other offers of marriage. You should be grateful for this offer rather than sorry. As for your mention of Cecilia's lack of love for Major Chilton, you surprise me. What has love to do with marriage? In France, marriages of people in our position in society are arranged according to suitability of rank and fortune. Love is a pretty sentiment, a luxury, and it may or may not come later. Why, look at your own parents. I understand their marriage was arranged by their families while they were still in their cradles.''

"You've chosen an odd example to prove your point, Bertrand. My mother deserted my father and eloped with her lover!''

"Precisely,'' Bertrand crowed with triumphant illogic. "Cecilia wouldn't be in the fix she's in if your mother hadn't fallen in love with Lord Rochedale!''

Mélissande laughed, her depressed spirits lifting at Bertrand's good-natured inanity. "That's true, if small comfort to Cecilia. If *Maman* hadn't eloped with Lord Rochedale, Cecilia wouldn't exist at all!''

Rising from a kneeling position, her back and knees registering a faint protest, Mélissande looked down with pride at the beds of daffodils, grape hyacinths, and snowdrops that she had just weeded. She lifted her head to sniff the fragrant air, redolent with the scent of lilacs just coming into bloom and the delicate odor of the apple and cherry blossoms in the small orchard just beyond her neat walled garden. Reluctant to waste even a moment of this tremulously lovely early-April morning by going indoors, she sat down on a rustic bench to plan mentally what spring vegetables should be planted in the central area of the garden that her handyman had just finished spading up the day before.

Her thoughts wandered from peas and marrows and beans. She was conscious of feeling more contented, more at peace with herself, than at any time in the past year and a half. Most of the problems that had plagued her during that period were now solved. She was no longer threatened by the specter of eviction from the Dower House. Nick was once more his cheerful, hard-working self. And Bertrand's vivacious, amusing presence was a continuing delight to Mélissande, especially since Nick, after an initial feeling of distrust, was now on the friendliest terms with her cousin. Earlier that morning they had gone off together, looking faintly guilty, and Mélissande suspected they were planning to attend one of the cockfights that she so abhorred. If only she could erase Cecilia's unhappiness, Mélissande thought, there would scarcely be a cloud on her horizon.

At the creaking sound of the garden gate being opened, she turned her head in surprise and some consternation to see Gideon, dressed in breeches and top boots, a many-caped driving coat, and a beaver hat. Painfully aware that she was wearing her oldest gown, now liberally splotched with garden soil, and a rather decrepit straw bonnet, Mélissande rose from the bench to greet him. She had not seen him for several weeks, not since the Assembly ball, and there was a note of constraint in her voice as she said, "Good morning, Gideon. Are you looking for Nick? He's not here, I'm afraid."

"No, I haven't come to see Nicholas. I wanted to speak to you." After a brief pause, Gideon asked abruptly, "Where is Cecilia?"

Mélissande tossed him a perplexed stare. "I don't see why you ... If you're really interested in Cecilia's where-abouts, she's visiting a former school friend in New Romney. She wanted to..." Mélissande cut short her reply. There was no reason to acquaint Gideon with Cecilia's problems, no necessity to tell him that her sister had gone away for a few days in the hope that, at a distance from home and family, she might better be able to decide if she should accept Major Chilton's proposal of marriage. "Cecilia wanted a little change of scenery. She doesn't have many friends of her own age here in Easton," Mélissande finished.

"I see. Then I fear I must tell you that this morning, as I was driving through Rye after spending the night with friends nearby, I saw Cecilia, accompanied by Stephen Lacey, driving out of town in a post chaise in the direction of

Tunbridge Wells. And since it was just two nights ago, at a dinner at Fiesole, that I heard Lady Haverford announce the betrothal of Stephen and Miss Augusta Millard, I confess I did wonder why Cecilia and young Lacey were taking a journey together. Are they eloping? And are they doing so with your knowledge and blessing?''

Pale with shock, Mélissande cried, ''Of course I didn't know that Cecilia planned to run off with Stephen. Gideon, how could you allow it? Why didn't you stop them?''

''Because Cecilia is of age, and I have no authority to stop her from doing whatever she chooses. However, I assumed that you didn't know of this elopement, and I thought it only right to inform you of it.''

''Since you've never had the slightest regard for your sister, I suppose I shouldn't be surprised to learn that you didn't lift a finger to prevent her from ruining her life,'' said Mélissande bitterly. ''You speak of an 'elopement,' but you know as well as I do that Stephen can't be thinking of marrying Cecilia, not after his betrothal to Miss Millard has been publicly announced. How could Cecilia consent to— but I'm wasting time talking about it. I'm going after her.''

As Mélissande rushed past Gideon, he caught her arm. ''Just how do you propose going about this rescue?''

Mélissande bit her lip. ''I—I'm not sure. I can't wait for Nick and Bertrand. I don't know where they went, or how long they will be gone. I'll have to drive the pony cart to Hastings. I can travel by stagecoach from there to Tunbridge Wells.''

''That's a hen-witted scheme if I ever heard of one. Ride a stagecoach to pursue a fast post chaise and four? Look, Mélissande there's nothing for it—I'll have to drive you in my curricle. Lacey and Cecilia may not be making for Tunbridge Wells at all, you know. We must stop at every posting inn along the way, to make sure they haven't turned off for another destination. Or, once arrived at Tunbridge Wells, they may well be planning to go on to London or to

Gretna Green in Scotland. You need mobility for a chase like this, my girl."

Unwilling to be under obligation to Gideon, Mélissande hesitated to accept his offer, but only briefly. Her pride could not weigh in the balance against Cecilia's welfare. "Thank you, Gideon. I can be ready to leave in ten minutes." She dashed into the house to tear off her gardening clothes and change into a gown of blue sprigged muslin, a darker blue pelisse, and a cottage bonnet. She packed her night robe and a few toilet articles into a small valise, though she fervently hoped that her search for Cecilia would not require an overnight stay away from the Dower House, and climbed into the curricle beside Gideon only a minute or two later than she had promised. The tiger jumped nimbly up to his perch, and Gideon put the team to a trot.

After stopping briefly in Easton to change horses and to arrange for Gideon's team to be sent back to the Priory, they drove in silence for some time before Gideon said tersely, "You realize, of course, that we may not be in time?"

Mélissande did not pretend to misunderstand his meaning, though her voice was almost inaudible as she replied, "Yes, I know. If we don't catch up to them before nightfall . . . It doesn't signify, however. No matter what has happened, I must persuade Cecilia to return home with me."

"Just so you understand," said Gideon, shrugging, and turned his attention to his driving. Mélissande was too preoccupied with Cecilia's danger to recall another occasion when she had been a passenger in this same curricle. Their first stop was at Robertsbridge. "I'm taking a calculated risk by not going all the way back to Rye," Gideon explained. "We would lose a great deal of time by doing that, and I feel sure in my bones that Lacey really is heading in the direction of Tunbridge Wells. If I'm correct, we needn't start checking the posting stops until we're on the direct road to the Wells."

At Hawkhurst, where they changed teams again, Gideon

reported to Mélissande with a grim smile that a post chaise carrying passengers of Stephen's and Cecilia's descriptions had stopped there several hours previously. At Lamberhurst, they received the same news. "So now we know they haven't turned off for Maidstone or Ashford. They can only be going to Tunbridge Wells. Would you like to stop here in Lamberhurst for a short rest and a light meal?"

"No, I thank you, Gideon. Please, let's push on."

They were passing now through a hilly, wooded district, but Mélissande was scarcely aware of the beautiful scenery that ordinarily would have delighted her. She sat tensely beside Gideon, her hands clenched tightly in her lap, relaxing only slightly when they entered the outskirts of Tunbridge Wells in its lovely natural setting enfolded by hills. Gideon drove into the town, drawing a blank at the first inn where he made inquiries. He then proceeded on to the Parade, pausing at an inn situated a short distance from the Assembly Rooms and the Pump Room. Emerging from the inn, Gideon said to his tiger, "We're stopping here, Rob. I don't know for how long. Have the horses changed and be ready to leave at a moment's notice." To Mélissande he said, "One of the hostlers tells me that a man and a young woman who must be Cecilia and Stephen Lacey arrived here in the early afternoon. Shall we confront the runaways?"

When they entered the inn, the proprietor greeted them with a beaming smile, a smile that faded somewhat when Gideon put to him a question about "my younger brother, Mr. Lacey," and a beautiful blond companion. "Well now, sir, I'd like to oblige ye, but I've no'un by the name of Lacey staying with me at this present. Fact is, I've only two guests, young Mr. Colwell and 'is bride, married in my best parlor not an hour ago!"

Mélissande drew a sharp breath, and Gideon gave her a surreptitious poke, remarking with an air of resignation, "Well, my dear, we were afraid of this. Those rascals were just too quick for us. I trust you'll agree that there's nothing for it but to give the young people our blessing, what? Where is the happy couple, landlord?''

"Having a wedding supper in that room down the hall there, first on the left." The innkeeper scratched his head. " 'Ere, sir, do ye mean to say that my Mr. Colwell and your brother be one and the same?''

"I certainly do. Come along, my dear.''

As Gideon took her arm and marched her down the hall, Mélissande whispered frantically, "Wait, Gideon. There must be some mistake. . . ." When Gideon opened the door and pushed Mélissande ahead of him into the landlord's best parlor, however, she saw immediately that there had been no mistake. Seated on opposite sides of a small table drawn up before a cozy fire, Cecilia and Stephen were enjoying what appeared to be a very tasty supper. They looked up in shock as Gideon and Mélissande entered. Cecilia exclaimed, "Sandy! What are you doing here? How did you find out about . . . ? Well, it doesn't matter a whit how you found out. You're too late. Stephen and I are married.''

"Married? Already? But how can that be? Gideon thought you might be eloping to Gretna Green, but . . .''

"Gretna Green! I should say not," declared Cecilia proudly. "There was nothing havey-cavey about *our* wedding. Stephen arranged for a special license and asked his friend, a newly ordained clergyman, to perform the ceremony.''

Mélissande's knees suddenly felt weak, and she sat down in the nearest chair. "I don't understand any of this. I thought Stephen was going to marry Miss Millard.''

Cecilia sniffed. "His parents were certainly pressuring him to do so, but he never cared a fig for Augusta. He never ceased to love me, so when I wrote to him a week ago to tell him that I was considering Major Chilton's proposal, Stephen suggested that we get married secretly and then wait in patience until Lord and Lady Haverford realized the futility of trying to force him to marry Augusta. I was planning to return home to the Dower House tomorrow and live there as usual with you and Nick until Stephen's parents came to their senses. So you must promise, Sandy, and you, too, Gideon, to keep our secret.''

A dazed Mélissande could think of nothing to say, but Gideon, who had been listening to Cecilia's account with narrowed eyes, now said softly, ''I can well understand your desire for secrecy, Lacey. It was only two nights ago that your parents publicly announced your betrothal to Miss Millard.''

Startled and angry, Cecilia turned on her lover. ''Tell Gideon it's a lie, Stephen.''

''Oh, it's true enough,'' said Gideon. ''I heard it with my own ears. How long did you think you could keep the news from her, Lacey?'' He extended his hand. ''As the head of Cecilia's family, I must now ask you to show me your special license.''

His good looks marred by an ugly scowl, Stephen spoke for the first time. ''I'll thank you to keep out of my affairs, my lord. It's very late days for you to be expressing solicitude for Cecilia as the 'head of her family.' ''

''Perhaps so, but I would still like to see that license.''

Cecilia said sharply, ''Show it to him, Stephen, just to satisfy my suddenly loving, big brother's curiosity.''

As Stephen glared at him in silent, sullen frustration, Gideon suggested, ''Make a clean breast of it, Lacey. There never was a special license, was there? Or an obliging clergyman, either?''

''Gideon! You can't mean . . .''

''Ah, but I can, Mélissande. I do. I submit that when Cecilia wrote to Lacey that she was considering the major's proposal, Stephen was faced by a cruel dilemma: he must either surrender Cecilia to another man, or he must brave his parents' ire by refusing to marry the wealthy heiress they had chosen for him. He apparently felt that he could have the best of two worlds by inveigling Cecilia into a false elopement before she could learn of the formal announcement of his betrothal to Miss Millard. Fortunately for Lacey, Cecilia had left the neighborhood for several days to visit a

friend in New Romney, so it was unlikely that she would
hear of the announcement until after she and Stephen were
'married.' By the time Cecilia realized the special license
was a useless scrap of paper and that the wedding ceremony
had been performed by a—was it an out-of-work actor,
Lacey, or perhaps one of your cronies with a bent for
practical jokes?—by someone, at any rate, who was posing
as a clergyman, it would have been too late for Cecilia's
reputation. For lack of any other option, she would have felt
constrained to remain in an illicit relationship, and Lacey
could marry his heiress while keeping a mistress on the
side."

Cecilia stood up, her hands clenched tightly together as
she stared at Stephen. She said in a shaking voice, "Tell me
it isn't so, it's just some Banbury story of Gideon's to keep
us apart. He's never liked me, or wanted me to be happy."

His face betraying his guilt and desperation, Stephen
clutched at her hand. "Cecy, love, I didn't mean to hurt
you, but it wasn't in the cards for us to marry. I can't bear to
lose you either, so what is so wrong about an arrangement
that would allow us to be with each other, to love each
other, even without an empty ceremony?"

Snatching her hand away, Cecilia covered her face, breaking into a fit of hysterical wailing. Mélissande rushed to her,
folding her into a comforting embrace, but the dreadful,
hopeless wailing continued. Finally, holding her sister at
arm's length, a pale but grimly resolute Mélissande slapped
Cecilia hard on both cheeks. Gasping with the shock of the
blows, Cecilia collapsed into a chair, subsiding into a bout
of quiet, dreary weeping.

Gideon surveyed Stephen with a cool dislike. "I won't
deny that I have a certain amount of experience in the
petticoat line, though you couldn't call me a loose screw,
precisely, but one rule I've *always* observed: lightskirt or
married lady of quality or country innocent, I never lie
about my intentions to females I hope to seduce."

Stephen's face flamed. He leaped from his chair and

rushed at Gideon, shouting, "It's time you learned that I won't submit either to your sermonizing or your interference, Rochedale."

Swerving his body, Gideon avoided his opponent's first headlong attack, and when Stephen, arms flailing, turned back to his tormentor, he was stopped short by a powerful and expertly aimed blow to the jaw. Seizing Stephen's legs, Gideon unceremoniously dragged the unconscious form out of the room and into the corridor. He returned to the parlor several minutes later, remarking, "It's been some time since I had a good mill, and I'm a bit disappointed that young Lacey wasn't handier with his fives. The errant bridegroom won't be causing us any further trouble, by the way. His aching jaw has quite taken all the fight out of him, and he's agreed to climb into his post chaise and return to the bosom of his family. Lacey has also promised to keep silent about the attempted elopement, and I fancy he will keep his word, as much for his own sake as for Cecilia's. He can't wish to have either his parents or the public learn about his shabby scheme to seduce your sister."

"Thank you, Gideon. I'm sure you did just as you ought," said Mélissande, but it was clear that she was giving him only part of her attention. She gestured toward Cecilia, who, though she had at last stopped crying, was now lying limply back in her chair, her eyes directed straight ahead of her in an apathetic stare. "It hurts to see Cecilia like this, Gideon. She actually looks ill, though I know she's just exhausted from sorrow and disappointment and resentment."

"Cecilia will be much more the thing, physically at least, after a good night's rest," replied Gideon calmly. "A failed love affair has never killed anyone yet, to my knowledge. But it's plain that she's in no condition to travel for the rest of the day. We must plan to spend the night here in Tunbridge Wells. I'll see the landlord to arrange for rooms."

Returning shortly to the parlor, Gideon lifted an unresponsive Cecilia into his arms and, showing not a trace of discomfort from his injured leg, carried her up the stairs to a second-floor bedchamber and placed her gently on the bed. "I'll order a light supper for us, Mélissande. I know you must be hungry as well as tired. Come down and join me for a meal when you feel you can leave Cecilia."

It was over an hour before Mélissande, looking drawn and tired, came down the stairs. She had helped Cecilia into her night robe, bathed her swollen, tear-stained cheeks, persuaded her to drink a glass of wine, and had had the satisfaction of seeing her sister rouse to an awareness of her surroundings and to a passionate gratitude for Mélissande's presence before drifting into an exhausted sleep.

When Mélissande entered the parlor, Gideon was lounging in a large wing chair, wineglass trailing from his hand, his feet propped on a footstool. "How is Cecilia?"

"She's fallen asleep, thank God. I think rest is the best medicine for her right now."

"It wouldn't do you a mite of harm either, my girl." Gideon waved his arm toward the table next to the fireplace. "I had the remains of the wedding feast removed in favor of some roast chicken, a joint of cold roast beef, and what our good landlord tells me is a very fine apple tart. And I can assure you that this is a quite passable Madeira. Let me pour you a glass."

Moving wearily to sink into a chair near Gideon, Mélissande caught the slightly slurred note in his voice and decided that he had probably been drinking steadily since she had gone upstairs to care for Cecilia. He was not castaway, precisely, just a trifle above par, and she reflected with a touch of surprise that she had not seen him foxed, or suffering from the aftermath of a drunken spree, since the memorable occasion earlier in their acquaintance when she had rid the Priory of his visiting London tarts.

She accepted the glass of wine that Gideon had poured for her, and by the time she had finished it, she was glad to observe that much of her weariness and tension had disappeared.

"Another glass, m'dear? I told you it was an excellent Madeira."

"Well . . . a half glass, perhaps."

They drank another glass of wine in companionable silence, with Mélissande growing more agreeably relaxed and Gideon displaying a tendency to doze off. At one point, rising to replenish their glasses, Gideon observed with a cheerful grin, "Well, we did reach the runaways on time, eh, Mélissande? And though I should have known that you are in no way a foolish female, I must say I was relieved when you didn't subject me to a fit of the vapors during the course of the chase."

"Doubtless my character has many flaws, but succumbing to the vapors is not one of them," retorted Mélissande. "But yes, we did get here on time, and I'm grateful for it, even though I suspect it will be many weeks before Cecilia fully recovers from the shock." She drank several more sips of wine and then put down her glass rather reluctantly. "I should be getting back to Cecilia. Your supper looks delicious, and it was kind of you to order it, but I'm really not very hungry." She looked ruefully at her wineglass. "Actually, I hadn't planned to stay down here this long. I came merely to express my appreciation for your help in rescuing Cecilia." To her horror, Mélissande found herself adding, "I've been wondering why you did it. You've made it abundantly clear that you are not overly fond of Cecilia."

"Well, I must admit that it would be much easier to like Cecilia if she occasionally displayed some sound judgment, or even common sense."

"I marvel then, at your strenuous efforts to save her from ruin," said Mélissande tartly. "But I presume you have some lingering care for your family reputation."

Draining his wineglass, Gideon said blandly, "Exactly so. And we can always hope that Cecilia will learn something from this experience."

Mélissande's eyes sparked, but she restrained her tongue

as she rose from her chair, saying, "Whatever your reasons for helping Cecilia, pray accept my thanks. Good night."

Catching her hand as she passed his chair, Gideon rose, pulling her close to him. She drew a quick, startled breath as she looked up at him, suddenly more conscious of his height, the width of his powerful shoulders, his aura of sheer masculine sensuality, than she had been since their first meeting on the rain-swept road near Fiesole.

"Gideon, please," she murmured, attempting to pull away.

Ignoring her, Gideon cupped her face in his hands, his gray eyes beneath the tousled dark curls gleaming with a fitful flame as he gazed down at her. "Come to think of it, my dear Sandy—isn't that what your brother and sister call you?—I shouldn't object to receiving a proper expression of gratitude from you. Of a certain kind, that is. From the first time we met, you know, I've been thinking what a remarkably beautiful woman you are, especially when you're angry, as you are at this moment. Your eyes are magnificent, like flashing black diamonds. And ever since that time, I've been longing to do this—again. . . ." He crushed her slight body against him, pressing his lips to hers with an insatiable pressure that steadily grew more insistent as he drained the sweetness from her mouth.

Mélissande made no attempt to break away. Floating on a clamorous, enticing tide of emotion that seemed to be bearing her into a flood of unimaginable delights, she felt her mind surrendering to her senses. Every nerve in her body was quiveringly alive. A burst of quicksilver warmth coursed through her veins, and she gasped as fiery arrows of unfamiliar sensations pierced her with an almost physical pain. Gideon lifted his head, the slight, knowing little smile that curved his lips revealing that he was fully aware of her response to him. But still Mélissande did not pull away. He brushed his fingers against her cheek in a gentle, sensual caress, murmuring, "Your skin is like rose petals, love, and your hair . . ." He buried his face in her dark curls. "Your hair is silky, the color of midnight, with gleams of shimmering silver like moonlight dusting the sea.''

Gideon pulled her more tightly against him, his voice husky as he whispered, ''Mélissande, you intoxicate me.'' His seeking lips traced a flamelike path across her cheeks, her eyes, the curve of her throat, and then, with a strangled moan, Gideon picked her up and carried her to the sofa. As she felt the weight of his body settling against hers, Mélissande gasped, like a struggling swimmer who had just broken to the surface of the water, and pushed frantically against his chest with all her strength. ''Gideon, let me go. I can't—I don't want this. . . .''

Surprisingly, he relaxed his embrace almost immediately and Mélissande jumped thankfully to her feet. Still trembling from the effects of the storm of unfamiliar emotions that had so nearly engulfed her, she straightened her disheveled gown with unsteady fingers and made an ineffectual attempt to smooth her hair. Though she was guiltily aware in one corner of her mind that she had given somewhat more than a passive acceptance to his advances, she steeled herself to say scathingly to Gideon, who was still sitting on the sofa, ''If that's the kind of thanks you want from me, my lord, I think you'll agree that I've been more than properly grateful.''

Gideon blinked. ''My dear girl, I had no intention of seducing you when I invited you to supper. Please accept my apologies. You were right, you know, that time long ago when you scolded me for drowning myself in a sea of spirits. I'm not really a gentleman when I'm in my cups.''

CHAPTER XII

Mélissande fastened the clasp of her necklace, put on the matching emerald earrings, and turned slowly in front of the cheval glass to check the hang of her gown. It was a new gown, the first new garment she had added to her wardrobe in many months, and it was very becoming, though she had sewed it herself. The dress was made of soft primrose-colored crepe, with long sleeves of spider net and a low square décolletage edged with delicate lace that Mélissande had salvaged from one of her mother's gowns.

Mélissande was happy that the dress had turned out so well. She knew how distressed and disappointed Aurore would have been had Mélissande appeared at Fiesole tonight in a dowdy or an out-of-fashion gown. For tonight would see Aurore's triumph, the long-awaited visit of the Comte d'Artois, a visit all the more eagerly anticipated because it had so nearly been canceled owing to the death, several weeks previously, of the Comte's beloved mistress of many years, the Comtesse de Polastron.

Aurore's enthusiasm for the royal visit had been contagious, Mélissande thought, smiling to herself as she picked up her shawl, her gloves, and her reticule. She, too, was looking forward with immense excitement to this gala event to which everyone of any social importance in the county had been invited. Including, Mélissande reflected with a little frown as she walked to the door of her bedchamber, the Marquess of Rochedale. She had not seen Gideon since the day following Cecilia's failed elopement, some two weeks previously, and she would have preferred to postpone their next meeting until she could be sure that the nagging, bittersweet memories of those moments in his arms had ceased to disturb her. Not that Gideon had referred in any way to that passionate scene in the inn parlor, when Mélissande had seen him the following morning. There had been an air of constraint between them, a marked tendency to avoid each other's eyes, but Gideon's manner had been icily correct as he inquired after Cecilia's well-being and insisted on sending the sisters back to the Dower House in the privacy of a post chaise and four.

Mélissande shook her head impatiently to dispel any thoughts of Gideon and walked down the corridor to Cecilia's bedchamber. When she found her sister still in her dressing gown, sitting disconsolately before the mirror, Mélissande exclaimed reproachfully, "Why, you aren't dressed, and it's nearly time to start for Fiesole." Since her return to the Dower House, Cecilia had largely confined herself to her bedchamber, except for an occasional solitary walk, and it had taken much time and effort to persuade her to attend the gala in honor of the Comte d'Artois.

"Sandy, I've been thinking. I really don't care to accompany you tonight. To tell the truth, I'm not very interested in meeting the Comte. I may *be* half French, but I don't *feel* French, and—and then Lady Haverford has never liked me anyway. You know she would be just as happy if I didn't come. So I've decided to stay home."

"Well then, I won't allow you to stay home. You can't mope in your bedchamber forever, Cecilia. You've had a sad experience, but there was no public scandal, and you should be grateful that you can put it behind you and get on with your life. You wouldn't want Stephen to think you were hiding from society to conceal a broken heart, would you?''

Cecilia stiffened. "Certainly not. He may have bubbled me, but I will not allow him to believe that I'm wearing the willow for a loose fish like him.''

"Exactly," said Mélissande, encouraged by this first show of spirit by Cecilia in many a day. If she could bring herself to call Stephen a loose fish, even if she did so out of wounded pride, it must mean that Cecilia's lovesick heart was mending. "Here, let me help you dress." After Cecilia had donned a gown of pale blue muslin embroidered in seed pearls, Mélissande skillfully arranged her short corn-yellow curls and threaded a ribbon among them. Then she draped over Cecilia's shoulders their mother's most expensive shawl of glowing Lyons silk.

"Are we going to a county party or to Versailles?" inquired Bertrand when he encountered the sisters in the hall downstairs. "My eyes are fairly dazzled by your beauty.''

"Stop throwing the hatchet at us, Bertrand," replied Mélissande with a mock-severe frown. "Your ordinary compliments are overpowering enough! Now, don't tell me that's another new coat?''

Bertrand pirouetted before them in a beautifully tailored coat of black superfine. "Couldn't resist the temptation. How often do I have the opportunity to be presented to royalty?''

"Well, it's not for me to tell you how to drop your blunt, but I will admit that your coat is in the first style of elegance. Don't you agree, Nick?" Mélissande added to her brother, who had just come down the stairs.

"Yes, by Jove, you're a regular out-and-outer, Bertrand," said Nick, without a trace of envy. He cared little for fashion himself, and even tonight his evening coat looked unbrushed and his cravat was carelessly tied. "Can't say I'm looking forward to this affair," he grumbled as Mélissande applied skillful fingers to his cravat. "All the high sticklers in the county will be there, I fancy.''

"All of whom you know, and most of whom are your friends."

"Yes, but dash it, Sandy, *Phoebe* won't be there. I still don't understand why you wouldn't ask your cousin Aurore to invite her."

"I've tried to tell you why," replied Mélissande, momentarily exasperated. "Aurore is not acquainted with Phoebe, and besides, the Wrights . . ." She bit her lip. She had been about to say that the Wrights were not in the Haverfords' social class.

"Don't bother to explain yourself, Sandy," Nick said with a suddenly bleak look. "I see your point about Mr. Wright. No doubt he'd feel out of place at Fiesole. But Phoebe! *She* could go anywhere! Are all of you ready to leave? I'll fetch the carriage." He stalked out of the house, and Bertrand, observing Mélissande's distressed expression, squeezed her arm in sympathy.

Arriving at Fiesole, the party from the Dower House followed a long line of guests up the staircase to the ballroom. As they neared the head of the receiving line, Nick muttered, "Is *that* the Comte d'Artois? I thought he was a much older man. Not very impressive looking, is he?"

As it turned out, the man standing next to Lord and Lady Haverford was not the Comte d'Artois but his son, the Duc de Berri. He was a clumsy-looking man whose near-ugliness was redeemed by an irresistible smile, much in evidence as he greeted each guest and even more so when he spotted Cecilia's blond loveliness. "My dear Miss Maitland, what a pleasure to meet you. I do hope you will save me a dance."

As she entered the ballroom, which was already almost uncomfortably full, Mélissande glanced quickly around, ignoring a stab of chagrin when she spotted Gideon's handsome head bent in animated conversation with one of the prettiest of the local belles. Almost as if there were a current of magnetism flowing between them, making Gideon aware of Mélissande's entrance into the ballroom, he lifted his head, a rather strained little smile on his lips as he nodded to her across the room. Returning his nod curtly, she turned her head away.

The last of her guests having arrived, Lady Haverford left the receiving line and joined Mélissande just before the start of the dancing. Their rift was now completely mended, and the cousins were back to their old close rapport, with Aurore carefully staying away from the subject of Stephen's engagement to an heiress. "I know, I know," said the Countess as she came up to Mélissande. "Like everyone else, you're about to ask me, 'Where is Monsieur?'" She used Artois' title of "Monsieur," reserved in the past for the eldest brother of the King of France, quite naturally, even though the Comte d'Artois' brother was merely an exiled claimant to a nonexistent throne.

"I'm desolated to tell you that Monsieur will not be with us this evening," continued Aurore with a sigh. "While my husband was showing him about the estate this afternoon, His Highness suffered a bad fall when his horse stumbled. He and Edmund had chosen to ride without attendants, so it was doubly fortunate that the accident took place just at that point where our estate borders on Priory land, and that Lord Rochedale chanced to be riding nearby. He and Edmund between them were able to remount Monsieur and convey him safely to the house. But the Comte has a badly bruised shoulder and an aching back, and he has chosen not to be present at the ball. Actually," Aurore added, with the slightly smug air of one privy to the private moments of royalty, "I think Monsieur was almost relieved to be able to avoid a large social gathering so soon after the death of Madame de Polastron. He said to me with such a sad little smile, 'If she could speak to me from the grave, I know my Louise would probably insist that I attend your ball, Lady Haverford. But then, she was a saint, a martyr to duty all her life.'"

Mélissande swallowed hard. Even though she was a lifelong, devoted royalist, she thought it odd to label as saintly a woman whose very public liaison with Artois had been a source of gossip for a generation.

"But you are not to feel too disappointed, *ma chère* Mélissande," Aurore went on. "The Comte has told me he will be very pleased to receive you and Bertrand privately, since you are both cousins of mine, and he knew your parents."

A little later, a somewhat nervous Mélissande and a distinctly nervous Bertrand were ushered into the book room, where both of them were instantly captivated by the occupant, a tall, handsome, elegant man with a smile of infinite grace and charm who sat in a comfortable chair beside the fire. He acknowledged Mélissande's curtsy and Bertrand's bow with a benign nod and asked them to sit down. At Mélissande's start of surprise, the Comte smiled, saying, "You are thinking of the strict court etiquette at Versailles, where only an exalted handful could sit in the presence of royalty. Exile has changed a great many things, I fear, etiquette among them." He put his hand to the small of his back, wincing. "In any case, I cannot stand at present without extreme discomfort, and I refuse to cause myself any more wrenched muscles by craning my neck to look up at you while we speak. So do please sit down."

The Comte directed at Mélissande a long and kindly but searching look. "Yes, you have the look of the Castellanes, my dear," he said at last. "I have fond memories of your father. We were close during his tenure as Governor of the Palace of Fontainebleau. I remember your mother, too. A very beautiful young lady, Jeanne-Marie de Gilonne." Artois shrugged, making a little moue of reproof. "Quite a naughty young lady, too, I fear, but we must put all that behind us! The death of the Duc de Lavidan—let me see, it was at the battle of Turcoing in Flanders during the campaign of 1794, *n'est-ce pas*?—was a sad loss to my brother and me." The Comte shifted his gaze suddenly to Bertrand. "Lady Haverford tells me you were a soldier of the republic, sir. Perhaps you, too, were at the battle of Turcoing?"

There was a look of embarrassment, almost of panic, on Bertrand's face. He lowered his head and muttered, "Yes, I was there, Monsieur." And although Mélissande had of course known that her father and Bertrand had fought on opposite sides in Flanders, she felt a shock as the thought crossed her mind for the first time that her cousin and the Duc might actually have exchanged shots with each other, that Bertrand, in point of fact, might have fired the bullet that . . . Mélissande hastily buried the thought in the back of her mind.

Mercifully, the Comte turned his attention back to Mélissande. She marveled at the effortless ease of his conversation and at his apparently encyclopedic memory for people and places. "I understand from Lady Haverford that your grandmother sent you to live in England at the start of the Terror. What a great lady she was, your grandmother. I recall seeing her at court when I was a young man. Those emeralds"—he motioned to Mélissande's necklace—"gave her a dazzling presence. But enough talk of the old days. I hear your life has not been very easy of late, mademoiselle."

"Oh, no, I thank you, Your Highness, but I am quite satisfied with my life."

Artois smiled. "How many times have I heard *that* story! I've long marveled at the courage of our émigrés, forever making the best of a bad experience, telling little jokes about the menial jobs to which they had to turn to earn a living when they fled from France. Some were hairdressers, other taught French or cooked in restaurants. One gentleman worked as a bookbinder! They did virtually everything except take a position as a servant. One Chevalier of the Order of St. Louis became a valet, and I was forced to order his court-martial!"

There was a decided undertone of sternness in the Comte's voice as he addressed his next remarks to Bertrand. "Your father, I believe, is the present Duc de Lavidan. It would be bending the truth if I were to tell you that I have fond memories of *him*!" As Bertrand reddened with discomfiture, the Comte's voice softened. "But there, I have no intention of raking you over the coals for your father's sins. Lady Haverford informs me that you have come to see the error of your parent's ways, that you wish to do what you can to redeem his actions, that, in short, you would like to attach yourself to me. I regret to tell you that at present there are no vacancies in my household. Such an appointment, in any case, would be very nearly honorific, since my purse is always close to empty! I will be delighted to receive you if you care to visit me in London, however, and I do occasionally require the services of—shall we say couriers? —to carry my messages back and forth to the Continent. Would you care to consider such an arrangement?"

"I should be honored, Monsieur," declared a beaming Bertrand. "When may I begin my duties?"

Artois laughed. "All in good time, M. de Castellane. All in good time. For the moment, my orders are for you and Mlle. de Castellane to enjoy yourselves at the ball."

As Mélissande reentered the ballroom, Cecilia hurried up to her. "Sandy, I've just spoken to Stephen."

Mélissande's heart sank as she observed her sister's flushed cheeks. Perhaps it had been premature to persuade Cecilia to attend a social function at which she was bound to meet Stephen Lacey.

"Yes, Stephen took me aside and begged me not to say anything about our elopement to his parents, and especially not to breathe a word to Augusta Millard," said Cecilia scornfully. Her eyes sparkled with fury as she added, "Would you believe it, he said not one word of regret or apology for the trick he played on me. What a poltroon he is, Sandy! Why did I ever think I was in love with him?"

"Why, indeed?" murmured Mélissande. At this rate, her sister would soon make a complete recovery.

As Cecilia went off on the arm of her partner for the next dance, Aurore came up to Mélissande. "*Chérie*, here is someone who would like very much to be presented to you. M. de Martigny is gentleman-in-waiting to Monsieur."

Mélissande liked Charles de Martigny on sight. Tall and slender, with friendly brown eyes, he was a man of about her own age. For the next several dances she thoroughly enjoyed his company, while fending off his graceful compliments on the elegance of her dress, her exquisite French, and her skill on the dance floor. He assured her, "I came here not really expecting to enjoy a stay in the provinces. Certainly I never thought to meet a young and beautiful and intelligent Frenchwoman!"

"Please stop, M. de Martigny, before you quite turn my head," Mélissande said, laughing. "And I can't allow you to malign, even by omission, the other French ladies at the ball. There are several, you know!" Her protests, as he knew perfectly well, were only half-hearted, and she felt a shade of disappointment when Bertrand claimed her for a dance. He was still ecstatic with joy over his favorable reception by the Comte, and he was chafing at the bit to assume his new responsibilities.

"I'm very happy for you, Bertrand, but I worry about you, too. Have you thought how expensive it will be for you to establish yourself in London?"

"Poof," said Bertrand airily. "I still have some of the money that I brought from France, and when it's gone I will paint portraits. You heard His Highness. I can work at anything useful to earn my bread except for becoming a valet or a footman, which I have no intention of doing. I'll miss you, though, Mélissande. I wish you could come with me."

After the dance, Bertrand went off to procure her some refreshments. During his absence, Gideon appeared next to her with a request for the next dance. He sounded oddly reluctant, almost as if he were asking her against his will, Mélissande thought resentfully. She edged away from him, uneasy about the insistent physical pull that she always seemed to feel in his proximity. "It's unnecessary, Gideon, to prove what a united family we are by asking me to dance.

Actually, I don't care to dance just now. I'm feeling somewhat tired.''

"You surprise me. I thought you displayed great vivacity
and energy just now when you were dancing with your
cousin Bertrand and that other Frenchman.''

"Doubtless it's my advanced age that's sapping my
stamina,'' retorted Mélissande, and promptly turned furious
when Gideon replied, "Ah, yes, I'd forgotten how old you
really are.''

Gideon glanced idly across the ballroom. "And how is
our Cecilia? She certainly shows little evidence of going
into a decline.''

Mélissande followed his gaze. Cecilia, in obviously high
spirits, was going down the dance with a young naval
officer. "Do you know Cecilia's partner, Gideon?''

"That's Lady Fenton's younger brother, just back from
the Channel Fleet. I believe his name is Gray, Julian Gray.
Now that it's evident that Boney is having second thoughts
about invasion, the navy seems to be granting shore leave to
its hard-pressed young officers.''

Mélissande realized with surprise that the invasion threat
had so lessened that she—and probably most of the English
people—had begun to forget from day to day that they were
in danger. It had now been some weeks since Mélissande
had searched the evening skies for a signal beacon.

"I think young Gray is safe enough, Mélissande, but I
noticed earlier that Cecilia was dancing with Artois' son, the
Duc de Berri, and she seemed to be enjoying *his* company,
too. If I were you, I would warn your sister that Berri has a
bad reputation for philandering. He might just try to take
advantage of Cecilia's ambiguous social position.''

"Your warning is quite unnecessary. Cecilia is no lightskirt,
to melt into the arms of the first personable man she meets.
She really loved Stephen Lacey, and had no thought but
marriage when she went off with him.''

"Even so, don't overlook Berri's charm, that same effortless charm all these Frenchmen seem to exert,'' argued

Gideon. "You apparently were feeling the effects of that charm yourself when you were dancing with the tall Frenchman, a gentleman in Artois' household, I believe."

Mélissande lifted her chin. "As a matter of fact, I find M. de Martigny *very* charming."

Just for an instant, a nettled frown appeared on Gideon's forehead. Then, shrugging, he said blandly, "Good. Lady Haverford will be pleased to hear it. She was saying just the other afternoon when I stopped by for tea that she wished so much that she could produce an eligible parti for you."

Speechless with rage for an instant at the thought that her personal life had been the subject of a discussion between Aurore and Gideon, Mélissande snapped, "I'm grateful to Lady Haverford and to you, too, Gideon, for your solicitude about my matrimonial prospects, but I must tell you I feel fully capable of taking care of my own affairs. I *will* say that, judging by at least one of the men with whom I've recently associated, I believe I would prefer to remain a spinster!"

Bertrand returned, glass of ratafia in hand, followed closely by Charles de Martigny, who asked, "Dare I hope for this dance, mademoiselle?"

"Certainly," replied Mélissande with a bright smile. She swept past Gideon, remarking over her shoulder, "Thank you for the ratafia, Bertrand. Perhaps you could offer it to Lord Rochedale. He appears to be in need of a little refreshment."

Martigny said in a low voice as they took their places in the set, "When I arrived here, I feared the days would drag interminably. After tonight, I know the days and the hours and the minutes will fade away like quicksilver, and soon I won't be seeing you again. His Royal Highness will be leaving inside of a week. Will you allow me to call upon you tomorrow? And the day after that, and the day after that?"

Mélissande's eyes sparkled with amusement. "You will, of course, be welcome at the Dower House at any time."

"You are more than kind, mademoiselle. Do you ever come up to London? I understand that your cousin, M. de Castellane, is planning to establish himself there in the hope of joining the Comte's household. Will you be visiting him?"

"I would like very much to visit London, but I don't think it will be possible."

"Anything is possible if one wants it badly enough. And so, if—no, when—you come, be sure to do so before the autumn, so I can have the pleasure of showing you the sights of London."

"You won't be in London after the autumn?"

"Oh, yes, but at the end of the summer I will be a married man."

Mélissande admired the delicacy with which Martigny explained to her how his financial circumstances required him to make a marriage of convenience with a wealthy Englishwoman. He made it quite clear that his heart was not involved with his future bride, and she liked him all the better for his gentle warning that he could not allow himself to be seriously interested in Mélissande. Much as she liked him, however, she knew that his unavailability would cause her no heart-burning, and she felt only a minor regret when he went off to take supper with the Comte d'Artois in the privacy of the book room. Mélissande ate the lavish supper provided by Aurore in the company of Cecilia and Bertrand and Julian Gray, a fresh-faced naval officer of medium height and build and no special claim to good looks except for his smiling, bright blue eyes that he could not seem to keep away from Cecilia's face.

"Oh, Sandy, Lieutenant Gray has been telling me the most fascinating stories about his service with the Channel Fleet," exclaimed Cecilia. "He says the gale winds were often strong enough this past winter to splinter masts and tear sails to shreds. And since they remained at sea for many months, they lacked fresh vegetables and fresh water, so many of the seamen contracted scurvy and ulcers. But

Lieutenant Gray solved that problem by growing a little garden of mustard greens and cress on the stern watch, and he says some of the men raised ducks and pigs on board, fancy that.''

"I'm sorry to hear you suffered such hardships, Mr. Gray," said Mélissande. "I'm also immensely grateful, because I know it was the sacrifices made by the officers and men of the blockading fleet that saved us from being invaded by Napoleon.''

"I think you for your kind sentiments, ma'am, but I'm not convinced that England was ever in any danger of a French invasion.''

"Mr. Gray, how can you say such a thing?" protested Mélissande. "For many months now, the entire population of England has been preparing for a French invasion.''

"Well, ma'am, I'm sure our government expected an invasion, but the problem, you see, is that the Prime Minister and his cabinet are none of them sailors. Just one look at those low, clumsy invasion barges, and any British seaman would know instantly that the French boats would capsize in the slightest sea. If Boney ever seriously thought he could transport half a million men across the Channel in those barges, I'll wager he's learned his lesson by now.''

Mélissande smiled, saying, "Whether or not an invasion was possible, Mr. Gray, nothing can detract from the gallantry with which the Royal Navy endured the privations of the Channel blockade.''

"How very true, Sandy," echoed Cecilia. "Mr. Gray was telling me that he has often found live maggots in his biscuits!''

"I don't like to accept praise under false pretenses, Miss Maitland," the lieutenant said merrily to Cecilia as he tackled appreciatively a bowl of the Earl of Haverford's hothouse fruit. "It's true that our food was often not very appetizing, but we were never in any danger of starving.

What really disturbed us most on board the *Centaur*, I really believe, were the rats who ate the bellows of a seaman's bagpipes so we could no longer enjoy the crew's dancing on Saturday nights."

CHAPTER XIII

To Mélissande's unaccustomed eyes, her small drawing room seemed almost crowded. Since they had come to live at the Dower House, she and Nick and Cecilia had largely fallen out of the habit of entertaining. It was not that their old friends thought any less of them for their forced move from the Priory, but they had hesitated to accept hospitality that was beyond their means to return.

Mélissande gazed at her visitors with a slight sense of unreality. Major Francis Chilton was a familiar figure, of course, though he appeared rather awkwardly out of place in this company, and she had by now grown used to Bertrand's amusing, vivacious presence. But never in her wildest dreams could she have imagined that one day she would be pouring tea for the Duc de Berri, who in better and happier times would be roaming the halls of Versailles as the next heir but one to the French throne. Nor had Mélissande really expected that Charles de Martigny, in view of his clearly stated intention not to lose his heart to her, would make more than a courtesy call at the Dower House. Yet he and the young naval officer, Julian Gray, had been daily visitors here since the Haverfords' ball a week ago.

She said now to Martigny, seated beside her, ''I can

scarcely believe my own ears, to hear French accents drowning out English voices in my own drawing room!''

"I wish you could live in London where, if you so desire, you need hear none but French voices, mine among them,'' murmured Martigny. "I know, I know, I shouldn't say things like that.'' He raised his voice. "All of us in the Comte's party are growing sad that our visit is coming to an end. Monsieur's grief for Madame de Polastron seems to have lightened a little in these beautiful surroundings, and I don't recall when I have seen the Duc de Berri enjoy himself quite so much.''

Mélissande looked across the room to where the Comte d'Artois' son sat to one side of Cecilia, with Julian Gray on the other, and breathed a little sigh of relief. The Duc had been pursuing her sister with ardor since his first glimpse of her at the Haverfords' ball, but Cecilia had scarcely seemed to notice. Her attention these days was entirely caught up in Julian Gray, who, as he so often did, was now regaling the company with an amusingly told account of his naval experience.

"Before I joined the *Centaur*, I served briefly with the fleet that was blockading the French naval vessels that had taken refuge in neutral Spanish ports. Our admiral was friendly with the Spaniards, even if they were sheltering French battleships, and managed to obtain a British anchorage at Betanzos Bay. There we rival lookouts met on neutral soil, even sharing the same windmill, with an English lieutenant—your humble servant—watching French port activity from one window and a French lieutenant keeping tabs on the British squadron from the other.''

Under cover of the general laughter that greeted Julian Gray's tale, Martigny said in a low voice, "His Highness can't match Mr. Gray's derring-do. The royal nose is quite out of joint.''

Mélissande laughed despite herself, but there was a certain tension in the room, and she was not really sorry when her guests took their leave. Martigny held her hands in

farewell far longer than necessary, and his eyes, if not his
lips, spoke volumes about his reluctance to part from her,
and the Duc de Berri's rather abrupt *"au revoir"* indicated
how little he relished his one-sided rivalry with Julian Gray.

The latter lingered after the other guests had left, requesting
Mélissande's approval of his scheme to take Cecilia driving
in a curricle borrowed from his brother-in-law. Mélissande
saw no harm in the excursion, and when Cecilia had hurried
up the stairs to fetch her hat and pelisse and gloves, Julian
took advantage of her absence to say hurriedly, "I say, Miss
de Castellane, do I have your permission to write to Miss
Maitland when I return to sea?"

"You do, though Cecilia is of age, you know, and doesn't
need my permission."

"I know that. Nevertheless, I should prefer to have your
permission—and your approval, too—because I would like
very much to marry Cecilia."

"But Mr. Gray—I hardly know what to say. You have
known each other for only a few days."

Bertrand was still in the drawing room. "Mélissande, if
you would like me to leave . . ."

"No, please stay, M. de Castellane," Julian said quickly.
"I quite regard you as a member of Cecilia's family, even if
you are not really related to her." His smile had a rueful
tinge as he continued, "We sailors must make the most of
our few precious moments of shore leave, although in my
case time had little to do with my falling in love. I was sure
of my feelings for Cecilia five minutes after I first met her. I
think—I hope—she will come to share my feelings. I've
even dreamed of being married on my next leave."

Mélissande said quietly, "Mr. Gray, I'm sure you know
about Cecilia's background. How will your family react to
her illegitimacy?"

"I know my parents will love Cecilia as much as I do
after they have known her for a scant five minutes," replied
Julian instantly. "But if by some chance they were to object
to my marriage on such flimsy grounds, I would simply

ignore their wishes. My desire to marry your sister is not subject to change by anyone or anything.''

''Your feelings do you honor, Mr. Gray, but are you also aware that Cecilia has no dowry? Oh, she has the promise of a few thousand pounds from her father's estate, but that sum may never be paid. Could the pair of you manage at all comfortably on your navy pay, which I am given to understand is very small?''

Julian Gray smiled. ''A doting—and childless—godfather recently died and left me five thousand a year. As my wife, Cecilia will never lack for anything—'' He broke off as Cecilia returned to the drawing room. A few minutes later, after Julian and Cecilia had departed for their drive, Mélissande sank into a chair in a sort of semidaze.

''What romantics you English are,'' remarked Bertrand in amusement, sitting down opposite Mélissande. ''Here's a young man so bowled over by the first pretty face he sees after months at sea that he proposes to plunge helter-skelter into a most unsuitable marriage.''

Mélissande roused herself to protest. ''I agree it's ridiculous to be making plans to marry after such a short acquaintance, but unsuitable? Why would a marriage between Cecilia and Mr. Gray be unsuitable? They both come from good families, he has a more than comfortable income, they like each other very well . . .''

''There you go, chérie, letting your fondness for your sister get in the way of your intelligence. In my opinion, it's very unlikely that Lieutenant Gray's family would ever sanction such a match. His parents will say—and quite rightly, I believe—that a young man of good family with a handsome fortune should look higher for a bride than a penniless girl of illegitimate birth. And supposing that Mr. Gray chooses to marry without his parents' consent? Inevitably he would come to resent a wife whom he could not present to his family.''

''Come now, Bertrand, don't borrow trouble before the event. I think you're being overly pessimistic. Mr. Gray's family may well consider his happiness to be more important than their objections to Cecilia's birth—*mon dieu,* what am I saying? I'm taking for granted that a marriage that was first mentioned only moments ago will actually take place! Mr. Gray is about to spend many months at sea, and by the time he returns, he and Cecilia may have forgotten all about each other. I refuse to worry about the situation until it becomes necessary.'' Mélissande eyed Bertrand with a teasing smile. ''You've made it very clear that you consider romance and marriage totally unrelated subjects. Considering your present reduced circumstances, I certainly hope you never have the misfortune to fall head over heels in love with a lady who has no fortune!''

''But I *have* fallen in love—madly, desperately in love— with the most beautiful, the most intelligent woman I shall ever hope to meet. . . .'' Bertrand broke off, looking aghast at his involuntary outburst.

''Bertrand . . . I had no idea. Who could it be?''

Bertrand threw up his hands. ''Good God, Mélissande, have you no eyes? Do you think if I had any choice that I would allow you to remain unmarried for one extra day?''

''I can't believe. . . What are you saying?'' said Mélissande in a faltering voice. It had never once occurred to her that Bertrand thought of her in a romantic way.

''I was saying some very foolish things, *chérie,* the stuff of boyish daydreams,'' replied Bertrand, his face relaxing into a somewhat strained smile. ''I suppose I meant to say that in a perfect world—prerevolutionary France, let us say—you and I might have been a perfect couple. Affairs being what they are, however . . .'' He shrugged, and a moment later he changed the subject. ''Did you and Cecilia finally make the all-important decision of what to wear to the hunting picnic at Fiesole tomorrow?''

Mélissande heard Bertrand's lighthearted question with a quick feeling of relief. She had never thought of him in romantic terms, but only as a delightfully companionable newfound cousin, and she now sensed gratefully that he would never refer again to the subject of love between them. "Cecilia has changed her mind at least a dozen times, but I *think* she has finally settled on a firm choice, her new sprigged muslin with the pink ribbons. Yes, Sally?" Mélissande looked up at her little maid, who had just entered the drawing room. "Miss Wright? Of course I will see her. Show her in, please."

Phoebe rushed into the room, dissolving into a torrent of tears before she could reply to her surprised hostess's greeting. With an admirable composure, Bertrand murmured, "My dear Mlle. Wright, you seem distressed. Pray allow me to retire." He headed for the door.

Urging Phoebe to a seat on the sofa, Mélissande sat down beside her, placing a protective arm around the girl's shoulders and waiting for the storm of sobs to subside.

"Are you feeling more the thing, Phoebe dear? Here, drink a little of this wine. Now then, do you care to tell me what's troubling you? You know I'll do what I can to help."

"I'm not sure that *anyone* can help," replied Phoebe drearily, mopping her wan face with the handkerchief she fished out of her reticule. "I just felt I had to talk to somebody. Do you remember George Mattson?"

"Mattson? I don't seem to recall . . ."

"Oh, you've probably never met him. He owns the large farm that adjoins our property to the south, on the Battle road. He and Papa have always been friendly."

"Yes?" said Mélissande, groping for understanding.

"Well, you see, Mr. Mattson lost his wife about six months ago, and since then he has taken to visiting us quite often. I didn't think much about it, except to feel sorry for him—he did seem lonely and he and his wife had no children. But I certainly never thought of him as a suitor. Why, he's *old*, at least thirty-five! Still, yesterday he asked Papa for my hand. And now—oh, Miss Mélissande, Papa is *pressing* me to accept Mr. Mattson's offer of marriage. Papa wants his grandchild—my son!—to become the largest landowner in the county by joining the Wright farm, which the child would inherit from me, to Mr. Mattson's property. After all the rest of us are dead, of course!''

"But I always thought . . .''

"You always thought I cared for Nick, and you were quite right.'' For an instant Phoebe's face brightened. "And Nick has come to care for me, too, and we've actually been talking of marriage someday.'' Her voice trailed off as her eyes once more filmed over.

"Then I don't understand at all. Mr. Wright seems so fond of Nick.''

"Yes¦ but now I'm beginning to think that Papa was just fond of Nick's title!'' said Phoebe bitterly. "He would dearly have liked to see me as Lady Nicholas, taking my place in county society. After Nick's father died, however, and the new Lord Rochedale came home, Nick's position didn't seem as attractive to Papa. Lord Rochedale appeared to *hate* Nick and Cecilia, and then there was that scheme to break the entail. Now Papa says that his lordship might at any time tire of his new arrangement with Nick, dismiss him from his post as bailiff, and attempt once more to break the entail. Then where would Nick and I be, Papa says, out of favor at the Priory and with no social standing in the county, because, without Lord Rochedale's sponsorship, who would be likely to extend invitations to a farmer's daughter, even if she was a lady?''

Mélissande listened in distress to Phoebe's rather disjointed remarks. "What has Nick to say to all of this?''

"Nothing! Nick never did actually ask me to marry him, you know. We—we just talked around the edges of the subject. So when I told him Papa wants me to marry Mr. Mattson, Nick just wished me happy and left the house. I haven't seen him since. Miss Mélissande, that's why I've come to see you. Won't you speak to Nick? Ask him why he isn't lifting a finger to keep me from marrying someone else.'' Phoebe swallowed hard. "Do you think . . . could he have fallen in love with another girl?''

"Oh, I feel positive he hasn't. Of course I will speak to

him." Mélissande paused at the sound of voices in the entrance hall. A moment later, Nick, followed by his half brother, entered the drawing room, saying, "Come have a seat, Gideon, I know I can lay my hand on that bill of sale in a trice." He jerked to a stop as he saw Phoebe, and the two of them stared at each other in speechless confusion until Phoebe, the tears once more raining down her cheeks, jumped up from her seat and rushed out of the room.

"Oh, that poor child," Mélissande exclaimed. "Nick, go after her."

Nick, his face wooden, turned to Gideon, saying, "Let me pour you a glass of this Madeira. I think you'll find it very tolerable. After all, it came from your own cellar! Well, Papa's cellar, actually. Sit down and have a cozy chat with Sandy while I look for that confounded bill of sale."

"Yes, I'll have a glass of that Madeira, Nicholas, and it's *much* more than tolerable. Our parent had an excellent palate. I regret extremely that there are only a few bottles remaining in the Priory cellar." Gideon spoke with a pleasantly casual air, but his eyes narrowed and there was a sharper note in his voice as he added, "But first, I think, Mélissande wishes to speak with you."

Nick flushed. He flashed Mélissande a defiant look, saying, "I don't wish to be rude, Sandy, but I can't talk about Phoebe."

"Nick, I don't understand you. How can you be so callous when Phoebe is in such great distress because of you? She asked me if you had fallen in love with another girl!"

"Then she's dicked in the nob. Fall in love with someone else, my eye and Betty Martin. I've never cared for anyone but Phoebe," Nick blurted, surprised out of his stubborn silence. Then he lowered his head, muttering, "But that don't signify. She'd best forget about me."

"Spare me a Cheltenham tragedy," said Mélissande impatiently. "What is so different about your situation and Phoebe's today—except for Mr. Wright's shatterbrained notions—compared to what it was a week ago? At that time I could have sworn that you and Phoebe would be married eventually and become the proprietors of the Wright farm when her father dies.''

Goaded, Nick exclaimed, ''Well, and so it may have been a good idea once, when Papa was alive and I could look forward to becoming bailiff of Easton Priory.'' With lines of angry hurt carved deep in his face, Nick glared at Gideon. ''But now, when my dear elder brother could become displeased with me at any time and send me and my sisters packing, I can't blame Mr. Wright for not considering me very good husband material for his daughter. He's determined to make Phoebe the mistress of the largest property in Sussex, and I won't put anything in his way. I'd rather muck out his cowbarn than become my father-in-law's pensioner!'' Nick treated his brother to another withering glare and stalked out of the room.

''May I ask what that was about?'' asked Gideon. ''Unknowingly, I seem to have done something heinous.''

''Oh, Phoebe's father wishes her to accept the marriage proposal of a wealthy farmer, a Mr. Mattson. Phoebe, of course, has adored Nick since she was a little girl. I think Nick loves her, too, but now in Phoebe's eyes he seems not only to be renouncing his own claims to her affections, but also he is urging her to follow her father's wishes.''

''Mattson. Yes, I know the name. Mr. Mattson is a very large property owner. If Miss Wright married him, she would be a lady of some substance. Not to sound cynical, Mélissande, but it is not uncommon for a parent to desire an advantageous marriage for his child. In any case, I fail to understand how Nicholas's problems of the heart can in any way be my fault.''

Gideon's calm reasonableness, his air of detachment, caused Mélissande's temper to flare. ''Where you *are* at fault, my dear Gideon, is in your failure to exhibit a little human sympathy for poor Nick. You must have a heart of stone not to see that he and Phoebe are really suffering.''

"Well now, I've been accused of many faults, but never of having a heart of stone," observed Gideon with an air of interest. He reached out to take Mélissande's hands and imprisoned them against his chest. "I wasn't mistaken, was I? You do feel a rather lively heartbeat?" He grinned as Mélissande, a bright spot of color in each cheek, snatched her hands away. Picking up his hat and stick, he said, "I'll try to be sympathetic to Nicholas, if you think it's indicated, but it's been so many years since I was a lovesick swain, I'm not sure that I can really enter into my brother's feelings."

CHAPTER XIV

Mélissande strolled slowly along the verge of the pretty little stream that edged the pleasant grassy clearing in the woods of Fiesole. She and the other female guests had driven with Lady Haverford in open landaus to the clearing to await the arrival of the gentlemen of the party, who were off with the Earl on a hare hunt, following the hounds on foot. Tables and chairs had already been set up on the grass for the "pick-nick," and footmen in the Haverford livery were even now setting out roast chicken, hams, ducks, and pickled salmon; custard puddings, gooseberry tarts, and assorted pastries; and mounds of pineapple, grapes, and cherries from the Earl's hothouses.

Pausing, Mélissande glanced around the glade to search out the delicate colors of the spring wild flowers she loved so much: the blue of hepatica and harebell, the yellow of kingcups and cowslips, a shower of white blossoms of the wood anemones. It was a radiantly lovely day in early May, and as a lover of the outdoors Mélissande ordinarily would have reveled at the prospect of an alfresco meal in such a beautiful pastoral setting. She had been able to summon little real enthusiasm for this excursion to Fiesole, however. Her mind had been preoccupied for the past several days with familiar worries about Nick, who had flatly refused to attend the picnic, and who had reverted to the brooding, uncommunicative behavior that had characterized him during that period in the autumn when he had been driven by his unhappiness to join the Easton smugglers. Mélissande had also found her thoughts turning all too often of late to Gideon, or rather to Gideon's newly acquired knack of goading her into resentful outbursts that shredded her normally dignified composure. She was helplessly and angrily aware that her sensitivity to Gideon's provocative words and actions would be alleviated only when she could blot out of her memory that passionate interlude in the inn parlor at Tunbridge Wells.

"This is a festive day, a gala day, and I won't allow you to keep yourself solitary," said a smiling Aurore as she came up to put an affectionate hand on Mélissande's arm. "I fear you are thinking sad thoughts, *ma petite,* and that you mustn't do. Today we must all of us put on our happy faces and try to forget that His Highness will be leaving us soon. You've enjoyed the Comte's visit, haven't you? I thought M. de Martigny was quite taken with you."

Mélissande chuckled. "Don't matchmake, Aurore. M. de Martigny is about to contract a marriage of convenience with a wealthy heiress."

"Oh, I hadn't heard. . . . The news hasn't made you too unhappy, I trust," said Aurore anxiously.

"Not at all. I understand quite as well as you do, Aurore, that impoverished young men of good family must find rich wives."

Lady Haverford flushed. "Really, Mélissande, how am I to take that remark? I hope you are not implying that Stephen is marrying Augusta just for her money. She is a lovely, charming young woman, and he is very fond of her. I'm only sorry that Cecilia's heart was bruised, but you'll see, she will soon recover from any hurt that Stephen may have caused her. She is still very young, and I would not be too surprised to find her making a suitable match one day.

Major Chilton, for example. I understand he has shown definite signs of interest in Cecilia."

Mélissande felt a sudden urge to deflate Aurore's complacent snobbery. "Thank you for your concern about Cecilia, but there is really no need." At the Countess's inquiring glance, Mélissande added, lowering her voice, "I know I can depend on you to keep this to yourself until the public announcement. Lieutenant Gray has offered for Cecilia's hand."

"Oh. I am so pleased for her. Of course, it won't be easy for her and Mr. Gray, living on his navy pay, but—"

Mélissande pushed firmly to the back of her mind her own misgivings about Julian Gray's precipitate courtship and said with a pleased smile not unmixed with triumph, "We liked Mr. Gray so much for his own self, but I won't deny that it was a delightful shock to learn that he has five thousand a year, thanks to a fond godfather."

Her mouth ajar, Aurore was incapable of speech for several seconds. "What wonderful news," she finally managed to say, adding hastily, "If you will excuse me, I must have a word with the housekeeper." She paused in midstep to stare across the clearing, where Charles de Martigny had just dismounted from his horse and was walking toward them. "But what are you doing here, monsieur? I didn't expect you so soon. Is the hunt over already, then? Will His Royal Highness be arriving shortly?"

Martigny bent his head over Aurore's hand and bowed gracefully to Mélissande. "*Pas du tout*. The Nimrods are still energetically slaughtering the poor hares. Myself, I find the pleasures of the chase a poor substitute for the company of beautiful and charming Frenchwomen."

"La, I had almost forgotten the outrageous flattery of you Versailles courtiers," teased Aurore. "You must be satisfied with the company of just *one* Frenchwoman for the moment, while I attend to my duties as hostess."

"I hope His Royal Highness won't chide you for derelic-

tion of duty, M. de Martigny,'' murmured Mélissande after
Aurore's departure.

"Have no fear. The Comte gave me permission to leave
the hunt. Since the death of his beloved Madame de Polastron,
he has been especially sensitive to an affair of the heart.''

Mélissande lifted a startled face to him. "Affair of the
heart? I should be very unhappy to think there had been any
gossip. . . .''

"No, no, there has been no gossip about you and me, but
His Highness has eyes to see, *tu sais*.'' Martigny tucked her
arm into his. "Come, let us take a little stroll by the side of
this beautiful brook.''

They walked along a path bordering the little river with a
sense of companionable pleasure, occasionally pointing out
to each other a nesting bird or a vivid wild flower. They had
gone well past the clearing, out of sight of the Haverford
guests, when Martigny halted, swinging around to face
Mélissande. His voice throbbed with emotion as he said,
"I'm obsessed with you, *chérie*. I can't get you out of my
thoughts. Last night, trying to fall asleep, I found myself
imagining what it would be like never to see your face
again. I can't live with such a prospect. Mélissande, I want
to spend the rest of my life with you.''

Half affronted, half flattered, Mélissande shook her head
at the tenderly smiling face so close to hers. "This isn't
Versailles, you know. Even if I were a respectably married
woman, I wouldn't consider becoming your mistress.''

"*Mon Dieu,* I'm not trying to seduce you! I want to
marry you!''

Mélissande stared at Martigny with a puzzled frown.
"You told me you were about to marry an English lady.''

"Until I came here, I had every intention of doing so.
Lucy—my affianced—is pretty and sweet-tempered, and her
fortune would allow me to live like a gentleman again,
without the nightmare of debtors' prison hanging over me.
But if marriage to Lucy means losing you, I'd rather go
back to pinching pennies. And who knows? Napoleon can't

last forever. One day you and I can go back to France with the heir to the throne, and then our money worries would be over."

"*Mon ami,* your heart is running away with your head," said Mélissande gently. "A marriage between us would be quite impractical, even if. . ."

Martigny smiled at her confusion. "Even if you loved me, which you don't, *n'est-ce pas? Eh bien,* it was just a dream, a mad, wonderful dream. I suppose I always sensed that you didn't love me. I could always feel between us the presence of another person. Who is he, this man who keeps me from my heart's desire?"

"There is no such man," said Mélissande curtly, angry at herself beyond reason because Gideon's cool, indifferent image had just popped into her mind. "I think we should go back, M. de Martigny. The gentlemen will soon be returning from the hunt."

Even before they reached the clearing, Mélissande and Martigny could hear the sound of horses and carriages, and by the time they had joined the female members of the party, the landaus carrying the gentlemen hunters had arrived.

The Comte d'Artois, moving rather stiffly, had just descended from a landau and was talking to his host when Mélissande and Martigny approached.

"Your Highness, I would not have had this happen for the world. I feel disgraced, not only for myself, but for the entire county," the Earl was saying. A placid man whose only real passions were for horses and hunting, Lord Haverford now sounded extremely agitated.

"Please do not distress yourself, milor' Haverford. You are not to blame for your guests' conduct. Let us speak no more of this matter," replied Artois soothingly. He turned to Mélissande and Martigny with an obvious air of relief at leaving a difficult subject. "My dear mademoiselle, you look more enchanting than ever today, if that is possible."

The Comte's inimitable charm had its usual effect, and Mélissande suddenly felt that her Leghorn bonnet trimmed with yellow roses and her straw-colored pelisse over a gown of pale green muslin were in the very forefront of fashion. She smiled, saying, "And how did the hunting go? M. de Martigny referred to you all as Nimrods!"

"Ah, you must not humiliate me with such a question," said Artois with a humorous grimace. "My shoulder and back are still not entirely recovered, and I fear my aim was sadly off. I did, however, greatly enjoy my excursion into your very beautiful countryside. We will miss Sussex, eh, M. de Martigny?"

"Your Highness, you must allow me to settle you in a comfortable chair and to procure you a glass of wine before supper is served," said the Earl. He and Artois moved off with Martigny in attendance.

"Sandy, guess what? Mr. Gray bagged more hares than anyone else today. *He* says it was pure accident, but *I* say he's being overly modest," exclaimed a smiling Cecilia as she came up on the arm of Julian Gray. She looked very pretty in a pelisse of lilac gros de Naples and a straw hat trimmed with matching ribbons. More than that, she looked radiantly happy. Stephen Lacey was standing nearby with Augusta, and Mélissande, catching a glimpse of his pinched expression as he watched Cecilia, was suddenly sure that she no longer need harbor vengeful thoughts against him. What more suitable punishment for Stephen than to watch Cecilia's happiness with another man?

"I wish I could pack up some of Cecilia's enthusiasm for my abilities and transport it to the Admiralty. Perhaps I would soon command my own ship!" joked Julian. His smile faded slightly as he said to Cecilia, "Would you excuse me for just a moment? I would like a word with your sister."

Pouting ever so slightly, Cecilia walked away. Lieutenant Gray's pleasant face was unusually grave as he said to Mélissande, "I feel obliged to tell you something. It is too delicate a subject to discuss in front of your sister. In fact,

God help me, I shouldn't be discussing it with *you*. But since your stepfather is dead, and your brother is so young..."

"Mr. Gray, pray do not keep me in suspense. What is this 'delicate subject' you seem to find so disturbing?"

"Well...to put it bluntly, your stepbrother and your cousin have quarreled, and M. de Castellane has challenged Lord Rochedale to a duel."

Mélissande's lips were stiff with shock. "When did this happen? How?"

"It was earlier this afternoon, at the hunt. Are you familiar with hare hunting? The hunters walk in a long parallel line behind the dogs, and since our muzzle-loading guns have a slow ignition and reloading takes a considerable time, there is a very strict gun etiquette. After each shot the hunter must halt and bid his dog to 'down charge' until reloading has taken place. Lord Rochedale physically attacked your cousin for careless shooting, claiming that M. de Castellane had walked ahead of him while his gun was being charged. Lord Rochedale knocked your cousin down, and M. de Castellane, perhaps understandably, challenged his lordship to a duel, to which the latter promptly agreed. Naturally, there was a tremendous commotion, with Lord Haverford suffering acute embarrassment because of the presence of royalty. To make matters even worse, it appeared to many of us that Lord Rochedale was foxed, an unforgivable fault in a hunter. Lord Haverford actually had to order him to leave the hunt."

"Mr. Gray, I simply cannot believe that Gideon would hunt while drunk, endangering the lives of everyone around him. Surely there must be some mistake."

"I don't think so. Lord Rochedale had shot the cat, or I've never seen anyone half seas over on Strip-Me-Naked." Looking acutely embarrassed, Gray burst out, "Good God, I know I should be drawn and quartered for talking like this to a female about a male relative's drinking habits, let alone his decision to fight a duel, but there's a time for strict etiquette and a time for common sense. It would be a tragedy for Cecilia—for all your family—if her half brother should kill, or be killed by, your cousin. Miss de Castellane, it may be beyond your powers, but I think you must at least try to persuade your cousin to withdraw his challenge.''

"Yes, of course," replied Mélissande numbly. "Not just try, but succeed. Surely, once he regains his temper, Bertrand will realize that he cannot fight a duel with my own stepbrother, whatever the provocation. Mr. Gray, it cannot have been easy for you to tell me this. I thank you. I know you will do your best to keep the story from spreading.''

"Well, as to that"—Gray spread his hands—"I fear the damage has been done. This very juicy bit of scandal will be all over the county by tomorrow.''

Trying to keep her behavior normal during the remainder of the afternoon, Mélissande pecked at Lady Haverford's elaborate supper, joined in the toasts to the Comte d'Artois and his son, and made determined small talk with those around her, all the while aware of averted glances and whispers that trailed away at her approach. She was thankful that Julian Gray whisked Cecilia away after the picnic to take tea with his sister's family, so that Mélissande and Bertrand were alone in the carriage on the return to the Dower House. As they rolled down the driveway away from Fiesole, she said tensely, "Bertrand, I know all about this monstrous duel. You must withdraw your challenge.''

Bertrand eyed her in sullen surprise. "How did you . . . ? *Mais, certainement,* that busybody, Lieutenant Gray, has been talking to you. I don't understand this England of yours. In France we don't tell our women about affairs of honor." His mouth relaxed in a smile as he took her hand in his. "I'm sorry. Please don't worry, not about me, at any rate. I am an excellent shot and a very fair swordsman. It makes no difference to me which weapon milor' Rochedale chooses." Bertrand broke into an uncontrollable chuckle. "Look at it this way, Mélissande: it would be all to the good if I disposed of this unkind stepbrother of yours, *n'est-ce pas*? Then Nicholas would inherit his father's title, and you and he and Cecilia could live again at the Priory.''

"Don't be ridiculous,'' Mélissande exclaimed angrily. "The very last thing I want is for either of you to be injured. Lieutenant Gray told me that Gideon was drunk when he picked a quarrel with you. I think that I—or perhaps Nick—can persuade him to apologize when he is sober, but first you must withdraw that challenge.''

Bertrand moved away from her into a corner of the carriage. "It's not a subject of discussion between you and me. I will not withdraw from an affair of honor.''

"Honor! What, pray, is honorable about shooting a fellow human being in cold blood? If you were to kill Gideon, I would refuse to see you ever again.''

"And would the reverse apply? If milor' Rochedale were to kill me, would you shut your stepbrother out of your life?'' Bertrand asked frigidly.

Mélissande clamped her lips shut in frustration. Perhaps tomorrow, when tempers had cooled, when Gideon was no longer in his cups, she could talk some sense into the combatants.

Arrived at the Dower House, Mélissande and Bertrand had just stepped into the entrance hall when they encountered Gideon coming down the stairs from the upper floor. Looking remarkably steady and clear-eyed for one recently so intoxicated that he had disgraced himself, Gideon said curtly to Bertrand, "Come into the drawing room. I want a word with you.''

"This is strange behavior,'' Bertrand said scornfully. "In France, we conduct affairs of honor correctly. There it is customary for the challenged person to send his second to the challenger's second to arrange the details of the duel.''

"And here in England we make it a point to keep our affairs of honor secret from our womenfolk,'' Gideon replied with a curl of his lip. "Incidentally, whom would you have sent to me as your second? My young half brother? I wasn't aware that you had any close friends in this district.''

"Gideon, enough of this, I want—''

"Mélissande, will you leave us, please? I wish to speak privately to your cousin."

"No, I will not leave, not until I've talked either or both of you into stopping this monstrous duel."

"Then you've no reason to stay. There won't be any duel."

"What is this, milor' Rochedale?" Bertrand exclaimed sharply. "You accused me of careless shooting and struck me in public, at which I challenged you to a duel and you accepted. Are you now crying off? If, *cependant,* you care to offer me an apology for your infamous conduct, I should be inclined to consider it in view of your close relationship with my cousin. I would much prefer, *naturellement,* not to cause her needless distress."

"What admirable solicitude," sneered Gideon. "It won't wash, Castellane. I know all about you and your schemes."

Bertrand's face became suddenly still. After a moment he said to Mélissande, "Perhaps milor' Rochedale is right. We should talk. Please excuse us." With a quick, formal little bow, he strode out of the entrance hall into the drawing room, followed by Gideon. Hesitating only for a second, Mélissande walked after them, her heart sinking as she eyed the two grim-faced men. She faltered, "Gideon, Bertrand, I know something is terribly wrong, something much worse than a silly duel."

There was a long, tense silence, and then Gideon said abruptly, "Very well, Mélissande, you can stay. You'll find out about this cousin of yours soon enough, unfortunately. You see, I accused him of careless gun handling only to avoid causing scandal in the presence of Lord Haverford's royal guests. Castellane's real offense was attempting to assassinate the Comte d'Artois."

Gideon swung on Bertrand. "I saw you take dead aim at the Comte. I firmly believe he would be a dead man if I hadn't leaped against you and jostled your arm. If you had killed him, it would have passed as an accidental death. There were so many of us in the hunting party, and we were scattered over so long a line in the forest, that it might not even have been apparent who fired the fatal shot. Even if the shooting had been brought home to you, you would have feigned the most abject remorse, and doubtless everyone would have thought how cruelly ironic it was that the very man whom you had forsaken your country to serve should have died at your hands. And then, after a suitable period, I daresay you would have faded quietly out of sight, with nothing to connect the death of the Comte d'Artois to the revengeful hand of your master."

Bertrand said incredulously, "My revengeful master? And who might that be, pray?"

"I have reason to believe that you were ordered by Napoleon himself to kill Artois, thus putting an end to the numerous attempts to assassinate Bonaparte, the most recent being the Cadoudal-Pichegru plot in which your great friend General Moreau was implicated, and during the course of which the Duc d'Enghien was executed. It's well-known even here in England that Artois has been the leader of the royalist plots to do away with Napoleon, and it was probably thought that, with Artois gone, the head of the snake would be crushed. At the same time, Napoleon did not want an out-and-out assassination, because he had just executed the Duc d'Enghien to a storm of protest from every government in Europe. No, he wanted the death of Artois to look like an accident. That was your mission, Castellane, and you very nearly succeeded."

"I think you must be mad. Either that or you are still intoxicated."

"I was never drunk. I merely pretended to be foxed so my behavior would seem scandalous but not alarming. I didn't want to throw the entire hunting party into an uproar with a public accusation that you had tried to kill the Comte, both because I hoped to spare Lord Haverford embarrassment and because I thought there was some chance that you might try to escape in the melee. No, I thought it better to keep you unsuspecting that your plot had been uncovered so I could hale you quietly into custody at a time and a place of my own choosing. That time is now.''

Bertrand turned to Mélissande, who had been shocked into a stunned, disbelieving silence. *"Chérie*, for some reason this stepbrother of yours wants to destroy me. Why else would he invent this calumny, this grotesque story, out of whole cloth, without a shred of evidence or motivation?''

"On the contrary, I had very good reasons to suspect you,'' Gideon declared. "I had an uneasy feeling about you from the first. It was hard to believe that a rising young French officer would suddenly abandon his career and his family for ideological reasons and defect to England just as the French army was poised to invade us. In my experience, young officers are far more interested in promotions and glory than political ideas! It was also too much of a coincidence that, arrived in England, you should head straight for the home of a distant cousin, from whom, by reason of a bitter family estrangement, you could logically expect nothing except distrust and dislike. The significance of the Comte d'Artois' imminent visit did not strike me until later. At any rate, my uneasiness prompted me, on the occasion of our first meeting at the Easton Assembly ball, to inquire about your military career.''

Gideon slanted a derisive little smile at Bertrand. "Do you recall our discussion of the battle of Hohenlinden? I commented on the brilliance of General Richepanse's turning movement of the enemy right. Not blinking an eye, you agreed with my opinion. Castellane, no officer who had served with General Moreau at Hohenlinden could have failed to catch me out. It was, of course, the Austrian *left* that was turned by General Richepanse. You didn't contradict me either, when I stated that the Austrians deployed against General Ney in the center of the line attacked from the village of Erding, which is miles to the northeast of Hohenlinden. Actually, the Austrians attacked directly opposite from Hohenlinden, at the village of Mattempost.''

Startled, Mélissande glanced at Bertrand, who had turned pale. "Bertrand, surely there must be some misunderstanding.''

"There's not a shadow of misunderstanding, Mélissande," Gideon broke in. "Let me go on, Castellane, to tell you how my uneasiness turned to active suspicion. After Artois arrived at Fiesole, I chanced to be riding nearby when His Highness took a nasty fall from his horse. Lord Haverford assumed that the Comte's horse had stepped into a rabbit hole, but I just happened to notice, tied waist high to a tree beside the path, a length of very strong twine, rubbed with blacking to make it invisible. I had no doubt that someone jerked the string against the forelegs of Artois' horse as it came abreast of the tree. I said nothing at the time, not wishing to distress His Highness, for I thought it likely that a prankish schoolboy, or an anti-French villager, had caused the accident. But then, on my way home I spotted you, Castellane, emerging from the wood where the accident took place, and suddenly I recalled the discovery of the Cadoudal-Pichegru plot in France a few weeks earlier, and the execution of the Duc d'Enghien, and I began to wonder if you were stalking Artois. At this point, I had no proof, so I decided to tell no one of my suspicions but to remain on my guard. Today, while we were gathering for the hunt, I noticed that you seemed to be very nervous, and it occurred to me that with so many hunters and guns in one place, it would be easy to shoot the Comte 'accidentally.' You certainly did your best, Castellane. If I hadn't broken your aim, Artois' son, the Duc de Berri, would be the next heir to the throne of the Bourbons, and Napoleon could breathe a little easier."

Still pale but composed, Bertrand said, "You must know that you have no proof to back up this insane accusation."

"Alas, that is technically true. Just before you and Mélissande arrived at the Dower House, I ransacked your bedchamber, and I found nothing incriminating."

"You had no right to invade my privacy! Your illegal search, however, reinforces what I just said to you: you have no proof of any wrongdoing on my part. You may *claim* that I shot at Artois, but I have scores of witnesses who will testify that you were foxed and your testimony therefore unreliable. Your accusations won't stand up in a court of law, but I presume that, to satisfy your sick whims, and despite all those great claims of English justice, you will hand me over to your secret police, and that will be the end of me."

Gideon laughed scornfully. "That remark certainly betrays your lack of familiarity with English customs. Here in England we *have* no police, secret or otherwise. Even in London there are only a handful of Bow Street Runners and a small band of parish constables assisted by a few venerable 'Charlies' to keep the peace. No, what I propose to do is to deliver you to Justice Banning in Easton. After a brief preliminary hearing based on my testimony, the justice will commit you to jail to await trial on a charge of attempted murder. Before you can be tried, there must be an indictment by a grand jury, of course. For that, I grant you, my unsupported testimony might not suffice. I'm confident, however, that when you are questioned by military experts it will be proved to the satisfaction of any grand jury that you have never served a day in any army, and that therefore your entire story is suspect. In fact, I think it probable you were one of Fouché's minions, before that unsavory individual's recent dismissal as Minister of Police."

"Enough of this," snapped Bertrand. "I deny your charges. They are outright lies, the figment of a diseased brain. I believe you have no legal standing, milor' Rochedale, so I will stand on my rights and refuse to accompany you to the justice of the peace until you can show me a properly executed warrant."

"By which time you would be well on your way to the nearest port," said Gideon grimly. He took a small pistol from the pocket of his greatcoat and trained it on Bertrand. "This is all the warrant I need."

"Gideon! I really think you must be mad!" exploded Mélissande, but Bertrand put a soothing hand on her arm. "It is all right, *ma chère*. I must yield to force, but you will see, nothing will be found against me. Milor' Rochedale, is it permitted that I have a private word with my cousin before we leave?''

Hesitating briefly, Gideon replied, ''Yes. Five minutes only. I will wait for you in the entrance hall.''

After Gideon had left the room, Mélissande said eagerly, ''Even if the justice actually commits you to jail, Bertrand, you mustn't despair. I will go straight to Lord Haverford— you know he's the Lord Lieutenant of the county. . . .''

''*Tais-toi, chérie,* we have so little time.'' Bertrand stepped close to Mélissande, speaking in low, urgent tones. ''Lord Haverford can't help me. Nobody can. It's more than likely that I will be convicted and hanged for attempted murder. We may never have another moment alone together, so I want to tell you now how much I regret lying to you, how much I regret betraying your trust.''

''Bertrand,'' Mélissande faltered. ''Are you saying you really are guilty of this terrible crime?''

''I tried to kill the Comte d'Artois, yes, but I am guilty of no crime,'' Bertrand said passionately. ''Rather, I tried to prevent a crime, the assassination of Napoleon. Over the years, Artois has fomented plot after plot to kill the First Consul. These plotters know that if they kill Napoleon, they kill the Revolution, because Napoleon *is* the Revolution. No, Mélissande, in killing Artois I am no more guilty of a crime than I would be in striking off the head of a venomous snake poised to attack me.''

''But you told me you had become disillusioned with Napoleon. You said you wanted to enter the service of the Comte d'Artois and work to restore the old monarchy in France.''

Bertrand spread his hands. ''All lies. I had to ingratiate myself with you, convince you that I was sincere, so that I could get access to Artois. Ah, yes, Mélissande, you were investigated thoroughly, you and Lady Haverford. We have known for many months about Artois' planned visit to Fiesole. You were a perfect cover. If you accepted me, you would introduce me to your cousin Aurore. Inevitably, I would be a guest at Fiesole during Artois' visit, where I was sure to have the opportunity to arrange for his 'accidental' death. Milor' Rochedale was quite right, *tu sais*. We wanted Artois dead, but without the world suspecting that Napoleon had any hand in the death.''

As Mélissande shrank back from him with an exclamation of horror, Bertrand said urgently, ''Mélissande, I was only doing my duty, exactly like a soldier on the battlefield, just as your stepbrother did his duty when he fought in India. I am only sorry that I used your friendship to carry out my purpose. Before we met, you see, you were only a faceless name, a fading childhood memory. I writhe now when I recall how I laughed at my superior's suggestion that I solidify my position with you by bringing you the Castellane emeralds. After just a few days here at the Dower House, I felt shamed by your warmth, your loyalty, your unstinting trust. After a few more days, I realized that I had fallen in love with you.'' Bertrand seized Mélissande's hands, pulling her close to him. ''*Ma chère,* dare I ask you not to think too badly of me? Won't you try to remember me simply as a cousin who loved you, not as your adopted country's enemy?''

Mélissande snatched her hands free, averting her eyes to avoid meeting Bertrand's pleading gaze. Her voice trembled as she said, ''How can you view yourself as a soldier? On a battlefield, soldiers like my father and Gideon kill and risk being killed in the face of the enemy. But you, disguised as a friend, you tried to shoot the Comte d'Artois in the back. Lurking in ambush, you attempted to kill him by causing him to fall from his horse. No, Bertrand, you were no soldier. I can only think of you as a common murderer!''

Her eyes swimming with tears, Mélissande rushed blindly into the entrance hall, where Gideon caught her into his arms. ''Mélissande, I'm so sorry to bring this grief to you.''

Touched by the sympathy in Gideon's voice, Mélissande rested her head against his shoulder and allowed the tears to flow freely for a brief moment. Then she straightened, brushing the tears away with the back of her hand. ''I couldn't ask you not to do your duty, Gideon. It's just . . . I've been so happy since Bertrand came. I had so little family, you know, just Cecilia and Nick, and then to come to know and love Bertrand, only to have him dragged away as an enemy spy. . . .''

"I know. It's very difficult for you." Gideon motioned with his pistol at Bertrand, who had just emerged from the drawing room. "Come along, Castellane. Let's not drag out this unpleasantness any longer than need be."

CHAPTER XV

Sitting in the morning room beside the dying fire, Mélissande stared blankly down at the open book in her lap. It was past ten o'clock in the evening, and she had read scarcely half a page in the previous two hours. Her mind had been too preoccupied with Bertrand, and the grief of losing him from the tiny circle of people she loved best, to concentrate on reading. She had earlier attempted with little appetite to eat a light supper with Cecilia, who had arrived home in high spirits at the attention shown her by Julian Gray's family. So engrossed was Cecilia in her hopes and fears for her own future—the lieutenant's leave, regretfully, was very nearly up—that she did not even notice Bertrand's absence from the dining table, and Mélissande did not have the heart to tell her about the plot to kill Artois. Cecilia would learn the news soon enough.

The door knocker sounded loudly in the silence of the house, and Mélissande, frowning slightly, hurried into the entrance hall to open the door. "Gideon!" she exclaimed. "Oh, how happy I am to see you. Come in, please. Tell me about Bertrand. Did Justice Banning commit him to jail? Would I be allowed to see him, do you think, before his trial? Because, no matter what he's done, he's still my cousin, and I can't just abandon him. . . ."

"Not so fast, Mélissande, you're way ahead of me," said Gideon, laughing. "Your cousin Bertrand is as well as can be expected, considering that by now he's doubtless on his way, trussed up and under guard, to a stay in a Sussex farmhouse."

At Mélissande's dumbfounded expression, Gideon added, "Yes, I brought him to Nicholas's old smuggling confederates in Easton. They happily agreed to keep him in custody until they can hand him over to the crew of the next boat to make a smuggling run to France."

Mélissande's stare was uncomprehending. "But why? What made you do it?"

"Well, we talked, Castellane and I, as we drove to Easton. It was clear that, in his own mind, he was acting from the purest of patriotic motives. It occurred to me, what purpose would really be served by putting him on trial? True, he tried to kill Artois, but he didn't succeed in his attempt. Also, let us face it, in the pragmatic sense Artois is important to England only as a pawn, a counterirritant, in the war with Napoleon. Why not avoid a notorious political trial? Why not spare you, Mélissande, the grief of seeing your cousin in the dock? The smugglers will prevent Castellane from any further attempt on Artois' life by keeping your cousin under guard until he can be dispatched back to France, where I fervently hope he will remain for the rest of his natural life!"

Suddenly feeling light with happiness, as if an impossibly heavy load had been lifted from her shoulders, Mélissande threw her arms around Gideon's neck, exclaiming, "What a wonderful thing you've done! I'll be thankful to you for the rest of my life." She pressed her lips to his in a quick kiss of thanks. He drew a startled breath and locked his arms around her, claiming her mouth in a long, bruising kiss that sent a familiar fiery sensation surging through Mélissande's body. Finally lifting his head, he said huskily, "I never meant to do that. I know you kissed me only because you were so relieved to hear that your lover was safe."

"My lover? But . . . I'm not in love with Bertrand. He's my cousin, a much-loved cousin, but no more than that."

A smile crept slowly over Gideon's face, a smile that reached the eyes that Mélissande had once thought so cold. "Then, my darling, my irresistible Mélissande, is there any chance for me? I've been fighting my feelings for you since the first moment I saw you, but I didn't realize how much I cared until that evening in the inn parlor at Tunbridge Wells. And I've been longing to do *this* again every minute of every day that has passed." *This* was another hard embrace and a kiss that turned Mélissande's bones to water. She relaxed against him with a sigh, responding to his lips with a passion that caused him to pull back, smiling shakily. "Was that your answer, Mélissande? Do you love me, just a little?"

"Oh, much, much more than that. Somehow, little by little, you've become my whole life, but I've simply been refusing to admit it to myself," replied Mélissande dreamily. "How could it have happened, Gideon? We've done nothing but argue and fly into rages with each other since the first day we met."

Placing gentle hands on her shoulders, Gideon pushed Mélissande ahead of him into the drawing room, where he sat down beside her on the sofa. Winding his arms around her, he snuggled her head against his shoulder and pressed his face against her hair. "When I came back to the Priory, I was so full of hate and resentment and disillusionment that there was no room for any other emotion. I had ruined my army career through my own stupidity, and the Priory was buried in debts and mortgages. I hated my father's memory because of his treatment of my mother, and I believe I hated Nicholas and Cecilia as much or even more. Then, slowly, gradually, I began to change as I listened to your solemn little lectures about the Maitland tradition, as I learned to know Cecilia and Nicholas and had to concede that they were in no way responsible for my father's actions, and most of all, sweetest Mélissande, as I saw the love and solicitude you seemed to extend to everyone around you, even to a drink-sodden lout who shot holes in his family's ancestral portraits!''

"That's enough humility, Gideon. I don't want you to turn into a completely different person," murmured Mélissande, burrowing her head deeper into his shoulder.

Gideon raised his head with a chortle of amusement. "Bless you, my love. Whatever else happens, we shan't bore each other." Turning serious, he added with a touch of anxiety, "It won't be a life of luxury that I'm asking you to share with me. It will probably be a very long time before the Priory is prosperous enough to allow me to pay off my father's debts, even if Nicholas as my permanent bailiff is able to put all his ideas into successful operation. I hope we can rub along comfortably enough, however, and I will certainly do my best to help Nicholas and Cecilia to be as happy as we are. Nicholas can have the home farm when he marries Phoebe—oh, yes, my love, I shall persuade Farmer Wright that he's a fool to prefer a rich yeoman to a lord for a son-in-law. We may need to invite Mr. Wright to dinner, perhaps to several dinners, but I think he will come around! And Cecilia will have a proper dowry if it means I must go further into debt.''

Mélissande sat bolt upright. "It won't be necessary for you to go into debt ever again. You forget that I'm a wealthy lady. We'll sell the Castellane emeralds."

"We'll do nothing of the kind," retorted Gideon, an angry frown driving the lighthearted gaiety from his face. "How could you even imagine that I would allow you to tow me out of the River Tick by selling a family heirloom?"

"Gideon, you fool, my happiness with you is more important to me than a dozen necklaces. No, we'll sell the emeralds, and when the estate is flourishing again, I will let you buy me the most expensive parure that you can find."

Mélissande raised her hand, gently smoothing out with

her finger the lingering frown lines on Gideon's forehead. "There's one more thing," she said suddenly. "In my relief at hearing about Bertrand's escape, I completely overlooked the fact that you've just ruined your reputation as a gentleman by allowing the whole county to think you were foxed during Lord Haverford's hunting party. There's nothing else for it: you must tell the Earl about Bertrand's attempt to assassinate the Comte d'Artois. You can say that Bertrand overpowered you and escaped while you were taking him to the justice of the peace."

"What a terrible female you are," exclaimed Gideon, breaking into a grin. "You think nothing of telling the most dreadful bouncers, you acquiesce in helping an enemy agent escape his just deserts, and I fancy you are about to turn me into the most henpecked husband alive. But I love you with every part of my being, and I will love you until I die."

"What's this, then?" Nick had entered the room to find his sister and his half brother so lost in each other's arms that they were unaware of his arrival. Nick looked unkempt, and he was not entirely steady on his feet. Mélissande suspected that he had recently imbibed far more Blue Ruin than was good for him. "Don't tell me that you two, of all people, have developed a case on each other," Nick said incredulously.

"We have, indeed, Nicholas," said Gideon. "You must plan to attend our wedding soon. Make that two weddings. No, three," he added recklessly. "Yours to Phoebe, and Cecilia's to Lieutenant Gray, if the Frenchies don't sink his ship before he can get leave again. We Maitlands must be the most romantic family in all of England."